Y0-CAT-047

The Last Frost Fair

JOY FREEMEN

St. Martin's Press
New York

Design by Paolo Pepe

Library of Congress Cataloging in Publication Data

Freemen, Joy.
    The last frost fair.

    I. Title.
PS3556.R3933L3 1985   813'.54   84–18310
ISBN 0–312–47084–3

First Edition

10 9 8 7 6 5 4 3 2 1

B00   5877

To Nita Holt

The LAST FROST FAIR

December 1812

ONE

Major John Ashton stumbled off a path leading from the Yorkshire spa of Harrogate and followed the rugged ground down to the edge of a small brook. He stood for a moment, then dropped despondently onto a boulder. It would be some time before the frigidity of its surface could be felt through his heavy woolen coat and thick leather breeches, but he was equally unconscious of the sharp westerly wind that was whipping cruelly round his hatless head.

He sat there, motionless, until an oath of annoyance intruded suddenly into his tangled thoughts.

A moment later, a low, clear voice floated down from the path, "Oh, sir! My papers! Will you kindly recapture them before they end in the North Sea?"

Jack Ashton was a well-traveled man of one and thirty. He'd encountered a great many beautiful women in his lifetime, but locked in his heart, as perhaps with all men, was a collection of features representing the one woman he could love. He had never seen her with his conscious mind. Until this minute, he'd been able only to sense how she would look.

Madeleine St. Cross, a magnificent specimen in her early twenties, was unmoved by a similar revelation as she beheld the dazed gray eyes that stared up at her. "My papers," she repeated, having to struggle a little with her patience. "They are blowing down the hill in your direction, and I mustn't lose them."

Even in his feverish condition, the major was unmuddled in his determination to know her. He gathered his wits. Just not enough to remember that his war-ravaged body was in no case to respond with the willingness of his spirit. Struggling to his feet, he lunged after the papers.

In the inevitable whimsy of a windswept article, one lay fluttering in its place until within inches of his grasp, then frisked away to flirt from another tempting distance.

As he pushed himself back from where he'd stumbled against the hillside, the major's brow was already dotted with beads of perspiration. He swayed twice before moving doggedly after it again.

"Oh!" Madeleine called from the path as the situation came home to her. "Great heavens, you are ill! Why didn't you say so?"

She began making her way down the slippery terrain. "*Stop*," she ordered with an edge of asperity. "Never mind it. Good God, it is not so important that you must do yourself an injury!"

She came up with him and tugged at his arm. "Stop, I say, you foolish creature. Here. Sit on this fallen tree."

She found her handkerchief and dropped down beside him, dabbing at his brow. "Why in the world didn't you just tell me to chase after my own papers?" she demanded.

Her dark hair was in a state of attractive disarray from the hood that had fallen back onto her shoulders. The major's attention fixed on this, but it seemed to Madeleine that he was merely gazing blankly into space. She tried to force his attention by turning his face briskly with one gloved finger.

He offered no resistance, merely continued his mute inspection, now wholly caught up in the fascination of her sea-colored eyes. She glanced nervously at the steep incline, thinking his inability to respond a dangerous sign.

Then quite suddenly he spoke. "God help me, I'm going to love you till the day I die."

Madeleine was certainly startled, but after a moment she said calmly, "I daresay your mind has been affected by your fever." Adding, more to herself, "I hope you aren't going to prove unmanageable now that I find myself alone with you down here."

"I couldn't harm you."

She smiled at that, wondering if it was his code of honor that he meant or merely that he wasn't up to the deed. From the look of him, she felt she might at least depend on the latter.

"Then I shan't worry any longer. But what am I to do with you?" She dabbed at fresh beads of perspiration. "It isn't good for you to remain in this freezing wind in your state."

"If you would kiss me . . ."

"No, no, I'm persuaded that wouldn't be of the least use. We must try somehow to get you up the hill. Are you putting up in the district?" When he nodded, she said thoughtfully, "You've come for the waters, I daresay."

She gave a soft laugh at the face he made, speaking soothingly as she pulled his arm about her shoulders and tried to help him to stand. "Yes, they smell only a little worse than they taste. It's hard to imagine their doing any good, but I hear many accounts of—"

An alarmed male voice from the path above broke in. "Mady! What is it? Are you in need of—?"

She looked up with relief. "Oh, Henry! *Yes!* Come down here at once! This poor gentleman is frightfully ill."

Henry Dunston, the son of a local squire and one of Madeleine's many youthful admirers, brought his horse down the incline, mumbling, "I'd thought at first—well, never mind."

Madeleine interrupted his attempt to dismount. "Now that you are here, we can sit a minute while you fetch my papers. They've blown off in that direction."

Henry returned, brandishing three large sheets of foolscap. "They look like drawings, Mady. Have you taken up sketching?"

In her concern, Madeleine had forgotten her own affairs. Dismay flitted across her features, but she said quickly, "Never mind that. Come down and help me to get him onto your horse."

The major fainted during their efforts to put him in the saddle. He lolled against Henry, who sat behind, guiding the horse. Madeleine walked beside, helping to hold him in place.

A short distance down the path, a manservant rushed up to them, exclaiming, "Aw, thanks be to Gawd! I've been hunting for me poor major this half hour past!"

"He seems to have come over with a shocking fever," Madeleine told him. "We were taking him to a physician."

"Oh, miss, me thanks to you, but 'tis a ball in his shoulder doing all the mischief. Stuck fast there these many weeks, only to be shook loose when the coach landed itself in a ditch. It's a surgeon that's wanted, and I've one now at our lodgings. It was when I went to fetch him that me master mizzled away."

Recalling his manners, he touched his cap. "The name's O'Hare, and with your permission, miss, I'll be taking over now."

Madeleine gave up her position beside the major with relief. For all the look of starvation about him, there was considerable weight in his tall frame.

O'Hare went on talking as they hurried along. "Ah, but it's past believing what me poor master has been made to suffer. Just after marching out of Madrid we set to storming one of them evil Spanish castles. And but for himself here, his lordship and the whole of the first division would have been trapped proper by sixty thousand of Boney's finest, as was slipping up behind."

"By Jove!" said Henry, looking with fresh interest at the unconscious form sprawled before him. "What did he do?"

"It's an intelligence officer that he is," replied O'Hare importantly. "He'd been off aspying out the land. That being his work, d'ye see. Checking on troop movements and smoking out their plans. Ay, and many's the time he's snabbled a uniform and gone right into their camps. Him being able to speak their heathen tongue as good as themselves."

"By Jove!" reiterated Henry.

Madeleine's thoughts wandered while O'Hare gave the fascinated Henry an account of the situation that had allowed the French to move up behind Wellington's position at Burgos. There was little she found so maddening as military gabble.

She spent the time pondering her own lucky escape. Thank heaven Henry hadn't made sense of the helpful comments scrawled beside the sketches he had rescued for her. For several years now, her family had been secretly engaged in the manufacture of hats and bonnets—a social sin of the highest order.

Not that there was any secret about the poverty that made it necessary. Nor the cause of that poverty. A cause too common to raise any brows. Madeleine's father had simply and selfishly wasted his estate through gaming and other excesses. Never putting back so much as a shilling until it was almost in ruin.

They had watched helplessly for years—his wife, his sister, his five children. Yet for all that, they hadn't a notion he had mortgaged it to the skies—*and* heaped up a mountain of debt into the bargain. Not until his death, seven years since.

They'd managed—just barely—not to lose the place by renting it out, and removing to Harrogate, in the hopes that Madeleine's elder brother, Patrick, could acquire the means to restore it and assume control. An endeavor, however, that all the hat-making in the world couldn't hope to accomplish.

There was only one way for any of them to regain their rightful place in the world. One of the children simply had to make a marriage that would guarantee a thumping great settlement. An impossibility for either brother. An unlikelihood in the case of Madeleine's elder sister, Dorothea. An attractive girl, but possessing nothing near the dazzling beauty of Madeleine. Jane, besides being no match for her either, was too young.

It had always been a dream of Claudia St. Cross that her extraordinary second daughter would one day acquire a title and a fashionable place in society. She saw no better prospect for reversing such financial ruin than to proceed with her plan to provide Madeleine a Season in London—long postponed, of course, while they struggled to accumulate the necessary funds.

It had taken seven years of struggle, combined with positively ruthless economy, but they had managed it at last. All was in train for Madeleine to set out in the spring. Claudia had located a distant cousin willing to help—not only in a few months with Madeleine's debut, but for the past several years by keeping them abreast of the latest fashions in headwear.

Now only their risky commerce seemed to hold any threat to their success. The barest hint of it could destroy their social standing for good and all. Genteel poverty was perfectly acceptable, but remained genteel only if one, quite literally, did not lift a hand to overcome it.

Madeleine couldn't suppress a slight shudder, her mind still dwelling on how unforgivably careless she had been to send Henry after those papers.

Soon, however, her thoughts were diverted again, as O'Hare got round to his master's part in the tale he was telling.

"We'd 'a ended our days right there," O'Hare was saying, "except that me major made a dash to bring us word. But the Frogs caught sight of him. He lost himself in the wood, but not afore they brought home two shots. And still he kept his horse astanding while he scratched out a message."

"And the horse got through to you," breathed Henry.

"Ay, caught up by our pickets. And thanks be to it, we was able to slip away afore the Frenchies showed their front."

"By Jove!"

"But your major," Madeleine demanded impatiently. "What became of him? Wounded and without a horse?"

"'Twas close on a fortnight afore his brother and me found him, miss. But thanks be to Gawd, he'd dropped off near to a stream and was able to keep himself alive. Having, as he did, all he wanted to drink."

"But nothing to eat in all that time?" Madeleine gasped.

"A mere few biscuits, miss, and what weeds he could drag himself about to gather. 'Twas another full se'ennight afore he could keep down aught but broth. And his victualing office ain't right to this day. 'Twas on that account the camp surgeon gave orders as he was to come and take of this water you have here."

Madeleine shook her head with a sense of uncomprehending sympathy. "Well, the important thing is that he is safely away from all that horror now. The waters may help him, of course, but I'm afraid he has no opinion of them."

"None at all, at all. It took direct orders from the chief himself to make him agree to it." O'Hare swelled visibly with a sense of vicarious pride. "But, you see, miss, his lordship says me master is worth a brigade to him. And he's wanting him back in good point for the spring campaign."

"Wanting him back!" Madeleine cried, glancing at the wasted figure. "Good God, hasn't he done enough? Surely there must be others who do that kind of work."

"Ay, miss, but none so nacky as the major."

Madeleine left O'Hare and Henry helping the major into his lodgings, her thoughts still full of the encounter. As for the major, she was of two minds. She would normally look gratefully upon any new arrival at this time of year. But a soldier—and fresh from the war! She made a face, envisioning the boring descriptions in store for her if she encouraged this conscientious officer, and was near to deciding that she would not. And yet there had been something engaging about him. She tried to recall what it was and couldn't.

After frowning over it for a time, she brushed that question aside. Not that it made any more sense to wonder whether he had a wife. If his qualifications as an agreeable flirt hung in the balance, in no way would he make an eligible suitor from the standpoint of their enormous need. Apart from his garments being sadly behind the mode, the fact that he was obliged to take lodgings with Mrs. Mogg ended all question of that.

Madeleine headed home, across the short path that ran between the vast cobbled yard of the Crown and the rear of Stone Cottage. Her mother didn't approve of this expedient. Or of entering the house through the kitchen door. A most ungenteel thing to be seen to do. And a dangerous one, if they were not to be discovered in the greater vulgarity of all but living in the practical comfort of this one room.

But Madeleine was chilled enough to risk a bit of censure. So she wooshed right in, causing a wild curiosity in her younger brother and sister over her appearance. After scrambling up and down the incline, her boots and gloves were soaked through and her cloak mud-spattered and a little torn where the pocket had caught on the shrubbery.

Nurse, who had reared four generations of St. Crosses, was interested only in divesting her of her wet things and bundling her directly into a hot tub. She shushed Lambert's and Jane's questions and waved away Madeleine's teasing reminder that it was neither of her days for the luxury of a bath. "Nay, lass, don't be fratching over sech. It's down with a lung tha'll be next."

Madeleine's Aunt Heartha gently upheld Nurse's views, but Claudia, returning from another part of the house, put an end to all discussion.

She turned instantly to Patrick and ordered him to draw off all the hot water from the huge kettle hanging from its idleback.

"Lambert will carry the tub into the washroom. Dorothea—quickly—towels and soap for your sister. Jane, you will run up and fetch dry stockings and slippers."

Madeleine, grateful but a trifle embarrassed, thanked them all and gave herself over to the delights of a hot bath in the small room built cozily behind the kitchen chimney.

It was hours later, during the bustle of readying the table for the daily project of hat-making, that Lambert groaned, "By God, Mady, I hope you mean to tell me about your major soon."

"Oh, such a bore, to be going over all that again," Madeleine teased. "The others had it from me already while you were off chopping wood."

"Since you are warming yourself from that very wood, you might think yourself obliged."

Madeleine laughed and nodded. She was aware that, to her army-mad brother, the story represented something of a high treat. But by the time she had been made to repeat and clarify the details of the major's heroism for the fourth time, she raged out, "Upon my soul, I cannot think *what* I would give if only the nuisancy creature had effected his cure at Bath!"

This put an end to all talk of the major, and she soon forgot her annoyance with him. Forgot him altogether, until three days later, when she caught sight of Henry Dunston standing once more with O'Hare in front of Mrs. Mogg's cottage.

She'd meant only to wave and go on her way, but suddenly she found herself crossing the cobbled street to join them.

Cutting short Henry's effusive welcome with a quick smile, she addressed O'Hare. "I hope this gathering doesn't mean that your major has come to further grief."

"Nay, miss, nay. 'Twas only this morning that he woke, but with the ball safe out now, he'll be up and about afore long."

"I say, Mady," Henry piped in, "he's a capital fellow. You should hear all the bold strokes he's brought off."

Just as she'd feared. Not only was the major going to be a bore about his experiences, but a boastful one into the bargain. Aloud she said, "He must indeed be on the mend, if he's able to relate a great many adventures so soon after waking."

"No, no. I got them from O'Hare. The major isn't permitted to discuss his work. Military secrets, you know."

"Is—is that what he told you?" Madeleine asked, biting back a laugh. Apparently she had misjudged the poor fellow.

"Well, it only stands to reason. Being an intelligence officer," Henry pointed out as he mounted his horse. "So you must be careful, Mady, not to ask awkward questions."

"Oh, I shall, I shall. To be sure, you may all rely on me."

"I'm just off to fetch some apples for the major," Henry added, gathering his reins. "While I have the key, I'll get some for you if you'll wait."

"It hints of dishonesty, but I'm too tempted to protest," she smiled. "You may be sure I'll wait."

As Henry galloped off, O'Hare turned to her. "Since it's waiting you've in mind, miss, you might just step into the warmth and say a few words to me master. Sure it's mighty pleased he'd be to see you."

"Oh! No, that wouldn't do at all," she returned on a surprised chuckle. "Besides, I'm sure he'd be better to rest quietly. Especially since I collect Henry has been plaguing him with a great many questions."

"Truth be told, miss, I'm thinking it's quicker he'll mend for another peep at that pretty face of yours."

Madeleine was too accustomed to compliments to pay them much heed, but this one tickled her sense of humor. "I'm sure I've never been prescribed as a restorative before. Unfortunately, I'm equally sure that Mrs. Mogg will never countenance it."

"Ah, now, if that be all, you just leave the managing of the Widow Mogg to me," he promised with a broad wink as he opened the door.

Madeleine paused, then shrugged and passed through, moving off in the direction he indicated. The door to the major's room stood open, but she tapped lightly on the frame, smiling a friendly greeting when he looked up.

There was a moment while he seemed to be accustoming his eyes to sudden light. But when he spoke, it was calmly enough. "You must forgive my staring. I was prepared for it to be Mrs. Mogg. You're not greatly alike."

Madeleine's mind flickered with sudden interest. Mrs. Mogg was a vast, hulking woman with straggling gray hair and a hatchet face. "No, I fancy I could give her a year or two," she replied with prompt cordiality.

She thought she saw a responsive gleam in the major's gray eyes but couldn't be sure. He still looked frightfully done up.

"Your man insisted that you wouldn't find a second caller too much a strain. You must tell me if he was being overoptimistic, and I shall go straight away."

"He was quite right," the major returned, arching his neck, to see behind her. He added, this time with an unmistakable gleam, "And so apparently was Mrs. Mogg."

"Ah, now that ends all doubt," Madeleine said, advancing into the room. "You must be in fairly good point, to lie there and insult your visitors." Tossing back the hood from her dark head, she removed her cloak and dropped it onto a bench. "I am very aware that nothing Mrs. Mogg will have said of me is less than an insult. But our acquaintance, sir, is rather short. I am positively quivering to discover just how you can be so cocksure that she was right."

"Why, because here you are without a companion."

"She warned you that I haven't the slightest regard for common propriety. You don't look shocked. Are you?"

"No, just curious. Sit down, won't you, and tell me—*have* you the slightest regard for common propriety?"

Madeleine perched lightly on the chair beside his bed. "Not to the point of making a fuss about a chaperone when a man is ill and tied to his bed and wanting company."

"Just impatient of convention."

"I daresay. Not that any amount of conformity would earn me a better opinion from the Mrs. Moggs of this town."

"Oh? And why is that?"

"Upon my word, O'Hare told us you are a spy. Is it merely a habit one gets into? You cannot possibly be interested in all this small-town tattle."

"If you'd rather not say. I don't mean to be impertinent."

Don't you, now? Madeleine thought in some amusement. Though you've no objection to being mighty provocative, if that smile of yours is anything to go by. . . . But there had been something in his expression before the smile. And there was really no malice in his roasting.

"Oh, well," she said, settling back in her chair, "we needn't think of that. I may wish to be impertinent myself before we've done. In answer to your question, it just seems that what may go unnoticed in another has always been unforgivable in 'that shocking St. Cross girl.'"

He appeared to consider this for a moment. "How extraordinary. Unless, of course, you mean 'what may go unnoticed in another' . . . less beautiful."

"Hmm, I see. Mrs. Mogg has also told you I am extremely vain."

That smile toyed with her again.

"Well, what more?" Madeleine invited. "We may as well have it all out at once."

When he would only shake his head, she said, "Craven? Or just suddenly too nice to be repeating gossip? Let me see . . . I don't suppose she'd miss a chance to say that I am dreadfully spoiled and pampered. Oh, and, of course, that I am flighty, wholly without accomplishments, and an incorrigible flirt."

"Not as thorough as all that. None of it true, by the way?"

"All of it, to be sure."

"If ever she raises a question of your honesty," he promised, laughter banishing the fatigue in his eyes for the first time, "I'll send her away with a flea in her ear."

"Thank you, major, and now I think we shall turn to the topic of yourself for a time. Only pray don't feel we need probe into all your faults right off."

TWO

Madeleine had already decided that she liked the major, but she was by no means swept off her feet, and only mildly interested in his background. Still, it was an unavoidable convention. So she confined her polite inquiries to his life before the military, preferring to add to her collection of facts about London. But this produced only a brief account of his estate in Ireland. She was surprised to learn that he was a man of property. Though her surprise evaporated as he went on.

"Unfortunately, the house was damaged and the rest of the buildings destroyed in a rebellious uprising while I was up at Cambridge. It was unfairly done. Or, perhaps, accidentally. The Ashtons have never been absentee landlords."

She hoped he wouldn't now dwell on the subject of country property, thinking that one of the most unfortunate things about being shut up in one room, winter after winter, with enthusiasts of any description, was that it quite wore out one's tolerance. Patrick, since inheriting their own estate, had filled far too many evenings with such talk, causing her to dread it second only to Lambert's obsession with the army.

Hoping at least to recapture the stimulation of frivolity, she asked, "Can it be that I am viewing the first black sheep in a long line of traditionalists?"

But the major, having shown himself perfectly willing to be frivolous over her affairs, frowned seriously. "I've wondered myself. Of course, having inherited an estate without income, there was really nothing for it but to seek other employment. I expect I'll rebuild one day."

Well, thank heavens he wasn't compelled to explain, with Patrick's endless detail, just how he planned to set about this rebuilding. The touching on *other employment*, however, brought them naturally round to the war.

Madeleine was somewhat impressed, because he made no attempt to recount his own exploits or even to reconstruct the battles for her. Unhappily, he found much to say regarding their objective there in the Peninsula.

It was slightly uphill work, trying to keep track of all the royal fingers that seemed to have got into the pie, but her irritation was growing from quite another cause. It was seeing him so pitiably torn and wasted as a result of these foreigners and their foolish bickering.

She continued to listen, her features set in the appearance of polite attention, until suddenly, to her own astonishment, she flew out at him. "Oh, dear God, what can it possibly signify *who* is king of Spain?" She made an impatient gesture. "Perhaps to a *Spaniard*. But for a young Englishman to be lying abed, looking like a death's-head on a mopstick over it, is foolish past permission. Get yourself well and leave them to fight it out for themselves."

The major's brows rose at the unexpected attack, but he was almost immediately caught in a paroxysm of laughter.

The quick succession of Madeleine's own reactions—remorse at having been so uncivil, relief that he hadn't taken offense, and finally concern for his health—left her in unaccustomed confusion. She leaned forward impulsively and pressed a hand to his chest. "Oh, do not! You must not! You'll set your wound to bleeding!"

For all his apparent weakness, the major had that hand locked in place with lightning speed.

His laughter settled into a warm smile. "No need to look so woebegone. I haven't laughed in some time. Even if it hurts a little, I'm grateful."

"Well, you look as though you may be coming on with a fever again. And if you do, I shall be responsible."

He smiled enigmatically. "On the contrary, I'm amazed at the rapid state of recovery you seem to be engendering."

Madeleine shook her head. "It's too soon for you to be having visitors. Strangers at all events. May I have my hand?"

"Only if you promise not to run away."

"Five minutes, then."

"Twenty."

"Ten and not a minute more."

"We'll settle on fifteen. To be socially correct."

Madeleine couldn't help laughing. "Then I should go at once. I've been here that long already."

"Beginning now. You owe me an opportunity to make amends for boring you."

She nodded absently, her thoughts turning from his health to her own unwarranted conduct. She was wholly at a loss to account for it. Many a gentleman who had provoked her beyond her patience—or her brothers, if she discovered them bent on some piece of masculine folly—had fallen under just such a tongue-lashing. But the major had in no way provoked her. Nor, she thought, with an inward chuckle, had he earned the right to be abused like a near relation.

"Well, I must certainly beg your pardon for that," she said. "But it wasn't that you were boring me." She broke off, a rueful smile playing on her lips. "Well, only a very little. I think perhaps I've heard too much of foreign wars that have nothing to do with me. Or *you*," she added severely.

"Then I promise to avoid the subject," he said, still smiling in that almost searching way he had. "Except, of course, to reply to your question. We concern ourselves only that the king of Spain not be an appointee of Bonaparte's. If he's allowed to swallow up Spain and Portugal as effortlessly as he might without British interference, we'd soon find ourselves having to lay England bare." He added, with a teasing note, "So, you see, it could have to do with you, after all. If we should fail, you might find yourself having to speak French everywhere you go."

"Quite impossible," she responded in the same spirit. "I made a perfect mull of the French lessons my mother was at such pains to provide me."

"Did you? I'd be happy to assist."

"Ah, yes, I recall now that O'Hare told us you were most proficient. No, it puts me out of all patience the way they insist on making such things as pencils a male or a female. Besides I—"

She broke off, for just then Henry bounded in, bearing two baskets full of apples. One he plumped on the bedside table. The other he bestowed more reverently in her lap. She thanked him and made a rapid calculation of its contents. There were eight—all maddeningly red and shiny, and she was free to take one.

As she sat, sunk in her enjoyment, Henry treated them to an account of his method of inveigling the key to the storehouse and his means of smuggling out the unauthorized fruit for her.

All of which, Madeleine began to think, bore a suspicious flavoring of what the major had been at down there in the Peninsula. Except, she decided, smiling at her own absurdity, not with regard to anything so practical as her delicious apple.

The major, also listening to Henry with only half an ear, was using the time to sort out his thoughts. He had a sketchy memory of those moments with Madeleine in the dell. And, much to his amusement, of his own conduct. There had been a muddled feeling that she had somehow cast a spell over him.

Civility prevented his looking pointedly away from young Mr. Dunston during the flow of his recital, but he had been keeping an interested watch on Madeleine out of the corner of his eye. She was every bit as beautiful as he remembered. More so, if it were possible. But not at all what he'd expected her to be like. Her undisguised pleasure in her apple was causing him no end of entertainment. What a thoroughly odd mixture she was. And something of a puzzle.

He had noticed right off that she endured a life of genteel poverty. But that was a long way from explaining why such a finished piece of nature hadn't been snapped up long before now. There had to be another reason for finding her still unmarried at twenty-odd years. He wondered darkly what it might be.

Just as Henry's tale was winding to a close, O'Hare came in and lured him away with a hint that his mare might be intending to develop a spavin.

The major's gaze followed their departing figures mechanically. Looking back, he found himself fixed by a droll stare and laughed. "No, no. I had no hand in that."

"I should think that makes it worse," Madeleine observed, "since it means your outrageous O'Hare is so accustomed to chicanery on your behalf that he needs no direction."

She dropped the core from her apple into the basket, wiped her fingers with her handkerchief, and sighed, "It must surely be that the most difficult thing in the world is to eat just one of anything."

"A few apples can scarcely threaten such a trim figure."

"It isn't my figure," she smiled, "but the apples that I am trying to preserve."

"Then you must have one of these."

"Good God!" she exclaimed, flushing slightly from a mixture of indignation and embarrassment. "Do you suppose I was cadging for yours?"

"I believe you know," he returned, unruffled and a trifle distracted by his consideration of the very slight cleft in her chin, "that I suppose nothing of the sort."

Her annoyance subsided under this casual disposal of the matter, but she shook her head. "I have my own and no right or reason to take any of yours."

"There's a reason, since you're wanting to save those. As to 'right,' you're infringing on mine to dispose of my property in a manner of my own choosing."

"Well, that is no doubt all very logical," Madeleine replied. "Too logical for my dithered thinking, I fear. Besides, you oughtn't to be so careless about your food. I'm sorry I called you a death's-head, but you are shockingly thin, you know."

"Just two. There are plenty in there. I could tell by the way he set it down."

Madeleine spoke more in manner of explaining to herself the cause of such bizarre habits of observation. "I fancy your work has taught you to notice things like that."

"Two."

"*No!*"

"Then one."

"None."

"At least one, or I'll order O'Hare to fling them into the snow."

"Upon my word, but you're a nuisance," she declared, snatching an apple from his basket. "Well, at least I should like you to understand that I am not hoarding these others up for myself. There are just enough for my family to each have one."

"Oh, well then, in that case you must certainly take two."

"*Major,*" she threatened in laughing exasperation, "I shouldn't at all like to hit you while you are so weak, but I shall if you say one more word on the subject."

He didn't, but continued to smile at her in a way she thought somewhat calculating.

After disposing of the second apple and exchanging a little less controversial conversation, she rose, saying it was already much later than agreed upon. When she'd got into her cloak and drawn on her gloves, she lifted the second core from her basket in a kind of salute, her lips forming a silent *thank you.*

He nodded. "I was hoping it would be sweet enough for you to forgive me."

She nodded back, her own slow smile just slightly teasing. "So completely that I am going to take Henry away and ensure you an undisturbed sleep."

Madeleine left Mrs. Mogg's cottage with a look of thoughtfulness that flashed suddenly into a smile and dissolved back again into frowning consideration. It had been a good many years since any from a legion of admirers had managed to fluster her so. The major had made a positive habit of it. She found it somewhat stimulating.

But although her thoughts continued to return to him over the next few days, she made no attempt to do so herself. Even if she hadn't been so unexpectedly charmed, she should have been willing to bear him company during what promised to be a long and tedious convalescence. But she knew very well that the fiercely respectable Mrs. Mogg would not be so easily cozened into permitting a second such visit.

In the event, it was four days before she spoke to the major again, and then it was with considerable displeasure. She found him drawn up in a rather disreputable-looking gig at the place where her lane gave onto the main road. Accustomed as she was to the foolishness of men in pursuit of a pretty face, she was still aghast at his having exposed himself to the full might of that particularly windy corner. And for God only *knew* how long!

Madeleine quickened her pace and, without pretending to misunderstand his presence, said, "Major, this will not do. You are in no fit state for such imprudence."

"I was hoping you'd agree to help me arrange a few subscriptions," he replied, passing over her rebuke. "I collect there's a circulating library. And, as you know, I was ordered here to begin a course of the waters."

"An excellent notion," she said, thrusting out her hand for assistance to board. As he helped her to arrange the rug about her, she went on, "I have errands in High Harrogate, but the pump room is along the way. And Langdale's—that is the library—is there in the upper town. Neither is apt to afford you much company at this season, but they *will* give you a place to sit out of the cold."

When he made no move to get underway, she cast him a wary glance, wondering if he had succumbed to another delirium. He looked to have his wits about him, so she asked, "Well, sir, why do we sit?"

"I've been wondering myself. You're on the driver's box."

"Oh! So I am. But *why* am I?"

"I was thinking you'd oblige with the reins. My left arm is of no use at the moment."

"Yes, of course. Stupid of me. But seeing you quite alone, I naturally assumed—Well, in any event, I fear my unhandiness in that regard rather does for your plan."

"How is this? I'd supposed that tooling a carriage was an accomplishment of every country lady."

"Possibly, but I am a country lady only by accident of birth. I've only one wish, and that is to pass the remainder of my days in London with a coachman at my disposal."

There was just the flicker of annoyance in the major's expression, but he spoke politely. "In that case, I shan't keep you sitting any longer." Thanking her for her kind intentions, he drew back the rug so that she could climb down.

"But you cannot *remain* here! In this abominable wind!" Giving him no chance to reply, she apostrophized him again as a nuisance and demanded, "Is this not Farmer Hutchin's Annie?"

"I believe it is," he hazarded, following her gaze to the ample rump between the shafts.

"Oh, very well," she exhaled on a defeated breath and unhitched the reins. "I daresay I can contrive."

But no sooner did the vexing thought occur that she must climb down again, in order to remove the full-length blanket from the mare, than O'Hare appeared, as though by magic, saw to this task, and slipped wordlessly away.

"Upon my soul!" she exclaimed when she could command her voice. "Why didn't you *tell* me he was about? I needn't have taken this on at all."

The major, observing her reactions in gathering delight, said kindly, "I'm not even going to mention that you gave me no opportunity. But no matter. Things have their own way of working out for the best, haven't they? Here. At least my whip hand remains in tact. Shall I manage that for you?"

Madeleine continued to eye him, once more with suspicion, for it seemed there might be a hint of mischief in that oh-so-charming smile of his. And possibly a good deal more behind his words. She found it impossible, however, to break his gaze of innocent inquiry, and surrendered at last to a soft, despairing laugh as she passed him the whip.

She held the reins gingerly in both hands as the carriage set in motion, and, only after picking her way in tense silence for some distance, was she able to trust that bolting off was the furthest thing from Annie's placid thoughts.

By the time they drew up in front of the Crescent Pump-room and Baths, Madeleine was relaxed against the backrest, but she could only wonder at herself in such a role. And chuckle a little, remembering the looks of incredulity that had marked their progress through the lower town. Yet, to say the truth, she was conscious of a rise in spirits since becoming embroiled in the major's mad-brained start.

They went into the impressive building together. Madeleine noticed that his leather breeches and top boots were of good quality, his earth-brown coat well cut—even if a few years behind the fashion.

The major put down his name and paid for a subscription but turned immediately toward the door.

"Major," Madeleine called, holding her ground, "when they ordered you take a course of the waters, they meant to *drink* it!"

He looked back, laughing. "But, Mady—May I call you that? I noticed Henry does. You must understand, Mady, that there is a matter of proper mental preparation. I never undertake a mission without it."

She could do nothing with him. He was far too adept at making her laugh at all the wrong times.

He did at least surrender eventually to her homily on the importance of rest to an invalid, allowing her, after an amusing hour spent at Langdale's, to return him to his lodgings.

But if she harbored any belief that he had taken her words to heart, it was banished as she entered the Crown, where a monthly ball was being held that evening. There, only hours after the exertions of the day, was her invalid.

She stopped to make him known to her aunt and sisters and

to introduce her brothers. (Claudia resolutely refused to appear in the outmoded evening dress they all wore.)

When the handshaking was done, Madeleine whispered to the major, "A ballroom seems hardly the place for you to *rest*."

"Oh, I mean to do no more than sit quietly and watch the dancing," he whispered back. "That is, if you will be kind enough to sponsor me for a quarter-year's subscription."

She replied aloud, once the others had moved away, "Since you've already shown yourself capable of learning where I live, at what time I usually reach the cross lanes in the morning, and when the Crown holds its assembly, I am ready to venture that you know perfectly well that they aren't so exacting about their winter subscriptions."

He laughed, making no real effort to deceive her over this ruse to become one of her party. Well, she was quite content to have him so.

The thought struck, however, as she laid her hand very lightly on his injured arm, that she would not be at all content to sit about in order to bear him company during his occupation of *just watching*. Of all things she loved most to dance, and looked forward to even these off-season affairs.

She hoped, as they stepped into the brightly lit ballroom, that he wasn't expecting it of her, and became vexed that such a consideration should have entered her head.

Yet she couldn't help a stab of concern as he moved aside to avoid the crush of gentlemen, all jostling and elbowing one another in an effort to secure her hand.

In the next instant, she was stepping through the crowd of young men that encircled her to where the major had taken a position beside a string of chairs.

"I shall save one to sit with you if you wish," she offered, wondering if she had suddenly run mad.

He regarded her for a moment. "Thank you, Mady, but I think it will give me greater pleasure to watch your performance."

"Truly?"

"Truly."

Madeleine nodded gratefully and was soon swept away as the music struck up.

She glanced over several times as she came down the line, meaning to reward him with a warm smile. But it wasn't merely that he was taking no pleasure in her performance. He was taking no interest in it whatsoever.

For a time, he gave his whole attention to Lambert's earnest talk. Next he was thoroughly caught up in conversation with her Aunt Heartha.

A brief feeling of pique gave way to a mild sense of apprehension. Her aunt was inclined to run on a bit and the major was quite a hand at drawing one out. Madeleine couldn't help worrying that the combination of these two, still with their heads very much together, might result in the major becoming privy to a great many family secrets.

But she forgot that and steeled herself for something of a dilemma when intermission was called. It was a point of agreement between all three sisters not to accept invitations in to tea, since the price of one shilling each made it impossible for their brothers and aunt to purchase tickets. Yet she was more than sure the major was planning to invite her.

But the major, anything but predictable, had claimed Aunt Heartha's hand for tea, giving her enough tickets to invite as many as she wished to join them. Madeleine tagged behind with her brothers and sisters.

She was almost overcome by a feeling of warm gratitude and a wholly illogical sense of pride in him. She supposed it was this silliness that caused her to promise to drive him to the upper town again the next day.

Not that there was anything in any of it to make her fear for her heart or her extremely necessary part in her family's plans. So she let herself be hoaxed, coaxed, or charmed into continuing to meet him, day after day, laughing herself into stitches at his efforts to get down four glasses of the foul-tasting water, passing a quiet hour over the London papers at Langdale's.

And after almost two months of this, she was still fully able to believe that nothing more had occurred than that sympathy and a little light flirtation had matured into a warm and close friendship.

Nothing more, she told herself. But naturally the comfort of such reasoning couldn't go on forever. It lasted only a few days more. Until the Wednesday, a market day at Knaresborough.

THREE

With Jack now fit to deal with the driving, Madeleine thought it a good opportunity to do her shopping away from Harrogate, where the hotels snapped up most of what little was produced in the district.

Unfortunately, a good part of the amusement to be found in a bustling market town was spoiled for them by the dark, windy day. Even the treat Jack arranged for their luncheon—pork roasted to a turn, moist and succulent, with a crisp, crackled edge, and a small jug of wine—was something of a trial in the sparse shelter available, and Madeleine soon became so chilled as to welcome an early start back.

Just short of Harrogate, however, the storm that had been imminent for some time burst with a clamorous din of thunder, followed instantly by a heavy fall of rain.

"Botheration!"

She drew her hood forward to shield her eyes as she scanned the fields to her left. "Oh, good. We haven't passed it. There, Jack. That old, disused barn. Turn off at the next track."

The ancient roof was leaking badly, but it was a spacious building with plenty of sheltered area for both horse and carriage. Jack dried Annie with a wisp of old hay and arranged her blanket while Madeleine paced about and commented inconsistently on the likelihood of a letup.

She had just turned away when she felt his hands, hard and compelling, on her shoulders. He spun her back and would have kissed her had she not thrust a small, gloved hand between his lips and hers in good time.

Jack caught hold of the hand and held it away, though he released her almost immediately.

Yet that instant, when it seemed he would make good his intention, left Madeleine oddly alarmed, and she raked him over with an accusing look. "I should never have suggested we stop if I'd known you couldn't be trusted not to take advantage, Jack."

"Then stop scolding and notice I am not taking advantage."

She stared back in some confusion. It was perfectly true. And true, as well, that she was making much too much of it. It was far from the first time she'd had to ward off a kiss. She moved away a short distance.

"Yes," she said with better command. "Yes. We shall forget it, shall we? I shouldn't have ripped up so. It was my surprise. I—Well, I'd just got in the way of thinking you different from other men."

"I hope you will go on thinking me different," he said.

She was feeling more herself now, so she let him take her shoulders again and just stood quietly.

"Really, I'm a little surprised by your surprise," he said, replacing a damp curl that had dropped onto her brow. "I've had the feeling for some time now that you were prepared for an expression of my love."

Madeleine's breath caught sharply and something deep inside seemed to melt and course warmly through her veins, only to end as a hot and painful lump in her throat. Wave after wave of feeling cascaded over her. Elation, tenderness, panic, despair. Oh, my God, is it possible? No! No, no, no, and *no!* In desperation, she snatched again at temper.

"Oh, *love*. The way you men toss the word about. Using it as merely a more respectable way to say what you truly feel."

"You imagine that to be—?"

"You know perfectly well! And if that is what we've come to—Well, it is just dreadfully disappointing, that's all."

There was a platform along one wall, with three broad steps leading up. Jack pulled her to it, swept an area with the wide brim of his civilian driving hat, and compelled her to sit in the place he had made for her. He seated himself sideways on a lower step.

"If you're suggesting that I desire you," he said, "I'm bound to admit that I do. Just how the devil *have* you been imagining me different?" He went on more gently, "Mady, it isn't in place of love, if that's what you're driving at."

"Oh, perhaps you see it so," she relented. "But don't expect me to be *pleased* about it. It's probably going to *ruin* our friendship. That was something new and special for us both."

Reminded by this of a convenient grievance, she added, "And neither can I be flattered by this desire of yours. Not when it makes me just another of the dozen or so that you have 'loved.'"

"Not dozens. Not even one, unless you're meaning the second housemaid while I was still in short coats."

Madeleine hesitated. It was wrong and probably ill-judged to pursue this course. Yet she was somehow impelled to it. Besides, it was comfortably familiar to be brangling with him in this foolish style. *And* decidedly safer! She couldn't think when she'd been so . . . so *overwhelmingly* touched.

She sighed, fanning up her irritation. "Oh, I realize it isn't the thing for me to have knowledge of your affairs. I daresay that is why you have denied them. But now I feel I must tell you—because I don't want you to *lie* to me, Jack—that I know all about your petticoat adventures."

Jack looked ready to break into a laugh. "No, I won't lie, but I will beg you not to make such preposterous statements. You couldn't possibly 'know all about my petticoat adventures,' because I have never discussed them."

"And what has that to say to anything? You have never discussed your war adventures either, and I know all about them. Heavens, you must realize O'Hare is ever ready to relate your conquests. And does—in *limitless* detail. He's told—well, I don't know who all—but he has certainly satisfied Lambert's deep curiosity."

It was Jack's turn to look skeptical. "And you'd have me believe that Lambert passed these on to you?"

"Oh! No, not intentionally. But I listened to an hour of uninterrupted narrative while he passed them on to Patrick. I was soaking in the bath, and they came into . . . the next room."

Jack's shoulders shook a little when he said, "I fear you must have become sorely chilled in that bath, Mady. If you managed to listen so long without making your own presence known."

Madeleine struggled to keep her features in order, but she burst out with what in anyone less lovely would have been a snort. "Oh—you—you *wretch!* How could you be so ungallant as to take me up like that?"

Her smile was almost dazzling with animation, but it softened, becoming tender as she turned her hand and gripped his tightly. "Oh, my dear, this—just as we are—seems so right for us. And good. Can you not be content with it? It would mean everything to believe you could. Jack . . .?"

He rose, leaving her free to examine the way the hair grew at the back of his neck. A rich, crisp brown. A trifle short for fashion. Just the hint of a curl at the ends. Not even enough to loop on a finger. It was no doubt all of a piece with the madness that seemed to be coming over her that she was sitting now, filled with a stupid longing to try.

It was almost a relief when he turned back to ask, "Mady, is it this nonsense from O'Hare causing you to shy off?"

"Oh, good heavens, no, no. I understand that you must all get on like that. Truly, you may be as outrageous as you wish, if only you will let *us* continue just as friends."

"You're saying you don't return my feelings?"

She flooded over with another bout of irritation. Yet she couldn't, in all fairness, expect Jack to understand. She had confided a good many things to him, but she hadn't told him the full extent of their financial difficulties or their plans for coming about. Those weren't personal secrets for sharing. They were family matters, somewhat embarrassing, and more than a little awkward to explain.

Jack broke the long silence. "Or is it that you're imagining a career of following the drum and dreading it?"

She glanced up, a little surprised. Visions of herself in the role of a soldier's wife had naturally never occurred. But they offered a straw for grasping. What she wouldn't hate about trudging behind him over foreign battlefields would positively terrify her. But before she could catch at it, he dashed it away, explaining that he had no intention of remaining with the army once Bonaparte was brought under control. He told her of the several good positions that had been offered him through his connections in the military. Acceptable positions with the government. At least two that would keep him in London and support a comfortable existence there.

She found herself listening as though it all made sense, her thoughts drifting off to imaginings of the sort of housing those positions might afford. Hired lodgings, surely. Furnished and not very large. And probably some distance from the really fashionable districts. Yet possibly something quaint. And near enough that she could take a hackney to the interesting shops. Just to look about while Jack was at his work. And he was clever, so very clever. He would advance, certainly, and they could begin to collect their own things and perhaps take a better place in a few years. One that she could decorate herself. Prudently, of course, but with taste and quality. And they would entertain the sort of persons who could help Jack in his career, and . . . well, not grandly, of course. But that wouldn't signify, because it would be such a snug home—and happy. Filled with laughter and—oh, dear *God*, what was she thinking?

"Jack, don't! It is that I've made plans for myself. Long, long before we met. But don't tease me about them. We've almost six weeks before you return to Portugal. I—I always think it so stupid to ruin good moments by quite useless efforts to make them more than they can reasonably be."

Jack studied her a little longer. "Mady, I've been hoping you would choose to discuss these plans with me. As it happens I am fairly well versed in them."

"Aunt Heartha." She sighed.

"Of course, and—if nothing else—we may be grateful that it places me in a position to stop you wasting the money that has been put by for this venture. I promise you, nothing could be more unlikely than the impressive title and vast fortune your mother has been envisioning for you. She seems to have got the idea that it needs only for you to appear in London and—"

Madeleine was still too preoccupied with newly discovered feelings for his words to have any real impact. She just waved away what she judged to be a generalized caution against setting one's hopes too high. "Well, if you know so much of our affairs, you must see that an impressive title is not a primary concern."

"No—but very much a part of this sleeveless plan to marry you off in the first circles of Mayfair."

"Oh, Jack, what are you about? A marriage of convenience is the usual solution in cases such as ours, and the first circles of Mayfair the place where they are most profitably made."

"And I will even allow that you are quite beautiful enough to make a fair portion of that set overlook your lack of dowry. That is if there was the least hope of a proper introduction to any of them. The one thing that seems to have escaped you all is your complete lack of connection. One lady to sponsor you is the very least that is needed in such an endeavor."

"Oh, but—"

"Are you going to tell me now of this Cousin Fanny of yours? From all I've been hearing, she sounds as far removed from that world as can be achieved within the confines of gentility." His tone altered, and he laid a hand softly against her face. "But, Mady, you must see that this discussion has no purpose beyond what consolation there may be in it for your family. It might help in some measure if they understood that there never was any great chance for these dreams to materialize." His fingers trickled down and caressed her throat. "The important point is that there can be no question of it now. Even if by some means or miracle you could have accomplished what was hoped, there is your happiness to consider now—and mine."

Madeleine had no need to think. Her response to such a moment had remained untested since she was a child of sixteen, but defense against it had been drilled into her brain every day since. Reaction was automatic.

"No! No, you imagine too much! On my part *and* yours! Promise me, Jack—Promise—I beg of you—that you will not press this matter further."

It was all Jack could do to keep from pulling her into his arms to make her see just how little he was imagining. But he controlled the urge, looking down with irrepressible humor. She had evidently been more clever by half at hiding her feelings from herself than from him. Yet that was the rub in a nutshell. He'd be pitting one very new and barely recognized fact against a lifetime of familiar dreams.

He sat below her again with a patience he felt deserved his warmest congratulations and took her hand. "No, I won't press you further, Mady. Not for the time being, at any rate. But I do want you to remember—by your own words—I've a fair amount of experience with females. Enough to know friendship or unvarnished desire from a feeling that embraces both and goes far deeper. It's that we are both feeling, you know, and I ask only that you will think about it a little now and then."

Madeleine did think about it. More than a little, more than now and then, and altogether more than she wished. Her mind was in a turmoil over it for the rest of the day. Then, throughout dinner and the hours after, she sat like someone stunned. At times there was a bittersweet pleasure in recalling Jack's words, but for the most part she could feel herself sinking lower and lower into depression.

There was just no place in her life now for the feelings he described. She'd given over believing in them long ago and had pledged herself to *accomplish* something with her marriage—satisfaction for her mother, relief and opportunity for her family. It was too late to turn back. Far, far too late. They had all of them abandoned any thought of separate pursuits in order to devote themselves to this project. A project that she alone could bring to fulfillment.

She tossed restlessly in her bed later that night, wondering how she could have been so stupid as not to have seen. She ought to have hedged off from those days with Jack weeks ago. Yet there had been nothing to warn her. None of that breathless eagerness when she went out to meet him. Nothing of those nonsensical flutterings she had experienced as a girl. Only peace and comfort and much laughter. It had seemed so surely just the way of good friends.

But wondering and repining would pay no toll. There were facts to face. The foremost: that she was well on her way to falling deeply in love. A situation that could hold only hurt and disappointment—and danger. She had already felt herself weakening, looking with longing at a life with Jack. She daren't risk another scene like that, and he had agreed to spare her only *for the time being*. No, it simply wouldn't do. Her family had worked too hard and too long for this chance. The *only* chance for her aunt and old nurse to ever return to the home of their birth and the only hope of respectable positions for her brothers or marriages for her sisters.

By morning she had reached a decision. She stayed in bed after Jane and Nurse, who shared the tiny chamber, had gone down to breakfast. Minutes later, Claudia arrived as expected, breathless with the fear that she might have become seriously ill.

"It is nothing—" Madeleine said with a meaning pause, "—nothing that a change of climate shouldn't put right. I've been thinking it might be well to arrange for me to go to Cousin Fanny as soon as possible."

Claudia was not unaware of Major Ashton. A name that had been cropping up far too often for her own peace of mind. She had tried now and then to hint Madeleine away from the association—but with rare discretion, for the last thing she wanted, at such a crucial time, was to set up her daughter's back.

Somehow she managed now to confine herself to a searching look and brisk nod before going off to make arrangements.

Madeleine climbed out of bed to begin her packing, not doubting that those arrangements would be swift and efficient. And, indeed, Claudia managed to convince young Henry's mother to set off immediately on a journey that the poor woman had been no more than contemplating vaguely for years.

Madeleine sent Jane with a message for Jack, claiming that she was feeling a trifle indisposed and would be keeping the house for a few days. She could only be grateful that they would be exhausting days, filled with the confusion of sudden decision.

They passed swiftly enough on that account, and, on the Monday, the Dunstons were there just after cock crow to take her up.

During the bustle of getting her baggage strapped to the roof of the coach, Madeleine read once more through the letter Lambert would deliver to Jack, then sealed it with one of the inexpensive wafers that were scattered among other odds and ends in a bedroom drawer. Her features were almost rigid with determination, for, along with it, she was sealing away those dreams—those foolish, foolish dreams that had continued to plague her.

She hurried down to the kitchen to pass through a line of tearful good-byes and then quickly out to the coach. There were more than two hundred miles to be got over and only seven or so of them could be got over each hour.

Long, tedious hours they proved to be, filled with regret that mingled more and more with apprehension as London began to draw near. Jack had by no means succeeded in convincing her of the hopelessness of their plans, but he had sown far too many seeds of doubt. There would be no rest until she could see for herself, and try, if there were difficulties, to overcome them. Yet whatever she might find in London, Madeleine remained convinced that the greatest threat to those plans was Jack himself, now safely behind her at Harrogate.

The third night found her finally at her cousin's house in Hans Place, still throbbing with the vibration of travel as she dropped wearily onto a comfortable bed in a spacious room, warmed by the luxury of a glowing coal fire.

Cousin Fanny had proved to be a small, round woman of late-middle years, neatly but unfashionably attired, with kind, though slightly startled eyes, and precisely, as Jack had predicted, the last person in the world to succeed in thrusting anyone into the exclusive circles so necessary to their goal.

Moreover, the briefest discussion as to Fanny's plans for her debut was sufficient to convince Madeleine that Jack had indeed been right on all counts.

Not that poor Fanny could be faulted for any of it. Evidently, she had been communicating her own doubts concerning Claudia's expectations for years.

It wasn't difficult to see how such efforts might meet with little success. Claudia had always been one-minded and a trifle unreasonable with regard to her scheme. Madeleine was momentarily prickled by an urge to write to the others and buffer them against depending too absolutely on her success. But it couldn't be done. Not without stripping them of every vestige of hope. And not without exposing her mother's folly and ignorance.

Yet she must do something. She simply couldn't waste every last farthing-piece they possessed on parties and gowns that could in no conceivable way profit them.

Yes, something, but, good God, what? She wasn't even mildly acquainted with the sort of matron Jack had said she must have for a sponsor.

Then, all at once, it occurred that she did, however, know somebody who was better than acquainted with such a person. Actually, a brother to the wife of Lord Hanbart at the war office. And, if his boastful comments could be believed, the positive darling of his sister's eye.

Yes, there was Charles. The Honorable Charles Morland, in whose tall, handsome person Madeleine had once imagined the embodiment of her every dream. Purely the product of youthful idiocy, of course, but she couldn't help a grim smile as the sixteen-year-old, alive somewhere within her, made haste to resurrect the romantic illusions of those days . . .

That first sight of him as he'd assisted an elderly uncle into the Crown. The way their eyes had locked so immediately in mutual longing. Time dragging so interminably until the next assembly, when the master of ceremonies could see to their introduction.

Yes, and from there on to a rapturous summer, marred only by the great pity she had felt for Charles's poor, ailing uncle—not expected to last the Season out. And naturally for poor Charles, so deeply attached to him.

"Stupid, stupid little ninnyhammer," Madeleine murmured, shaking her head at this younger self. For his uncle was soon pronounced wholly recovered, causing a rude awakening for her.

Charles had assured her, of course, while making quite another offer, that marriage had certainly been his intention. . .
"But the devil's in it, Mady. With the old man apt to drag on for years now, I've got to have a dowry or face getting right down to bedrock . . . Dash it all, must I tell you how much I regret this?"

Plainly he had seen that he must, for he had told her and told her, until she managed to break free and run home. And still not content, he made it a point to stop at Harrogate—never less than twice a year—to renew his offer and tell her again.

Madeleine, musing over this, was in some doubt whether *poor Charles* could ever be brought to any purely unselfish act. But she had to try. So she sent off a note immediately, desiring him to call in Hans Place.

He was prompt to respond. Only hours later, Fanny's young maid swept into Madeleine's chamber. "Oh, miss, the most handsome gentleman to see you—and looking as impatient as may be!"

"Thank you, Atty. You can be describing none but Mr. Morland," Madeleine said, smiling at the girl's excitement.

Never since that first occasion had she treated Charles or his disreputable pursuit as anything but a joke. It might have begun as just a painful masquerade, but in less than a year she had realized she was laughing at him in earnest. If Charles realized it, too, his only reaction seemed a more fevered resolve to bring her to terms, if he achieved no other goal in life.

Madeleine hurried down to the small drawing room and found him waiting—tall, well-made, and most exquisitely attired in every fad and fancy known to Bond Street. But seeming to her not so much impatient as a trifle apprehensive.

"What the devil brings you to London?" he demanded.

Madeleine accepted the carefully manicured hand, guessing that it didn't suit his purpose to find her escaped from her backwater resort, where an impoverished female of any attraction learned swiftly to endure such offers as his.

"I believe I told you that we've been saving to give me a Season one day. My cousin has been good enough to have me here."

"Daresay you did. But I hardly expected you to raise the wind so soon."

No, but then, of course, he was hardly aware of their hat-making enterprise.

He glanced about the modestly comfortable room, and suddenly his countenance lightened. "Yes, I see. So you sherried up to Town and discovered that the parcel of nobodies your cousin is able to collect for you is no better than what you might have found in Harrogate." He dropped onto the chair she indicated, opposite her own. "Well, no harm done. As it happens, I've had a change of circumstances and should have brought you from Harrogate in a week or two anyway."

Madeleine never had been able to convince him that her unwillingness to become his mistress was owed to anything but the limited rewards he was able to dangle before her. He usually kept her in a state between laughter and rage with his excuses, a prime favorite being that his estranged wife's fortune was tied up in the children, and he had access only to the income.

Today, however, he assured her right off that she might now depend upon a carriage and coachman of her own.

She frowned curiously, then exclaimed in sorrow, "Oh, has that dear old man finally died?"

"*What* dear old—oh! Expect you mean my Uncle Collier. No, daresay he'll see us all put to bed with a shovel. If you're wondering how I come to be in high water, it's that I've had a run of luck with the bones."

He went on to enhance his proposal with an annuity that would provide her a "reasonable" income for life.

"I was wondering how you planned for me to contrive once the dice turned back on you again," Madeleine said dryly.

"You don't poison luck with that kind of black-thinking. I was just offering some sort of security for . . . your future."

"Ah, yes, to be sure. A little something for when you've grown too young for me."

"Oh, the devil. Are you going to make a grievance out of that? I didn't invent the arrangement."

"Not at all. A quite typical arrangement."

"Then it's settled."

"I fear not."

"Damn it, Madeleine, you've run me as high as I can go! You'll have to close with my last offer, so let's leave off wasting time!"

"It is you that is wasting time. For six years now I've tried to make you understand what I feel about an arrangement of that kind. The only offer I can or will consider begins with a respectable marriage and includes—God send—a settlement large enough for my brother to recover his estate."

"Then why in thunderation did you *send* for me?"

"Because I need your help," Madeleine returned in a voice slightly less audible. The hands resting quietly in her lap seemed to have become riveted together. But she overcame her pinching pride and went on, "You are quite right in saying that my cousin knows no one likely to answer our need. But your sister, Charles, might easily introduce me to somebody who does."

"By God, that's a new come-out! Are you actually expecting *me* to help you into another man's . . . arms?"

"Oh, for heaven's sake, what can it possibly signify? One way or another, I shall marry before this Season is done. I must. The only thing to the point is that you have it in your power to help me achieve something genuinely worthwhile for my family. Nothing but the most unconscionable meanness could make you refuse."

Charles was perfectly capable of such meanness, but he saw no profit in insisting on it. "And all in the name of good fellowship," he retorted bitterly.

"Yes. Or if you like—to give evidence of that devotion you've been laying claim to all these years."

He could at least see some value in that. Once married and in London for a time, he mused, she'd be bound to forget her missish ways and be as ready as any to take a lover. If he refused to help her now, he'd be right out of the running when the time was ripe.

Still, it had never occurred to him that he might end by having to share his prize. He tried to console himself with the theory of half a loaf, but just the thought of it filled him with rage. Later, perhaps, but—*blast* it all!

He lounged back in his chair, pondering and frowning, but after mulling over the matter for a few minutes, he suddenly sat forward. "Very well, I'll do as you ask." He eyed her with something that seemed quite removed from devotion, adding, "Since nothing else will convince you, I daresay I have no choice."

Madeleine was so relieved that she agreed instantly to the long list of rules and restrictions that would be in force during the project of finding her a husband. Nothing signified except that one indeed be found to meet their needs.

At last Charles rose, asking for an exact accounting of those needs. He choked and stared a little but just nodded, saying that he was off to a couple of house parties in the morning, but would call round again on the first of April.

"Too early in the year for the marriage mart just now, in any case."

FOUR

Madeleine settled in, but life in Hans Place was even more uneventful—if anything could be—than Harrogate before Jack. There could be no question of walking out alone and little hope of company to make it "proper and safe." Her cousin's comfortable form told, without her having to, that she was not up to regular exercise. Nor, just as obviously, could she spare either of her maids to the project of daily walks.

It didn't take long for Madeleine to realize that Fanny was barely making ends meet with the soaring prices caused by the war. Or to learn that the fire in her chamber was merely a generosity afforded her as a guest.

Well, it was pleasant and very welcome, but she was used to a much more rigorous existence and insisted, if she were to feel at home, that it must be stopped.

Naturally, Fanny no longer kept horses or a carriage. But she assured Madeleine that they would be able to go shopping in Town by the Chelsea coach. "Although I had expected it to be a deal warmer by the time you arrived, my dear."

Madeleine assured in turn, if somewhat mendaciously, that no more did she wish to brave these damp, winter days.

Consequently, nearly a fortnight passed with her living on the edge of London and seeing no more of it than had been visible through a window in the coach that had brought her.

Most of her entertainment since had centered on what might be viewed through various other windows in the house, and so she stood this morning, as she did each daybreak, watching the activity in the square as the vendors wheeled in their carts and the kitchen maids hurried out with lists. Then, suddenly, she drew a sharp breath. Was it? Could it be? It *was!* O'Hare, of all unlikely people! Flirting out there with a young maid in a mob-cap so huge that she seemed in danger of toppling over. Madeleine's eyes scanned the area excitedly. And there *he* was. Jack. Astride a tall bobtailed gray, and plainly with no idea in which house to find her.

She had not acted so impulsively in her entire adult life. In less time than it would have taken to think about it, she was down the stairs with the front door flung wide.

He saw her and dismounted leisurely, strolling over as though it were a quite commonplace time to call. But as he walked up the few stone steps, their eyes met and held, and it all came back to her. The reason she had fled. That terrible determination lying just beneath his smile.

His movements still seemed leisurely, but he had set her gently aside, stepped in, and closed the door before she could take it all in.

"It's been some time since I was last in London," he said placidly, "but I doubt things have changed so much that it has become acceptable for a young lady to appear in a dressing gown."

Madeleine glanced in the entrance way looking glass, as though unsure of what young lady he meant. Yes, there she was. A dressing gown and tendrils of hair escaping from a morning cap. He had lost none of his ability to turn her into a flustered, empty-headed chit.

"How did you find me?" she asked.

"Since the members of your family had evidently been sworn to secrecy, there was nothing for it but to await the return of Mrs. Dunston and Henry and discover your general whereabouts from him. Their disappearance at just that time made it a safe guess as to who escorted you into Town."

"But Henry was also instructed not to inform anyone."

"I'm sure he is quite unaware that he did. But let us not waste time on that. I came to—"

"Jack—If it is to go on with our last conversation, I beg of you—"

But Jack had no intention of flushing his bird again so soon.

"I was merely going to say that there is still more than three weeks of my leave. I'd hoped you would agree to pass them with me, seeing a few of the sights."

The combination of Jack and London was almost irresistible, but Madeleine stood fast. At length, she asked meaningly, "As friends, Jack?"

"As friends, Mady."

"If you mean it—*truly* mean it—then nothing could make me happier."

"Then I shall have to mean it, because to make you happy is my greatest wish. Now I suggest you go upstairs before you are discovered in this state. I will return at a more seasonable hour and pay homage to propriety by asking to see your cousin and obtaining her permission to take you for a drive. Shall we say at two?"

Madeleine shook her head slowly, then let the smile that was already filling her heart break through. "Sooner. Much sooner."

"That will not alarm your cousin?"

"Everything alarms my cousin. But she loves of all things to be accommodating. I promise you we have no other plans for the day."

Jack returned at ten in a smart curricle. He was outfitted in an approved mode of Town dress, straight trousers worn over his military boots and a morning coat of deep blue.

Madeleine came out of the house with him, exclaiming over the carriage. "Oh, what a stylish turnout! And you." She looked him over again. "What is it that Lambert says?—'Looking as smart as a carrot new-scraped.'"

He laughed. "Thank you, but you had better spare your cousin the shock of such phrases on your lips."

Madeleine laughed back. "It must be a sad trial to be so easily shocked and to have me in the house. Poor woman. But I do like her immensely and try very hard to keep the rules. Now tell me at once how you have come by all this finery."

"The carriage is borrowed, the horses hired, the clothes purchased off the rack in Cranbourn Alley. My uniform is still a good bit too loose, so I brushed down there for this rig."

"Well, I hope you may not have left yourself a bankrupt, but it is rather splendid to be able to cut such a dash on our first day in Town."

There was an expectant pause following her words. When he said nothing, she sighed. "Though you haven't mentioned my appearance. And I was thinking all the while I was dressing how glad I was that you'd be able to see me in something other than those same dreary gowns. These have been waiting in silver paper for almost a year."

She indicated the white pelisse draped over one arm and the crisp, jonquille walking dress, caught just under the bosom with a lacing of white ribbon. Jack took in the pose with a smile, scanning her elegant form right up to the wide brim of a charming cottage hat.

It was one of their own kitchen-creations, but Madeleine saw no reason to mention that.

"And still you say nothing," she accused.

Jack laughed. "I can't help thinking you must become bored, hearing over and over how lovely you look—in *anything*."

"Hmm, you must not be a very intelligent intelligence officer if you have been thinking anything so silly as that," she returned, favoring O'Hare with a wink, as she made her way up to the seat of the tall sporting carriage.

She waved away Jack's advice that she wear her pelisse, but the early March weather was laced with a penetrating chill, and by the time they had pulled up the steep hill to Hyde Park Corner she begged him ruefully to stop and help her into it.

As he was tying the ribbon at her throat into a jaunty little bow, he asked where she wished to go.

"Oh, I wish to see everything," she said.

Jack soon discovered that she had spoken no more than simple truth. They spent the first several days just weaving endlessly through the streets and mews of every district.

Her greatest interest naturally centered on Mayfair—the land in which all her childhood fairy tales had been set. But her curiosity about life in the metropolis as a whole was almost boundless. She wanted to see the City, the riverfront, even the back slums of Westminster. "Everything, Jack!"

By the time they had been all through the parks, including day excursions to Richmond, Kensington, and Hampton Court, Jack was able to assure her that they had driven the equivalent in miles to Yorkshire and back.

She was ready then to get down to more specific sightseeing, and suggested the London Museum, the Tower, and various plays that were showing during the afternoons.

Then one day she came out of the house armed with a list of linen-drapers and shops, claimed by Cousin Fanny to be establishments where one might meet with many fine bargains.

Jack frowned at the list, and Madeleine laughed. "I merely wished to look these places over. But if a day amid female furbelows is too daunting, we needn't."

He regarded her thoughtfully, then shook his head and drove her without further comment to one after the other, standing by patiently, sometimes in high amusement. She had absolutely no head for figures.

She compared roll after roll of dimity or sarcenet with various muslins. English poplin at four and six with the Irish at six shillings the yard. Throughout, she flicked over her fingers, mumbling amounts, only to end by turning to him in exasperation.

"Oh, for goodness' sake, Jack, what *will* it be if I need seven yards for a gown? And this? And this?"

She marked it all down in a small pocketbook, adding, as she went along, the various prices of ribbons, lace, and feathers, silk stockings, cotton stockings, sandals, half boots in kid, half boots in jean, long gloves and short gloves . . . "Dear me, only four shillings. I wonder if they will stand up under washing."

But at Grafton House in Bond Street, she became so excited at finding silk stockings for only twelve shillings the pair that she decided to purchase on the spot. Jack took her firmly by the hand and guided her out into the street.

"But, Jack, they were sixteen or more everywhere else," Madeleine protested. "I could probably get . . . five pair for the price of three!"

"Four," he said, tucking her hand in his arm. He informed O'Hare, who was in charge of the carriage, that they would be walking to the top of Bond Street.

"Well, even at that," Madeleine said.

"Even at that," Jack repeated. "Mady, you've come to a point of making plans that I feel should include me. For one thing, I don't want you spending the money your family saved to send you here. I shall buy your stockings and gloves and—"

"Jack!—"

"Quite honorably. After we are married. Which, with a special license, need only be two days from now."

"Oh, Jack, Jack, I thought we had done with this," she moaned. "Why can't you understand?"

"I do understand, the only issues of importance. I love you, and you love me, and you wish to help your family out of their financial difficulties. Naturally, I wish that too. What you evidently don't understand is that I am in a position to do it."

Madeleine looked up at him, startled. He nodded and went on. "Given the chance, I should have explained all this to your mother or brother or both of them together. You are remembering that I mentioned having no income from my estate. Until recently, you've seen me going about in clothes that had been packed away since I was a lad of—oh, Lambert's age. Apparently the two together have fixed you in the belief that I have nothing but a Rochester portion."

"I—I don't know what that is," Madeleine said, her breath almost suspended.

"Two torn smocks and what nature gave," he smiled.

Madeleine was incapable of returning the smile—or of making any response at all. But he continued without pause. "I don't mean to give the impression now that I can lay claim to vast riches. I cannot, of course. But I've been saving for some time. One of my economies," he smiled again, "was not to have a new wardrobe made up for what I knew would be very temporary measurements. At any rate, I've a total of sixteen thousand. Ten left me by my mother. The rest accumulated. I've been reinvesting the income, along with half my pay. So, at this stage, it is bringing me eight hundred a year."

Madeleine breathed again. What, in heaven's name, had she been expecting? That he was going to suddenly reveal himself as a wealthy nobleman in disguise? Not that it wasn't a deal more than she had been imagining.

"Mady?" Jack's voice broke in on her brown study.

She looked up, shaking her head. "Jack, I've never doubted that you would be willing to help. What you don't realize— even if you were to strip yourself to nothing, which I could not in any event permit you to do—it wouldn't begin to cover what is needed. Our estate must be restored from one end to the other—besides being heavily, heavily mortgaged. I'm sorry—sorrier than you will ever know—but what you suggest won't answer. I simply must—"

Jack cut her off. "I cannot believe you would trade away the rest of our lives merely as an expediency. Repairs and mortgages can be dealt with over a period of time."

"Oh, Jack, it is far from a case of mere expediency. Patrick has been waiting seven *years* to take up his rightful place as squire of the district and master of the hunt. And there are my sisters. Marriage—at least for a female—cannot just be put off until convenient. And Lambert. He must be started in a profession if he is to have time to make anything of himself. And Nurse can think of nothing but returning to the country of her birth to—" her voice failed slightly "—to pass what little time she has left."

"Well, Mady, I have answers for these things, if you will open your mind and listen." After a crackling silence, he asked, "Are you saying you won't even do that?"

"Oh, I don't know," she breathed on a weary sigh. "I just don't know. It is more complex than you imagine, Jack. I must think how to explain it properly to you. But you've taken me unawares with all this, and suddenly I feel pulled to death. Take me home. Grant me a night to go over it in my mind."

But the night brought only sleepless conflict, leaving her little better prepared for such a debate when the sounds of Jack's carriage penetrated Fanny's snug little breakfast parlor the next morning.

Madeleine set down her cup and went to the door, convinced that her unhappiness was complete. But no. Apparently it had been Charles and not Jack she had heard a moment ago.

"Oh, how is this?" she demanded, as she crossed the railed area fronting her cousin's house. "You said you would be tied up with country parties until the end of the month."

"Measles," Charles replied succinctly, holding the low, iron gate for her. "Come along. I'll take you to meet my sister."

"Indeed, no! I am engaged for today, Charles."

"Suspected as much. Is it that duke of limbs I saw dragging

you up Bond Street, or have you been gathering every tag-rag in London for your court? Whatever the case, leave word that he's seen the last of you. We've an agreement, remember."

She did, but only then. She had stipulated to see just those gentlemen recommended by Charles or his sister. It hadn't seemed important at the time.

She tried to calm him by pointing out that their agreement was not to begin until the first of April, but Charles was having none of it. His attractive brown eyes narrowed in warning, and she sighed. She resented his using his power over her in this way, but it was going to make no real difference. She had already decided not to go on seeing Jack. There was just no other way.

"Oh, very well," she said dully. "But you must grant me a few hours to explain to him."

They both looked away at the sound of another carriage swinging into the square. Naturally it was Jack, just in time to make things thoroughly awkward.

It was impossible to avoid an introduction, but to her horror, Charles shook hands, saying, "Fear you're in for a disappointment, Ashton. Mad'leine didn't expect me back in Town just yet. Naturally, she'll be engaged to me from now on."

She stifled a gasp. "Jack, I must explain—"

"A tinker's budget, old girl," Charles drawled. "A man whose been about the world long enough to earn the rank of major don't need such things explained to him. Am I right, Ashton?"

Jack's hard, questioning stare settled on her like a hundred-weight, but if she dared to challenge Charles now—to make a mockery of his words—his stupid jealousy might carry him to any extremes. She mustn't. She *couldn't*. There was entirely too much at stake for risk.

"It would appear so," Jack said finally. He was replying to Charles's question but speaking directly to her. After another long pause, he added, "I trust you know that you are giving me no alternative but to take my leave."

"I—I'm sorry, Jack."

He made her a curt bow and turned back to his carriage.

It took every scrap of resolution not to rush after him—not that she had the smallest intention of letting it end this way. She was already making plans to pursue him into the very chamber of his inn, if he would hear her no other way. However disappointing he might find her decision, it was as nothing to what he must be imagining now.

She turned to Charles, struggling to show no more than cool disdain. "Well, having caused all this unnecessary unhappiness, perhaps you'll take yourself off for a while. I must change into something more suitable for a morning call."

"You're fine as you are, and I'm not the flat you seem to think me," he said slowly, a searching frown in his eyes. "Climb aboard, unless you're ready to exchange a rich husband for that rattle-boned soldier."

She had no alternative, but he kept her away until minutes before dinner. She was almost feverish with impatience by the time she could dash out a note to Jack. Her cousin's manservant took it round to the Fox and Bull, but too late. Jack had settled his reckoning hours ago and gone off with no word of his plans.

And with the entire metropolis now at his disposal, Madeleine could think of nothing but to mount slowly to her chamber and cry herself to sleep. Fortunately, after a night's rest, her mind became more productive. "Imbecile!" she abused herself, hurrying to dress in the cold room. "Lord *Hanbart!*"

It had suddenly occurred to her that there must be some official that Jack kept informed as to where he could be reached. And who, for heaven's sake, was in a better position to advise her than Lord Hanbart? Lord Hanbart of the *war* office! And she was to meet him that very night at dinner.

The hours between seemed something of an eternity, but at last she was making her curtsy before him—a plain man, thickset, and considerably more than double his wife's three and twenty years.

He greeted her with a little reserve, but few men managed to remain so in her company, and it was no time at all before Madeleine felt free to present him with her problem.

"Well, of course, my dear," he assured her, after hearing her out, "I shall be most pleased to make inquiries for you. Unfortunately, I shan't be in Town again until the day after next."

Madeleine curbed her impatience. It would doubtless take her treble the time without his help.

But those two days cost her her last chance. Lord Hanbart reported apologetically that Jack had left London just the night before, and the country, on the morning tide.

"Oh, but how can this be?" she demanded. "There was almost a fortnight of his leave remaining. Only four days have passed."

"Unfortunate. Most unfortunate. And difficult, I know, for a young lady to comprehend these matters. But, my dear, Lord Wellington is winding up to begin his spring campaign. Naturally, in his position, Colonel Ashton must be heavily involved."

"Major," Madeleine corrected distantly.

"Ah, well, here I am able to be the bearer of a little good news. Your major was promoted to lieutenant colonel in response to a recommendation by Lord Wellington himself. A decided honor that. You may be very proud of him."

Madeleine nodded politely, but she had no appreciation for military achievement and should have preferred him to be a major and comfortably within reach.

Glancing up, she saw that his lordship was observing her with a degree of sympathy. He said, "I should like to make up a little for your disappointment, my dear. I shall engage to include a letter in the dispatch case leaving for Portugal—provided, of course, you can get one together for me now."

Madeleine assured him that she could, and he rang for his butler, who showed her into a small saloon, equipped with an elegant escritoire and a large branch of candles.

But after one or two strokes to the cleft in her chin with the feathery tip of her pen, she saw the complete hopelessness of trying to make Jack understand with a hastily written letter.

She must see him once more—if never again. So she wrote only:

"Jack—if you truly love me or ever have, you will not deny me a hearing. You are wrong, you know, in what you suppose to be my relationship to Charles Morland. Just as there are reasons, very powerful reasons, why I couldn't marry you. I am begging that you will grant me one more opportunity to explain it all to you properly. Promise that you will contact me the very instant you are next in England."

With ingrained economy, she snuffed out all the candles on the desk and conveyed her letter personally back to Lord Hanbart's austere office at the extreme rear of the house.

Coming away, she paused to think that if Charles's imbecility hadn't interfered, she'd meant to end things with Jack that day. Would she have seen as swiftly as she did now that a future with no Jack was an unbearable thing to contemplate? Even a future that left them so little held some comfort and reason.

Yes . . . but for the moment she was conscious of only a deepening sense of deflation. There had been so much tense relief in having some means of communicating with him that she hadn't stopped to realize that it would take weeks for him to receive her letter and weeks more for her to receive his.

Yet there was nothing to be done about it but make a dissatisfied face and continue along the spacious corridor. At least she *would* hear. There was no longer a question of that, and it was something. In the meantime, having done all she could she would simply have to give some of her attention to matters at hand. For the next several days, this centered mainly on a more careful analysis of her new sponsor.

She found Lady Hanbart, if a bit of a quiz, not nearly as shatter-brained as her fondness for Charles had seemed to suggest. Beyond allowing him to run tame in her house, disrupting arrangements with his erratic habits, she maintained a fairly efficient establishment. Or as efficient as was possible, with Charles taking his dinner there almost every evening. And not only his own dinner, but including one or more of his cronies.

Mostly they were younger fribbles like himself, but among them, now and then, was the excessively arrogant French Baron de Beauvoir of just slightly fewer years than Lord Hanbart.

Madeleine couldn't help remarking, one evening after rising with her hostess to leave the men to their port, that it was rather surprising for Charles to have such a friend.

"Oh, but quite suitable company for him," Lady Hanbart assured her. "I desired Hanbart to look into his background, for I must own that I was a trifle surprised myself. However, his lineage is both impeccable and impressive. One of the *ancien régime*, you know." She paused and shrugged. "Still, at present, one cannot think of him as really much more than just another of the many *émigrés* waiting out the war. Naturally his lands have all been confiscated by the Bonapartist government."

"Well," Madeleine remarked, choosing one from a group of straw-colored chairs in her ladyship's enormous drawing room, "he has at least solved the riddle for me as to why Frenchmen are sometimes called Frogs. To be sure, he looks a little like one. Long legs, short, squat body, and great bulging eyes."

FIVE

If Madeleine was able to count her Season a success on the grounds of popularity, it threatened to pass without so much as one suitable prospect, and left her, by the end of May, facing the terror of total failure. Then, suddenly, she found herself confronted by a rather drastic half-solution in the form of a proposal from a wealthy merchant, met quite accidentally in Grosvenor Square.

She returned from this interview, a trifle stunned, to Lady Hanbart's drawing room, where her hostess was busily acquainting Charles with news of this development.

"If you marry that damned cit," Charles raged before Madeleine had even taken a seat, "you'll be throwing away everything we've been running wild to achieve. And what the devil, I should like to know, did Hanbart mean by making such a rum touch known to you?"

"Oh, Charlie," Lady Hanbart intervened, "he cannot be blamed, truly he cannot. Well, I ask you—what *could* he do, when we ran flat up against them in the hall, and Mr. Toggle would just stare, trancelike, at her? Hanbart daren't offend him just when he is negotiating for his ships to carry supplies. And—well, he *is* rather a good sort in his way."

She sighed heavily and turned to Madeleine. "But it is true. So very, very true. You'll not set foot in another fashionable salon if you *marry* him. I mean . . . well, I need scarcely explain. Oh, indeed, Madeleine, you must wait and hope that someone more suitable will happen along."

Madeleine lifted her eyes from a somber contemplation of the figures on her skirt. "If in all this time no one more suitable has happened along, it would be madness to bank on it now. No," she said flatly, "I simply cannot let this opportunity slip by."

"I'll tell you what you *will* do," Charles retorted, scraping back his chair. "You will wait until I can speak to Menard."

Madeleine stared blankly, then gasped, "The *Frenchman?* The one you've been dragging to dinner all these weeks?"

"Oh, your pardon! You forgot to mention that this husband was to be young and handsome, as *well* as a damned Croesus!"

"Don't be absurd. Mr. Toggle is far from young or handsome. It is that your baron is uncommonly repulsive—and more in manner than appearance." She took the cup Lady Hanbart passed to her. "Besides, this is nothing to the point. He is plainly in no position to—"

"Oh, he's well up to your price, Madame Gilflurt. Just hasn't been counting your worth as high as you. Why the devil do you think I *have* been 'dragging' him to dinner?" he growled, slamming out of the room.

Madeleine looked after him and shook her head, sure that

nothing would come of this flight. The frightful baron had had ample opportunity to pursue the matter himself had he wished. Yet, by the end of the week, she was somewhat shaken to learn that he was now prepared to come down with the full amount.

"How the devil you can sit there humming and hawing is more than I can say!" Charles seethed. "It offers everything you dashed well wanted."

"Except that I shall have to live the rest of my life in a foreign country."

"Oh, the devil! So far as society's concerned, you'd as lief live on a desert island as with Toggle in the *City!*"

She needed no reminder of this. Claudia had belabored the point at such length that her bulky letter had cost almost the last penny Madeleine possessed. And no more did she need to be told now that there was no real choice left to her. Not if she were to provide a respectable address from which Dorothea and Jane could make their own marriages.

So, on the twentieth of July, in two ceremonies to satisfy the separate religions, Madeleine became the Baroness de Beauvoir. But there was no consolation for her in a title so glaringly foreign. She stood composedly throughout the long bride's reception, but, if not *Lady So and So,* in the English fashion, she would have much preferred a simple *Mrs.*

"But baroness you are and baroness you will remain," she said a short time later to a mirror image of herself at her new home in Leicester Square. She was still ravishingly gowned in a robe of Brussels point lace. Lady Hanbart had insisted on giving her this luxurious bridal ensemble for a wedding present.

Madeleine started as her new maid, a flamboyantly pretty creature known as Beker, indicated that she was ready to help her undress. Madeleine submitted without comment, but her thoughts flew off immediately to Jack. He had not written with the promise she had begged of him. And now, of course, he would hear of this marriage and possibly never understand or even care what it had cost her to turn from him to a husband she thoroughly detested.

Apprehension soon mingled with revulsion when she was left

to pace the coldly impersonal chamber that seemed wholly dominated by its out-sized bed. Yet she couldn't help a wintry smile as she caught sight of herself once more in the ornate looking glass. There, at least, was a familiar sight. The old nightdress that had seen her through many a summer at Harrogate. Beker had gasped in horror at the mere sight of it.

Madeleine studied its faded pattern. Well, she had had neither the funds nor the inclination to purchase the sort of nightwear that bold French maids might think appropriate.

Time passed with agonizing slowness. She had no way of judging how much, except that her legs had begun to stiffen from the tense exercise, and a great fatigue was beginning to war with her agitation.

She approached the bed, slowly, ambivalently. The thought of being caught off guard had seemed unbearable, but she was beginning to wonder fancifully if the odious little worm would just go away if he found her asleep.

At last she gave in and slipped beneath the somber counterpane. Yet each time sleep came, it was driven off by one of the many creaks and stirrings of the hundred-year-old mansion.

By morning, she was so fatigued as to actually wonder if it could possibly be a French custom to spare the bride that particular misery on the night of her wedding.

Madeleine might have been grateful, whatever the baron's reason, had his consideration extended to sparing her such torturous anticipation, as well. She was now so worn down as to doubt her ability to remuster resolution for the night ahead, and she found herself beginning to think irrationally of flight.

An insubstantial French breakfast did little toward restoring the tone of her mind. She waved away the chocolate, asking that tea be brought instead, and found herself against a stone wall.

Beker, she knew, did not speak English, but apparently no one did. No one except the baron, who had already left the house. Well, she was too relieved about that to wish for his aid, but she'd forgotten, if she ever knew, the French word for tea.

Finally she went down to the kitchen herself, and found the

area where vast amounts of chocolate and coffee were stored. "No tea?" she gestured. "No *thé*," she was assured.

Luncheon, though a trifle strange to her taste, was a more supportive meal. But no sooner had she retired to the drawing room than the butler threw open the large double doors for the announcement of Monsieur Morland.

Madeleine turned to him, her expression decidedly vexed. She had not thought to inform the butler (if indeed it would have been *possible* to inform the butler) to refuse all visitors.

"I hope you had enough sense not to ask specifically to be shown in to *me*," she said when left alone with Charles.

He threw himself onto the sofa. "Are you playing off airs, or is it possible you haven't realized yet that the baron is well up to the rig?"

Madeleine's thoughts began running riot. He was as much as saying that the pair of them had *planned* a sharing of her.

Charles, watching the wariness come into her eyes, spoke up. "Now don't be looking as if I'd come to rob the house. It ain't as though you didn't know this was a marriage of convenience."

"Yes, but what I wish to understand is why he should be making it so *convenient* for you."

"Part of the terms I'd arranged, naturally. Said you wouldn't accept him without a nod from me."

"I see. And he believed you. And I, of course, have no difficulty believing you capable of it. But that still leaves me to wonder why he ever *agreed* to your terms—if, as is becoming apparent, he didn't want me himself."

"Don't be a featherhead," Charles bade her kindly. "Of course he wants you. It's—" He broke off to gesture. "It's as though you were that chair there. Some sort of French antique. Once the old boy took it into his head to want it, he ended by outbidding everybody to get it. But it wasn't because he planned to *sit* in it."

Madeleine widened her eyes, and he shrugged. "Just his way. Likes to be envied his possessions. Just as he once took pride in being at the head of society. In France, that is. Don't much like the English. But he likes less being at the back of things, and with the war dragging on, he decided to shove an oar in. For that, he needs a hostess. An English hostess. Once he'd made up his mind to it, he wouldn't hear of anything less than a veritable diamond. It's as simple as that. You're it!"

Madeleine sat quietly, one brow raised, as she digested this. It was at last becoming clear why Charles had been so eager for her to accept the baron. But as it fully sank in that the baron had no intention of *ever* sitting in his expensive chair, she became so giddy with relief that she might actually have embraced Charles in sheer gratitude, except that it was necessary to make him understand that he couldn't sit in it either.

The next several minutes gave her less cause to be grateful. For Charles had kept a few cards back. Part of the terms he had imposed on the baron had been that he must keep a tight rein on his new wife.

"I have no intention of allowing poachers on my preserves," he added with cool finality. "No lovers, no flirts, not even cicisbeos. No freedom of *any* kind, but what I choose to sanction. And I'll tell you right now," he continued, rising, "the baron don't care for anything but political dos. So, as far as the amusing affairs about Town are concerned, you'll go with me or not at all."

He left her then to consider her situation.

She did, and took the first opportunity to see if Charles had been speaking the truth. She was outraged to discover that he had. Not that the baron admitted to the unsavory arrangements. He merely replied crisply that, yes, certainly it was true that he had no intention of entrusting his wife to any but his good friend Charles.

"This is positively gothic. Can you really be saying that I am to be kept a prisoner in this house?"

"Madame, do not disgust me with the language of your English stage. When I choose to accept an invitation into mixed company, you will naturally join me. During the day you will be free to pursue any activity that does not require the escort of a gentleman. We have already established that you may accompany Charles to such affairs that do. It is as much freedom as any wife has a right to expect. We will not discuss this again."

Madeleine saw the uselessness of trying to win him over and swirled away, hoping that he was better pleased with his ugly old chair. She had never felt so despised in all her life.

But she decided philosophically to devote her free evenings to thinking up menus and making plans to redecorate the house. During the day she would visit various furniture warehouses and—dear God, yes!—*Twinings*, to get in some tea.

She was at least permitted to order her tea. Not personally, of course. There was a housekeeper for that. As for interfering in the management of the house, there was the baron's cousin, a darkly attractive woman, whom Madeleine discovered at dinner would continue to reside with them. Nor did the house require furniture or new hangings or paint. Marie had seen to that. The baron was pleased with the result.

And there's an end to that, Madeleine thought with an apologetic glance at Marie. But apparently the baron's translation to his cousin had not included those tactless references to her taste, for she showed no resentment at all.

A few days later, Madeleine ordered her new carriage and directed her coachman to Hans Place. Fanny rushed out of the house to greet her. After an exchange of affectionate hugs, Madeleine signaled to the tall footman, standing on the rear of her carriage. "In here, Roget."

He carried in a large basket, laden with pounds of tea and sugar—both outrageously priced commodities since this latest war with America.

"And you are not to run the tea through twice anymore, Cousin Fanny," Madeleine said. "I shall see you have all you wish while I remain in England."

She had brought monetary gifts for the three servants—all so kind and helpful during those Spartan months. But by the time she had succeeded in banishing Fanny's grateful tears, Madeleine felt she could endure no more affecting scenes and left the gold coins in folded notes to be distributed later.

But there had been great satisfaction in being able to make

these gestures, and soon, of course, there was the first letter from home.

"Hunterfield in now wholly free of encumbrance, and Harrogate left behind us forever," Claudia wrote. "Your sisters and I are putting up at the White Horse while repairs are underway at the house."

Madeleine smiled to think of them. Nurse determinedly ensconced in her old quarters, alternately caring for and bullying Patrick, who was already deep in the business of getting the estate in order. Aunt Heartha temporarily with Mrs. Micklefell and delighted to be "home at last."

And if each plus seemed to have a minus these days, at this stage, it was merely that Lambert, whose recent arrival in Town had brought so much comfort, had used his share to buy into a regiment that was bound almost immediately for the Peninsula.

"Just think, a fighting regiment, Mady!" he said, downing a third cup of chocolate. "Oh, not cavalry, but that isn't everything, after all."

She had certainly believed it to be, so often had he bored her with talk of it. But he was pleased with his choice and almost beside himself to be going, and for that and for him, she was happy too.

"Well, then—" He seemed suddenly a little shy when he rose and came over to kiss her cheek. "Well," he said again, "I shall take my leave now. And thank you, old girl. It could never have been without you. Don't think I forget it."

He paused again. "Er—you are pleased with your own lot, Mady, now that you've settled in? I mean it *is* what Mama and you were always used to say you wished. This London high life. The title and carriage and all that?"

She thrust him toward the door. "Don't be a goose. How could anybody with a title and carriage and all that be less than pleased? Why, my quarterly pin money is more than you shall earn for sleeping in tents and risking your neck the year-long."

His face brightened. "Can't argue with the truth of that," he returned with boyish pride as he crossed the checkered marble floor and accepted his hat from the porter.

No, even she couldn't argue with the truth of that, Madeleine thought, refusing to succumb to memories of Jack. They haunted her constantly throughout the long, empty evenings. There had been no sign of Charles since that first day, and she wondered if he had guessed the effect of leaving her to the loneliness of this cold, French-speaking house, just when she had been depending so heavily on diversion to see her through.

There was some relief, of course, for she did entertain; if not with frequency, with a fair degree of regularity. It was the one area in which she was allowed to exist in Leicester Square. And the one atmosphere in which she could lose herself.

She had full charge of these affairs. No one interfered except regarding the guests themselves. Naturally there was always a list of stuffy political cronies to include. But in his position as spokesman for the Royalist *émigrés*, the baron felt it his duty to show appreciation to the men in arms against Bonaparte. So she was ordered to extend general invitations to the officers of such regiments and ships, as well.

Nothing could have suited Madeleine more. They were mostly a gay and charming lot, and there was the decided solace of being able to dance now and then. Still, she wasn't too surprised to discover the inevitable worm in the rose. She noticed that Marie seemed always to be hovering near. Madeleine would move casually away, only to find her at her side once more.

Madeleine shrugged it off with the rest. The language barrier made it impossible for Marie to interfere beyond assuring that she didn't slip from the room with one of those eager young men—something she had not the slightest wish to do.

A week later, during one of these affairs, Madeleine glanced up and saw Charles shouldering his way into the circle gathered round her.

"Tempted to suspect you've been having an uncomfortable time of it while I was at Brighton," he said, drawing her away from the group, his deceptively innocent brown eyes betraying an unkind amusement.

Madeleine kept her temper by wondering how he had contrived to remain so pale down there in the seaside sun. "And obviously you hurried off to Brighton to assure that I should," she replied, with no sign of the violence she was feeling.

"Well, it seemed a good notion to give you a taste of how things might be if you were to disappoint me into staying away for good and all. However, there's the Carver ball at the start of the week, and I knew you shouldn't wish to miss that."

She met his gaze squarely. "If you are inviting me in the belief that I am now ready to become your mistress, Charles, you will be well advised to withdraw the offer."

"No, no, the offer stands. And others, as well, if you like. It's time for a new lesson. A taste of what you've been missing. You've seen society only as a debutante—with all the restrictions that a married lady needn't endure. If not before, I'm betting you won't think twice if it comes to spending the spring Season as you've spent the summer."

Madeleine glared at him. She would not think twice; she would not think of it at all. Her family would be down for the spring Season. Then let the baron explain to Patrick, if he dared, that he could not entrust his wife to the escort of her own brother. After? Well, with reports of Wellington's victories all the talk in town, the spring might be her last few months in London. In any event, the time to worry about was *now!*

They went on famously for a while. Charles escorted her to every conceivable function. And he had changed. Almost, but not quite, he had hidden himself behind the agreeable pretender she had known as a girl. She suspected that his object was now to try if he could seduce her with charm. He'd catch cold at it, but it was decidedly more agreeable to deal with his false charm than his honest roguery.

As autumn drew to a close, however, a squabble broke out. Madeleine became filled with a desire to visit her family during the fortnight before Christmas. The baron would be entertaining on Christmas Day, but she promised to arrange everything beforehand and to be back in good time to hostess the party.

When the baron refused, after a day's consideration, Madeleine went straight to the source. "Why, in heaven's name, did you say I mightn't go?" she demanded of Charles as they set out to attend a play. "You'll be away with your own family for Christmas."

"True, but there's no saying that's really what *you've* in mind."

"Oh, great heavens. If that's what you think, escort my coach. You were always used to stop in Yorkshire in the past."

"At Harrogate. Miles and miles of difference. Besides, I haven't kept you wrapped up and new all this time, only to turn you loose among the haylofts of your youthful flirts."

She argued through all three acts, but nothing would convince him that there was no cause to think of such things. He seldom thought of anything else.

This time, however, Madeleine was determined not to be herded about as though she had no more rights than a dumb beast. When the time came, she simply sent Beker to hire a chaise and joined the vast parade of traffic rattling along England's Great North Road.

It seemed an incredibly short ten days later that she was once again viewing the same scene, for she was heading south again by the twenty-second of December.

She had drawn reluctantly away from the new splendor of her girlhood home just as all the preparations for the gala Christmas celebrations neared completion. But she had promised herself that she would break only the unreasonable rules of her marriage. The party in Leicester Square was her first responsibility.

However, shortly after crossing into Bedfordshire on the twenty-fourth, with a good six hours of travel between them and London, Madeleine and Beker were tumbled violently across the front seat and kept jolting there until the postilions managed to bring the team of alarmed horses to a stand.

Madeleine paid no heed to the long, technical explanation concerning her mishap. It was enough to know that something-or-another on the carriage had broken in two and that progress would be impossible until it could be replaced.

After considerable delay and much confusion, a local gig was acquired to convey Beker and herself to the Cock at Eaton Socon. But nothing Madeleine could do would get them farther. It being Christmas Eve, no one could be found willing to make the repair. Nor, with Sunday coming right on the heels of Christmas, was there any hope of help for the next two days.

With every conceivable form of transportation booked for the holiday, there was plainly nothing but to bespeak rooms and wait out her time at the Cock. Unfortunately, Fanny, knowing her plans, would be on thorns over her failure to appear. So Madeleine posted a letter first thing, giving a full explanation of her dilemma and promising that she was perfectly safe and comfortable.

She was indeed that, if excessively nettled to have sacrificed the fine Christmas she'd helped to prepare at Hunterfield only to drift aimlessly from a cheerless bedchamber to a small private parlor that she had been lucky even to get.

Finally, on the Monday, Madeleine received word from the wheelwright that her carriage was ready for the road. However, with dark coming on so early these days, nothing could be gained by setting out before the next morning.

So she tried for an early night. But the inactivity of the last days made her entirely too restless. With a murmured oath, she pitched out of bed and dressed herself again to go down to the parlor.

Just as she approached the first landing, she was swept by a rush of chilled air, as the front door burst open and an army officer, wrapped from chin to ankle in a heavy, dark gray cloak, pushed into the empty hall.

Madeleine rounded the bend and stood stock-still, poised just as she had halted, one gloved arm resting along the banister, one small, slippered foot ready for descent. Her dark head, held high a moment ago with cool assurance, tilted a little in uncertainty. Then the very room seemed to brighten with the breaking of her smile, and she began to grope for her skirts.

"Jack!—Oh, Jack, it *is* you!"

SIX

There was no answering smile, but Jack was forced from his unreceptive position, for she was all but flying down the rest of the way. He shot forward, snatched her from the fourth step, and swung her to the floor.

"In the name of God, Mady, you'll break your neck, running like that on the stairs!"

"No, no," she laughed, her head flung back. "Nothing bad could possibly happen to me now!" She closed the fingers of both hands tightly over his arm. "I couldn't be sure! And then I couldn't *believe* it! But this cannot be a coincidence," she said breathlessly. "Yet?—Oh! Cousin Fanny, of course. She's had my letter."

"Cousin Fanny, to be sure, but she's had no letter. I found her in a rare taking, imagining you'd been abducted or robbed and left by the road without a meg." He studied her a moment, then said, "I collect you're on French leave, so she was afraid to contact . . . anyone else about the matter." Glancing off at the sound of footsteps, he said with unfamiliar harshness, "But we shouldn't be discussing all this in a public room."

"Oh, no, no, you're right, of course," Madeleine agreed, still laughing from her excitement. "And doubly foolish, since I have a private parlor just here," she added happily, while she waited for him to gather up his hat and gloves from the floor near the fire.

Once inside the small, paneled room, Jack unfastened his cloak and cast it over a chair. Madeleine ran a swift glance over his white, leather-cuffed trousers, then let her gaze feast on that rather dazzling scarlet and gold taper, from wide shoulders to a trim, white-belted waist.

"Well, it's small wonder I had difficulty recognizing you," she said. "I expect it's just that you've recovered your normal weight, but you seem so large from what I remember. So tall and broad and with a look of power about you that is"—she gave a little shrug. "Well—*almost* frightening."

Madeleine was still too overcome to realize that much of this impression sprang from a stern, unrelenting countenance—despite the fact that she was studying it, as well. In a thinner state, the weather-toughened skin and small, crinkling lines about his eyes had make him look a trifle haggard and somewhat older than his years. But now, combined with that healthy, squarish face, they struck her as devastatingly attractive.

"And I've never seen you in your uniform. *Most* dashing," she said, catching his hand. "But come. Sit down. So I won't be thinking you are going to vanish at any second. I am really all on end. There must be a hundred more important things, but I can think of nothing but to ask—if my cousin *didn't* receive my letter, how you knew where to find me."

He let her draw him to the fire but, ignoring her invitation to sit beside her on a small sofa, took a chair opposite.

"Is it truly going to amaze you to learn how few unescorted ladies—even without notable beauty—have passed through the toll gates of the Great North Road? *Or* booked rooms at a posting house, long-known as a favorite haunt for sporting bucks?"

If the sting in his words didn't wholly deflate Madeleine's euphoria, his next remark did.

"Of course, I had only your cousin's word that you *were* unescorted on this spree."

Madeleine caught her lip between her teeth, her mood plummeting with the recollection of how many long, unpleasant explanations stood in the way of the happy reunion she'd been envisioning.

"Very well, Jack, I am more than ready to own that my spree, as you call it, was imprudent in a great many ways. But don't expect me to regret it. Not when it provided the very means that enabled you to find me." She fixed him with an inquiring glance. "I trust you are convinced now that I *am* alone?"

"Since the breakdown of your carriage, at any rate."

"The object of this journey was solely to visit my family," Madeleine returned, holding her temper.

Her thoughts flooded with a consciousness of how foolishly

she'd behaved in the face of their situation. She cast him a glance from under long, dark lashes. "You must have been thinking me quite absurd these few minutes. It's just that there have been so many months of believing I would never see you again."

"A logical end in the circumstances," he remarked. "Except that your letter was phrased in a way to make that impossible— as plainly you'd intended it to be."

"Yes, I hoped it would have that effect. But then you didn't answer . . ."

"Well, you needn't mourn for your effect. I am answering as promptly as could be expected. I received your letter less than a month ago."

"A month," Madeleine gasped, startled out of her depression. "But—good God! Lord Hanbart assured that you would have it by May at the latest."

"Hanbart? Of the war office?"

"Yes, he was very kind and—"

"That at least explains how your letter came to be in a dispatch bag."

"He told me it would leave England sooner that way."

Jack nodded wryly. "I expect it did. Unfortunately, it fell just as quickly into the hands of a Yankee privateer."

"The Americans!" Madeleine exclaimed with vexed enlightenment. Yet, after a moment, she asked hesitantly, "Are we not still fighting with them?"

There was almost a smile when he replied. "We are. But apparently there's another romantic in their own war office. I received your letter with a note explaining that the seal had been broken in the belief that it was one of our official documents. I can only guess that it must have been put into the hands of one of their naval officers, with instructions to pass it along. It reached our navy through a Portuguese fisherman."

Whatever misunderstandings might still exist between their two countries, Madeleine had just made a private peace with her transatlantic cousins. She said wonderingly, "They must have seen how much it could mean to me if you failed to recieve it."

If there had been any lightening in Jack's mood a moment ago, the steel was back in his gray eyes when he spoke again. "It escapes me why it should mean anything to you at all— *baroness*."

"Oh, Jack, as to my marriage, I explained so much of that already. I thought you understood a little."

"Did you? I wonder why, when I told you that I did *not* understand. *Or* agree that such a sacrifice was justified." He paused, his whole manner condemning. "But then, 'sacrifice' is the telling word, isn't it? Lambert arrived in Spain with apparently little else in the way of conversation. So God knows I've heard enough and to spare about your great satisfaction over this conquest."

"Jack, that isn't fair. What else *could* I say to him, when he was going off to war, worrying that his happiness might have been bought at the expense of mine? Whatever disappointment I was suffering was no concern of his."

She came almost out of her seat to reach across and cover the hard fist resting on his knee. "Jack, if you've come in response to my letter, it was to let me explain. Then let me."

The hand moved under hers in a curt gesture of consent, but he drew back, folding both arms across his chest and stretching out his long legs, almost as if to form a barrier between them.

Madeleine sighed and settled back herself. At least he was here and willing to listen. It was more than she had dared hope for some time.

"You see," she went on in a low tone, "Lambert had a right to all that came to him from this—this 'conquest' of mine. They all had. I know you were thinking that matters could be dealt with another way—with compromises and a slower progression. But it was too late for that, Jack. Years and years too late. Because, by then, everyone had been scrimping and slaving away with something altogether different in mind. And—and I had already promised myself to them. Not just once but a hundred times and in a hundred ways."

She raised a hand in an unconscious gesture, then paused and extended it for him to examine—smooth and soft, with creamy white skin and long, beautifully manicured nails.

"You've paid me compliments on these hands. Did you never stop to think how it was possible to keep them so? We had no servants, you know. Whom do you suppose saw to everything? The cookery, washing up, scrubbing, laundry, firewood. All the thousands of little things that constitute keeping house and caring for a large family. You must certainly realize that none of it could have fallen to me."

She let the hand drop into her lap. "And there is something else I never told you. Those papers that I begged you to retrieve for me on the very day we met . . . They were sketches and notations from Cousin Fanny to guide us in our manufacture. Yes," she nodded as his brows drew together. "By night, our kitchen became a factory for the production of ladies' hats. Willow shavings, you know—or more probably, you don't—can be purchased, ready-woven into flats, for just a shilling. But Patrick learned how to procure the willow and weave them himself. Dorothea shaped them into bonnets and hats, and Jane—from the time she was scarcely ten years old—tied and clipped each one before Lambert painted them—well, it was actually a dye, but he had to apply it tediously with a brush. All this time, Nurse and my aunt sat by, sewing endless ells of satin and other materials into caps. And my mother trimmed the whole."

She gestured again. "In the matter of the hats, I was permitted to help a little. I shopped for supplies and knotted a few ribbons. But the others saw to everything else. Everything! Working as servants during the day and laborers by night. Earning, saving, doing without. Without heat and even proper food much of the time. And all the while I was forcibly pampered— left only to watch and wait for the time to do my part. Jack, do you not see? Surely you must. *Could* I—if I would—just drop a note from London saying that I no longer cared for the bargain? That instead of all the things they had been working for, I meant only to give them another opportunity to scrimp and toil again—this time on the estate?"

She fell silent and watched him, seated there as though he had been cast in stone. At length, he asked in a voice rigid with control, "And what had Morland to do with all this?"

"He had everything to do with it, Jack," she said tensely. "I needed his help. Desperately. It was when I realized that what you said was true—that I couldn't succeed without a sponsor of greater connection than Cousin Fanny, that I thought of him. Of his sister, really. You see, she is Lady Hanbart."

Jack's eyes glided back to her. "And—" he prompted with a hard, steady look.

She turned her gaze to the fire, smoothing the soft fabric of her gown over one knee. "I swear to you, Jack, he only made you think there was something between us, knowing I didn't dare contradict him. And I *didn't* dare! Everything was depending on his sister putting me in the way of the right people."

Madeleine waited expectantly for a time, but needing to break the heavy silence, she insisted, "Jack, you are too reasonable and fair not to understand. Say that you do."

For the longest time, he just sat, staring back at her expressionlessly. Finally he flicked a hand in a gesture of futility. "I understand that the walls about you were too solidly built to have ever been breached. That you yourself were too well primed to have acted other than you did. Is that fair and reasonable enough?"

It was. Just that and no more. She supposed she ought to be satisfied, but she couldn't help herself. "Jack, if you can allow my provocation, can you not forgive me, as well?"

He rose wearily. "I daresay. Can it possibly matter?"

"It matters all the world to me," she said, reaching out and closing her fingers over his wrist. "Don't stand. Sit here beside me, Jack."

He tensed at her touch. For all the changes he had been observing, she had lost none of her magic, her power to enchant. But he'd come expecting as much. Young officers by the dozens arrived at the Peninsula, toasting her charms.

Not that he'd needed these reminders to know that he still loved her—probably always would. But those same young officers also had plenty to say of her obvious position as Morland's mistress. She'd explained Morland's hold over her before her marriage, but that could have nothing to do with after. And talk of them, seen constantly together, had become too un-varied to be doubted.

He was forced, nevertheless, to gather some resolution. A circumstance that was making him as angry with himself as with Madeleine. His tone was cutting as he pulled free of her. "Obviously your husband is astonishingly complacent, but I hear that your lover is not. Aren't you being a trifle rash? Or are you expecting me to play Jeremy Sneak for Morland's benefit?"

Madeleine sprang to her feet, her own temper breaking out at last. "I don't care what you've heard. I explained about Charles, and I have no lover, drat you! Nor is my husband complacent. Why do you imagine I have been put to such shifts merely to visit my own family?"

"I *cannot* imagine. It is just one of the reasons I am finding it so hard to believe it *was* just to visit your family."

"Oh, no. It is that you are finding it hard to believe *anything* to my credit. What hope have I against such an attitude? Plainly there is nothing I can say to convince you."

She moved abruptly to the door and spoke to someone in the passageway.

"What the devil are you at?" Jack demanded.

"I have sent for my maid, hoping that you will be able to accept from *her* the details of my 'spree.'"

"Don't be stupid," he lashed back.

But Madeleine was already waving Beker into the room. "The colonel wishes to question you. Answer truthfully," she ordered as the girl stepped interestedly in.

Beker took leisurely stock of the situation, then broke into a delighted smile as she exclaimed, in the painstaking French she used when conversing with her mistress, "Ah! But all be-comes reasonable now! I tell myself, not truly does madame *la baronne* arrange all this just to visit Mama!"

Madeleine drew in an outraged breath, then released it in exasperated relief. There could be no denying that the abom-inable Beker had, in her way, supplied the very vindication she had been seeking. There was even the ghost of Jack's old smile as he spoke to Beker in her own language.

Madeleine waited while the two indulged in a long dialogue, too swift for her to comprehend. When at last Jack closed the door behind Beker, she demanded, "What on earth were you two discussing at such length?"

"Owing that you said I wished to question her, I thought it best to do so. I asked what she thought of the English countryside. She doesn't care for it. You'll be relieved to know, however, that she has no objection to the country inn. Although she suspects this may be only because the ground is presently too hard for hunting."

Madeleine smiled faintly. "The aforementioned sporting bucks, I take it."

He nodded. "She is also pleased that you are now to have some amusement, as well. It seems that you have been something of a crosspatch since the breakdown of your carriage."

"Yet she must surely believe that I contrived that breakdown in order to arrange this assignation."

"No, in light of your impatient efforts to find other transportation, she believes we were to have met elsewhere and that it has taken me all this time to find you. I explained, of course, that there was no assignation. That I was merely sent from London to effect a rescue." He shook his head. "But I shouldn't stake a groat that she believed me."

"Capital. Now perhaps you will understand how vexatious it is to be doubted when speaking only the simple truth."

"If you will allow that your own witness justified that doubt by sharing it herself."

Madeleine's smile became steadier. It was almost as though no time lay between them any longer. She nodded. "Yes, I can do that. Partly because I know the whole world would support it—given the opportunity."

"Evidently you mean them to have that opportunity," Jack returned. "A truly mad-brained start, to have made your maid a present of this situation. I might have slipped off to another inn and no one the wiser."

"To another inn?" Madeleine shot back. "No, no. We cannot

be wasting time while you hunt hopelessly for a place at this season. You must make do with this parlor for the night."

Jack just shook his head. "There seem to be no bounds to your capacity for imprudence. Don't you know, or don't you care about the repercussions that could arise from such a thing?"

Supposing her own bridges already burned, Madeleine wasn't concerned for herself, but it occurred to her that those repercussions might easily fall on Jack. If the baron could be persuaded to bring an action against him . . .

"Yes," she said, speaking out of her reflection, "but there's no need to use your true name."

This actually surprised a short laugh from him. "I'm beginning to think I've wandered into one of Sheridan's plays. It was of your reputation I was thinking. Do you never think of it yourself?"

"To what purpose?" she asked with a sigh. "I have it on your word that such things are already being said of me. The important thing—for us *both*—is that without a genuine person to accuse, no open scandal can result." She added wryly, "Nor, for that matter, will it make sufficiently interesting gossip to survive the week out."

"Let us return to the things already being said of you— which *do* involve a 'genuine person.'"

"Oh," she sighed again, "very well, but only while I assure you that they have no more basis in fact than Beker's conviction that I came away on this journey to meet you. I expect it is just human nature to try to make things more interesting than they are. But, don't you see—that is why we mustn't concern ourselves with what they have been saying. Or with what they are apt to say simply because we have passed a few hours under the same roof. Let them. I care only for what you believe."

"And I take it you are wanting me to believe that Morland is not and never has been your lover."

"Yes."

"To just accept that on faith and say no more about it."

"Yes."

He had been watching her closely, but at this he looked down, gazing intently at the space between his boots. When he raised his eyes again, he said, "Do you have any notion how hard that is? Flying in the face of all reason? Of so much evidence to the contrary?"

"Isn't that the purpose of faith? At all events, we must come to it in the end, Jack. I have no one to speak for me in that regard." She paused, her eyes intense and searching, a deep green in the subtle lighting. Finally she said, "Jack, I *promise* you I have no lover."

He nodded after a moment, his own look as penetrating as hers. "Just a husband who is not complacent."

"But not in the sense you are thinking! He has no *feeling* for me. Not a jot. I am no more than an ornament about the house. And not one he admires overmuch at that. It is just that he restricts my freedom so unreasonably. No, no. Let us not go into that either. It is the very reason I am begging you not to waste this opportunity, Jack. You can have no notion what a miracle has arranged this comfortable setting for us. Do let us leave all these tiresome explanations for a less perfect moment."

Jack smiled openly for the first time. Except for her fine feathers, perhaps she hadn't changed so very much after all.

Madeleine smiled back in relief. "Come, let us make this into an adventure. You are used to going about incognito. Now I may share in the fun. What name shall we have for you?"

She sank down onto the sofa, insisting that he not disturb her while she gave the matter careful consideration, then decided almost instantly that he should become Colonel Edelmar Croft. She laughed at his pained expression, but before either of them could speak, there was a knock at the door.

Madeleine looked up with alarm, but it was only Beker, come to tell them that it would soon be too late to get food from the kitchen. "If the colonel is hungry? . . ."

"Yes," Jack said, thanking her. He followed her from the room, adding to Madeleine that he would use the time before the meal to inform O'Hare of the plan.

Madeleine paced about, waiting for him to come back, too filled with undefined need to sit quietly. But his return brought no relief. The waiter, bearing his meal, followed almost immediately on his heels and began busying himself with the large table in the center of the room.

She moved away to a smaller one in the corner and remained there, toying with the bits of stiff paper spread over its surface.

Jack poured a glass of wine and joined her.

"Isn't it strange?" she asked, indicating her project on the table. "It's a map that has been cut into hundreds of fragments. The object is to piece it together again. I've been finding it quite compelling."

"And making excellent progress," he observed, "for one bent on introducing China into the West Indies."

At last the door closed quietly and they were alone. Without conscious thought, Madeleine turned herself into his arms, her voice little more than a low, pleading whisper. "Oh, Jack."

He held her so tightly that the tips of his fingers bit into the slenderness of her back. "Mady, Mady, what a damnable tangle you've made for us."

She pressed her face deeper into his shoulder, unable to command her voice. Finally she drew back, whispering, "Your food will get cold."

He shrugged.

"Flattering but impractical," she said softly. "Come. If you've been searching the North Road all day, you must be in need of something hot and nourishing. Furious with me as you were, I'll wager you didn't stop for a proper meal."

"Scarcely the thing when off on a mission of rescue," he agreed, following her to the table.

Afterward, he joined her on the sofa, propping his boots on the seat of a straight-backed chair and lying back. Madeleine sat quietly beside him while he sipped his wine, then snuggled under the arm he used to draw her nearer.

An hour or so passed comfortably. Tender talk and tender kisses. But then Madeleine found herself becoming a little unnerved by the arm that held her close—or rather the hand attached to it that caressed her own arm. So large a hand. Properly placed one minute and, with the barest movement, alarmingly intimate the next.

It was becoming all too plain that she was heading rapidly for a predicament. She knew that for a married lady of her world such a progression was not only accepted but expected. But she was not a married lady. At least she didn't feel like one. And besides, she hadn't been reared in that world. Nor, if it came to that, had Jack. Of course, men went on quite as they pleased in any world, but one would *think* he'd recall how furious he had been just minutes ago, when he'd suspected her of having a lover. She was glad to have recalled it herself, for it would make it easier to deal with a situation that was fast becoming decidedly worse.

"Jack," she said, shifting away from him a little. "Pray don't spoil our lovely evening by flying into a pet, but this is not at all the thing."

He stared at her, a little stunned, then incredulous. "Mady, what the devil *is* it that you want of me?"

"I—There is only one thing left for me to want, Jack."

"A trifle ambiguous that," he replied, "but I expect you must be harking back to that business of wishing us to go on merely as friends."

"Yes, of course," she said, coloring slightly.

"I wonder if you have the smallest notion of how thoroughly unsatisfactory such an arrangement would be to me. Rather, I must say—how thoroughly impossible."

"Jack—Oh, I daresay I can understand that you might feel so just at this moment," she said, vexed with herself for having let things get so far. It hadn't occurred to her to be seriously concerned. Jack had mentioned his desire in Squire Macey's old barn, but it hadn't struck her as an overly strong emotion. It was just one of the things that had made him seem so wonderfully different from other men. She loved him no less, but she couldn't help thinking it a great pity that he must turn out to be so very like them after all.

She laid a hand on his arm in appeal. "Won't you try to think differently on calmer reflection? Perhaps it will be best if we discuss it in the morning. I—I think I should go up now, if you don't mind."

Jack looked even more disbelieving. "If I don't *mind*—?" he repeated, a touch of fantasy in his tone.

Yet out of this frustrated fascination, something else emerged. An easing at the back of his mind. A slight elation. He had agreed to take her on faith concerning Morland, but it came to him now that he must have continued in vague doubt. These rather unrealistic notions of hers, however maddening, had at least removed that doubt. Not that *he* had ever entertained notions of this arrangement. Not before she had left them no alternative. Nor had he meant to tolerate it any longer than necessary. If there were a way in the world, he intended to find it and marry her yet. In the meantime . . . Well, the matter of Morland made it a good bit easier to summon his patience.

He kicked away the chair he'd been using for a foot prop and stood, smiling down with a little effort. "No need to look so Friday-faced. I shan't spoil the lovely evening. Very well, we'll go on as you suggest. At least until I've had time to think how to rectify the situation. In the meantime, I very definitely agree that it would be best for you to go up now."

Madeleine flashed a look of concern over what he might mean by *rectify the situation*, but she was not about to prolong *this* one herself. She smiled gratefully and took hold of the hands he extended to her.

SEVEN

Whatever else her failings, Beker was skilled and efficient in her work and had her mistress up and ready to depart for London in good time the next day.

Jack was waiting at the foot of the stairs when they came down, Madeleine outfitted for the raw weather in a traveling habit of deep blue, her hat spilling a feather of the same color down one side of her face.

She waved gaily to O'Hare as she stepped into the waiting carriage, then made room for Jack under the heavy lap robe. Beker had already settled herself on the forward seat.

They set off a cheerful, talkative party, but as the day became steadily colder, Madeleine found herself less and less inclined for conversation. She almost sighed aloud when they reached Baldock and Jack ordered the postboys, now so thoroughly muffled up that only their eyes were visible, to gather up the bricks from the floor of the carriage and have them reheated.

While fresh horses were being poled up, O'Hare darted into the tap room and fetched out a tray of steaming mugs for them all. Madeleine made a slight grimace as the fumes of strong spirits assailed her nostrils, but she drank hers down fatalistically. It was hot, and that was all she could bring herself to care about at the moment.

Jack, meanwhile, had managed to purchase a blanket from the reluctant innkeeper—a frightful old rag, which he cut in two. He gave half to Beker, then, placing the other over Madeleine's shoulders, set about bolstering their spirits for the chilling stage ahead by pretending nonsensically to be very much grieved that it didn't match her feather.

They made good time for the next hour, but, as they neared London, the clipping pace of the horses began to slow more and more perceptibly. Madeleine had been watching the great tails of fog floating about the carriage and didn't wonder. But when the horses were eased to a walk, she stared out in dismay. There should have been a good hour of strong daylight left, but nightfall seemed to be overtaking them by the minute. Finally, an impenetrable blackness brought their progress entirely to a halt.

"How strange it is," she said in an awed whisper. "One can almost *feel* the darkness."

Jack produced a tinderbox and lit a small, fixed lantern, then made to open the door. Madeleine caught his arm.

"I shan't go far," he promised. "But you must see we cannot simply sit here. I wouldn't hazard a guess as to the temperature, but it is easily the coldest in memory."

She let her hand fall. "Yes, of course. It's just I have never seen *black* fog—and this strange, strange cold. It's fanciful, I know, but it makes one think there mightn't *be* a world out there anymore."

"I promise you there is. And 'dear Edelmar' is going to see you safely through it."

She laughed. She had been teasing him with the name during the first part of the journey.

Apparently Jack found the postboys in the same state of awe as herself. Madeleine heard his rallying voice chiding them through the darkness. "Come along, lads. There's nothing for it but to get down and lead 'em along. One of you walk ahead to be sure we keep the road. Talk as you go—or sing, if you like—so your chum can follow the sound of your voice."

Then he called into the nothingness behind the carriage. "O'Hare, are you there?"

"That being jest what I was wondering meself," a disorientated voice called back.

"Tie your mount to the carriage and bring yourself forward. We've work to do."

Madeleine drew the tattered blanket more closely about her and settled back with a smile.

Soon the chaise began moving again, adding to the comfort of Jack's matter-of-fact handling of the affair. But after a half hour at an inching pace there was a new terror. A crude face suddenly pressed itself flat against the carriage window, causing both Madeleine and Beker to start violently.

But no sooner had its distorted features appeared than they were jerked roughly away.

Beker, crouching in dumb fear, began what promised to grow into unrestrained hysteria.

"Don't be absurd," Madeleine said sharply, doubting that

her own nerves would stand up to such a display. "There is nothing to fear. Can you not see that the colonel has attended to him?"

"*Le colonel* cannot be in all places at once," Beker whined reasonably, her scared eyes fixed on the opposite window.

Lilting accents sounded as if in response. "Ah, would you?" There was a ghastly thud, a grunt, and O'Hare's voice again. "And maybe one day you'll be telling me how you like the touch of good Irish oak."

"There," Madeleine said. "The colonel is quite accustomed to planning in such situations."

Another hour dragged by before the monotony was relieved by a new collection of sounds. The first was a spate of furious oaths from their foremost postboy, when he discovered an approaching coach halted right in the center of the road. Thanks to his loud, if inelegant speech, both vehicles were spared collision.

Then there began the constant cries of foot passengers, calling out in a well-founded fear of being run down. "Who is coming—" "Mind!—" "Take care!"

Next there was the sound of more scuffling nearby. All ears within the carriage were on the alert, and Beker's scream ready in her throat as the near door was flung open. But it was only O'Hare, bearing his master's compliments. He spoke to Madeleine as he walked beside the creeping carriage, his useful shillelagh ready in one hand, an enormous pistol tucked reassuringly into his belt. "Me colonel was just wanting to assure your ladyship that he'll be up with us in the twinkling of a bedpost."

Madeleine had kept her composure through all else, but the news that Jack was no longer with them was quite another matter. "Where *is* he?" she gasped.

"Ah, now, he's but a few steps behind, me lady. Him having a couple of ruffians in tow and wanting to tie 'em to a lamp post so they won't be atroubling us again. Nothing to be concerning you or the mamzell. Only a pair on the rattling lay."

"What in heaven's name is that?" Madeleine demanded, glancing apprehensively over her shoulder.

"Just the business of slipping up behind the slower coaches and cutting away the baggage, me lady."

"I see," she said, considering this, then voiced another concern. "I expect they'll be found before long. It's so terribly cold."

"Oh, aye, me lady. They'll set into bellering once they reckon me master is safe out of tongueshot."

Jack, with more consideration for the ladies' nerves, announced himself before pulling open the opposite door. O'Hare gave a nod and shut his.

"Oh, J—my dear," Madeleine said, catching hold of his hand. "I am grateful, of course, but if we should encounter others who will be content with the baggage, do let them have it. You mustn't risk yourself in such a cause."

"There was no question of risk," he said calmly.

Madeleine smiled at this new facet of him, but said in a rush of feeling, "I can't even think what should have become of us if—Yet how horrid and uncomfortable for you. Having to—"

"If you feel sympathy is due me, promise never to go off like that without an escort again."

Madeleine nodded, and he squeezed her hand and closed the door to resume his post beside the carriage.

Such dangerous progressions were taking place all over what would soon be known as "the lost metropolis." At much the same time, three other gentlemen, each well-known to Jack, were suffering much the same hardship. The Prince Regent, proceeding toward Hatfield, was obliged to turn back after several hours, his extensive cavalcade managing to get no farther than Kentish Town, where one of the outriders ended in a ditch. The Secretary of the Admiralty, on a journey northward, made a progress of only three or four miles before putting back. Of them, only Lord Castlereagh, owing to an early start, succeeded to the continent, where he was at last to begin peace talks with the Bonapartist government.

Jack, drawing heavily on his every resource, managed, after many, countless hours, to deliver his own party safely to Leicester Square. When the correct house number had been located with the aid of a linkboy, he tapped gently on the carriage door and swung it open.

Madeleine awoke with a start and ventured a hand outside her muff to take the one he offered. "Goodness, I'm not certain I can move. Beker, if you can, run into the house and send out one of the footmen to carry in the baggage."

Beker nodded but took the time to deliver effusive thanks to the brave colonel, so strong, so wise, so gallant.

Madeleine followed her down onto the paved walk, laughing uncertainly. "Well, only fancy, my feet *are* still there. I expect I shall find that my ears are, too."

It had been agreed that they would meet in Hans Place on the following day, but Jack said quietly, "You mustn't go out of the house until the fog has lifted, Mady. This whole thing is having its effect on the superstitious and impressionable. I've been hearing such phrases as 'the portent of doom' as I walked along. In that kind of atmosphere, even the usually harmless will commit acts of mayhem. There have already been accounts of females coming to grief on the streets. Agreed?"

"Agreed. Very well, then—if not tomorrow, the day after," she whispered and hurried to her door.

But there was to be no question of tomorrow or the day after or the day after that, and she soon fell into a perfect fret. Charles was due back and would learn of her unauthorized journey into Yorkshire. She'd been prepared for a reprisal—had even faced that it might take the form of restricting her to the house during the day. It had seemed well worth the risk at the time, but that was before there had been any hope of spending those days with Jack.

Then the fog disappeared as mysteriously as it had come, yet left her no better off, for it snowed incessantly, a heavier fall than could be remembered by London's eldest citizens. Next, a short thaw left the streets over a foot deep in mud and snow and all but impassable, so that by the time the weather made it possible for her to reach Hans Place, the new year was well underway and Madeleine found only a note from Jack, saying that business would now be demanding his time for a while.

She could see only one piece of good fortune out of it all. Charles, along with hundreds of others, had been kept snow-bound in the north.

Surprisingly, however, Charles proved no problem when at last he called. Madeleine pondered this, but supposed she ought to have guessed that the baron might prefer to conceal his own inefficiency in the matter of her escapade. Not that it wasn't a relief, whatever the cause, but new concerns had already begun to replace the old. Weeks had slipped by with no word of Jack, and by the end of the month she could keep back no longer from applying to Lord Hanbart for news.

He was willing enough to oblige, but Jack's mission had been of so secret a nature that even his lordship found it hard to get anyone to admit he had been in England at all. In the end, he could learn nothing except that Colonel Ashton had left the country more than a fortnight ago.

Madeleine forestalled depression by indulging in a towering rage. The stupid, stupid—*stupid* war!

But Jack had not returned to headquarters as supposed—merely undertaken a rather tricky mission in Paris. He was back, and trying his best to reach her through the great snows long before Lord Hanbart had discovered he was gone.

He arrived on the evening of February fourth and had himself driven to Leicester Square, where he scribbled out a message to Madeleine, saying that he would await her at the usual place in the morning but couldn't depend on being in Town for more than a day. Smiling a somewhat humorless smile, he signed himself as "Edelmar," then lounged back in his hackney carriage, a watchful eye on the servant's entrance.

Not long after, a small fellow, probably a page, hurried to-ward the house. He took the note, but admitted that he could do no more than try to pass it on to the *baronne*'s maid before he retired. "*En vérité,*" he added, accepting Jack's coin with a sly grin, "it isn't hopeful that she *will* return in time, that one."

Beker, Jack gathered, made a habit of slipping off on ama-tory adventures whenever her mistress was from home. But it offered the perfect opportunity to assure that his message was delivered before morning. He settled back for another long wait.

It was just after one o'clock when he caught sight of Beker making for the house. She was willing enough to do whatever he wished, but told him that he could easily deliver his message himself. It had been the *baronne*'s intention to attend the Frost Fair directly after her musical party.

"And where, *mon amie*, does one find a frost fair?"

Beker laughed and explained that a part of the Thames had frozen solid and become the center of a gala entertainment. Anyone in London could direct him to it.

She pocketed the coin he pressed into her hand but protested that she had done too little to earn such a handsome fee. With a seductive glance at the coach, she added that they might safely depend upon the *baronne* to remain quite late at the fair. Naturally, she would not wish to overlook any of the activities.

Jack laughed at that. Certainly not if he knew his Madeleine at all. But he merely recommended that the lively Beker get into the house before she caught cold.

He learned from his jarvy that the Frost Fair was being held on the stretch of river between London and Blackfriars bridges and asked to be taken to the best inn nearest there.

A short drive saw him settled at the Queen's Arms in St. Paul's churchyard, where he dismissed O'Hare to his own pleasures and set out on foot for the river. It was close at hand, and in less than a minute he could hear the mingled sounds of merriment.

Just as the street joined the Thames, there was one sign announcing a safe footway across the river and another, more colorful, designating this temporary crossing as FREEZELAND STREET.

But a gateway had been erected at the waterstairs and an "ice toll" of twopence was being exacted by the watermen. Jack queued up impatiently behind a pair of citymen who were disputing the charge.

One of the larger watermen came forward, booming hotly

that the river was their livelihood and they weren't about to be done out of it just because it had become frostbound. "Hire a boat or pay the toll," he challenged, planting great square fists on his hips.

Jack tossed him a coin. "Let us through."

"Right you are, general," the waterman chuckled, catching it deftly. "A sow's baby opens the gate for three."

Waving away a lecture on "The Principle of the Thing," Jack pushed past the two outraged citizens and proceeded over the ice. A pathway, strewn with ashes, twisted between vast heaps of snow left by the shovelers and the jagged mounds of ice upheaved by the river in its final bid for freedom.

This led him to a grand mall, complete with another signpost proclaiming it THE CITY ROAD. It ran lengthwise down the center of the river and was bound on either end by the great, snow-laden bridges dramatically outlined in the moonlight.

The entire way between them was packed with ornamental tents, sutler's stalls, and entertainment booths—all gaily decorated with brightly colored flags, streamers, and signs. Jack walked along, amused by the selection. Booths for bakers, butchers, and barbers sprinkled amid stalls offering books, toys, and trinkets of every description. And each item fixed with a label stating that it had been BOUGHT ON THE THAMES.

Behind the central stalls he found more novelties. Swings, plays, Punch shows, skittle alleys, sliding barges, and round-abouts with gaily painted steeds. But most popular at this hour, of course, were the drinking tents—filled with wild young men and women dancing reels to the excited strains of fiddles—and the inevitable booths offering gaming in all its varieties. Everything from EO or *Rouge et Noir* tables, to teetotum, pricking of the garter, and wheels of fortune.

After a few minutes, Jack stopped to take stock of the situation. At this point, he'd have been better pleased to forgo the chance of seeing Madeleine tonight rather than think of her exposed to such a set of company. Young bucks and beggars alike had drawn their last sober breath hours ago. The "women of the town" had begun to romp in and out the drinking tents with their bullyboys or tipsy gentleman, and there was no reason to suppose that thieves and rogues of every description weren't working their way most profitably through the crowds of fuddled merrymakers.

But he couldn't help a slight smile. There was even less reason to suppose that Mady had seen the state of things and gone prudently home. No, she was out there somewhere, enjoying herself to the full.

But finding her was going to involve a closer, more methodical search. So he marked his location and set out again, stopping to examine the crowds packed in and around each display, cursing himself all the while for not thinking to ask Beker what her mistress was wearing in the way of outdoor garments.

At intervals there were printing presses—Jack counted at least eight—all cranking out ballads commemorating the Great Frost Fair. Or, if one preferred, other documents, on which one's own name could be printed as a testament to his presence at this rare event. Everything, sacred or profane, was eagerly purchased as soon as it could be set and rolled from these enormous presses.

A sheep being roasted on the ice seemed to be another great attraction. Jack shouldered his way among a large, noisy group who had paid sixpence just for a glimpse of the spectacle. The meat itself was being sold under the name of "Lapland mutton" for a shilling the slice. Or, at a nearby fire, one was invited, for the price of a few pence, to "Fry your own Sausage in the middle of the Thames."

The savory aromas teased Jack's nostrils, reminding him that he'd had no dinner. He moved on with small hope of being allowed to forget it. The place abounded in savory aromas. At every turning he seemed to encounter a perambulating pieman or a hawker of hot gingerbread or oysters at a few pence the dozen. Yet, as tormented as he was becoming by it all, he was determined not to stop for a meal until he had found Madeleine.

He frowned down a side path to his left, doubting that even she would have ventured into the drinking booths to stand cheek-by-jowl with the majority of London's muslin company. But knowing her love of dancing, he headed at once for a vast barge. He found a good-size orchestra and dozens upon dozens of performing couples, but no Madeleine.

On his way back, he was accosted by a peddler of confections and surrendered to a small sack of brandy balls. These he could at least pop into his mouth while he continued his search.

Then suddenly there she was. On the back of a small donkey, trotting toward him at a nimble pace.

When she caught sight of him, her smile of amusement burst into one of the greatest joy, but she tugged on the reins with no effect. "*Stop*, you nonsensical creature!" she commanded in laughing exasperation.

Jack, laughing himself, was forced to act swiftly, for the young animal was clearly bent on rushing her right past him. He swung to the side, catching a rein with one arm and Madeleine with the other, as she flew from her seat, partly in eagerness, partly as the result of her mount's abrupt halt.

"Jack! Oh, Jack. Oh, I was so unhappy, thinking you'd returned to the army! But how——? Well, it could only be Beker," she exclaimed, taking advantage of her loss of balance to hug him briefly. Steadying herself on his arm, she glanced down, laughing in the way she did when she was excited. "Isn't he the dearest creature? Do you think he will return to his master if we just release him? Oh, never mind. Here he is just coming."

The donkey's attendant came up and took the reins, but lingered, working the leather in his hands, obviously bewitched. Jack watched him with sympathetic amusement. Madeleine was indeed looking very like an enchanting snow queen, cloaked as she was in flowing, scarlet velvet, all trimmed with white fur. He was even more amused by the matching hat, set at a rakish angle and bearing strong resemblance to a French busby.

She gave the fellow an inquiring smile, and he mumbled that she'd not 'ad 'er shilling's worth of ride.

"Oh, but I have," she returned, catching Jack's eye merrily.

"He has taken me, like a magic carpet, to precisely the place I wish most to be."

Her beautiful face still aglow as the young man led his donkey away, she said, "Really, it is a little like magic, Jack. I was just thinking how desperately I wished you were here to share this with me, and suddenly you appeared. The most wonderful thing! And— But, speaking of wonderful things, what have you in that intriguing sack about to tumble from your pocket?"

He told her brandy balls, and she gave him a quizzing smile. "So, you've been succumbing to some of the pleasures already." She accepted the sack and fished one out. "Um, yes, excellent. I have been planning to sample the gingerbread as well. Only it is all so fascinating. Just fancy, Jack—a fair right in the middle of the river! And the last we are ever apt to see, by all accounts. They say there hasn't been one in over seventy years."

"Yes, I've heard that mentioned some thousand times or more. Er—may I have my brandy balls—or at least one. There's every danger that I may die of starvation. Also in the middle of the river."

Madeleine gave a startled laugh and passed him the sack. "But, my dear, how is it possible? With such a collection of foods so readily to hand? They are roasting a sheep somewhere—right on the ice! And sausages. And there are hot pies. Steak or mutton or kidney. And—well, just everything."

She took his arm. "All the same, I cannot help but be glad you haven't eaten. Now we may do so together. I haven't myself. There has been so much to see and do. I found a gypsy to read my palm. And I wished to try my hand at skittles and the coconut shy. And, of course, that darling little donkey. And I am still wanting, of all things, to take a turn on the roundabout and—But never mind that. We shall get you fed."

Squeezing his arm, she added happily, "I am so pleased. Not only that you are here, but now, instead of using this delightful affair merely to overcome my disappointment, we shall have it to remember together. You do think it madly exciting, don't you?"

"I do. What's more, I shouldn't doubt there are those who would think it too exciting for the eyes and ears of a gently bred female."

"Oh—but truly, Jack, everyone has come to it. The most respected of persons."

"I daresay. I expect it's merely that you've chosen an unfortunate hour. The atmosphere has become decidedly bawdy, and the not-so-respected persons are beginning to display themselves rather—Hmm, and, I think perhaps that is precisely what you have been finding so fascinating."

She gave him a look, half-playful, half-sheepish. "I must own I have. Well, one can scarcely help being fascinated by bits of life outside one's own rather narrow—Now, Jack, you aren't going to say that you think it wrong—?"

He shook his head slowly, his expression teasing and affectionate. "How can I? It's too much you." But the gentleness went out of his tone. "What I *do* dislike, and more than half, is that you've been in danger of receiving the grossest of insults— or worse. I assume you're here with a party, but I cannot help thinking them a devilish loose set to have left you to wander about on your own like this."

The color drained from Madeleine's face. The frantic mood of the fair, the sheer joy of Jack's unexpected appearance, had driven all thought of Charles straight out of her head.

She saw that Jack was watching her closely, a questioning frown deepening the creases at the sides of his eyes. Then, as if reading her mind, his gaze swept the area and fixed on a distant view.

She turned but without needing to. Yes, there was Charles, with all the untimeliness of death, standing in front of the gaming booth where she had left him.

"Jack," she began hurriedly, for Charles had seen her and was stalking over. "You must realize that there has been no opportunity since that first night to explain about him." She managed no more before her words were drowned by Charles's rantings, already well in progress.

". . . damned dependence on you," he ended as he reached

them. "What in hell do you mean by brushing off the minute my back was turned? You set down the wine I gave you to hold and when I wanted it, some crusty beggar was lapping it up. And you fouled my luck. How many times have I told you, when the luck is running, the least alteration can—"

Jack's presence at last penetrated his consciousness. Charles stared, his beautifully sculptured lips pursed in an effort of memory. "Acton—no, Ashton," he said, apparently weighing up the improvement in physique and costume, the dashing angle of Jack's cocked hat, the badges of office on his long, elegant military cloak. "Colonel now, is it?" Charles muttered. "And a top aide of some sort into the bargain."

These observations did nothing to improve his temper. "Good to see you again, Acton. You'll excuse us now," he said, taking firm hold of Madeleine and glaring down into her face. "Well, you've managed to queer all my pleasure, damn it, so come along and ride your rubbishing roundabout."

Madeleine had become paralyzed by the expression on Jack's face, one she had never seen before. But the harsh contact of Charles's hand brought her shocked senses to order. She gave her arm a quick jerk. But his hold remained fast. "It's no good, Charles. You may inflict what punishment you wish in the future, but I intend to remain with Colonel Ashton now."

Charles kept her arm, saying slowly and with heavy meaning, "Now, now, my lovely. I advise you to give a little thought to all those long, lonely nights and recall how sorry you'll be without me after you've come to your senses."

EIGHT

Before anyone could say more or even think, Jack broke the hold Charles had on Madeleine's arm and brought home a flush right to his handsome jaw.

"That was entirely for my own satisfaction," he hissed back at Madeleine as Charles sprawled over on the ice. "You are too obviously accustomed to his foul speech and rough handling."

He spun abruptly away, but Madeleine clung frantically to his arm. "No! Jack, I shan't let you go off from me like this again. You must let me explain."

"Explain?" the word exploded from him. "Explain what, confound you? If I haven't been listening to a man and his mistress enjoying a domestic squabble . . . No. Morland said it once, and rightly. I need no explanation. *And* no more of your damned lies!"

"*Jack!* My God, how in the world can you possibly doubt what you mean to me?"

"Oh, I don't," he returned with a look near to hate. "It's all become perfectly plain. You wanted a richer husband, a handsomer lover, and me as an amiable lapdog to round off your collection. Well, I don't fancy the role, so do as your *protector* bids and say good-bye before you lose him to a chill. I don't think he means to stand while I remain."

He tore from her grasp and strode off. She would have rushed after him again, but Charles caught at her cloak so viciously that she landed in a heap beside him.

She called to Jack in pleading desperation, but he didn't look back. The sounds of his furious pace enclosed him completely in a world of his own misery. Heels cracking hard on the ice, his long, heavy cloak slapping in violent rhythm against the cold leather of his boots . . . so completely that it was several minutes before he realized that he was heading away from his rooms at the Queen's Arms. His eye fell on a drinking booth. A hastily erected building, claiming to be the temporary annex of the Feathers in High Timber Street.

A full measure of brandy suddenly seemed the only worthwhile thing in life. But even this was not to be had. The publican had removed his regular store of drink some time ago. There was nothing but a quartern of gin left behind for the personal use of his help. The cheerful individual in charge set up a glass, urging Jack to settle for a little of the blue ruin instead.

He downed it with indifference and tossed another coin on the counter. A second dram was measured out, but he left it merely as the focal point for his unseeing gaze.

Suddenly it skidded down the length of the counter and crashed to the floor. In the next instant, Jack himself was thrown down, only to be bounced to a perfect upright again.

The attendant staggered toward the door to discover the cause. Jack, thinking he knew the cause, was before him. Only a narrow fringe of ice surrounded the booth.

"Gawd save us!" the attendant exclaimed in an awed whisper. "The ice is broke up. We're adrift!"

He set up a cry for a pair of colleagues, sleeping in the back beside a warm stove. But they were in no need of his warning. They'd been flung from their cots and only narrowly escaped the red coals cascading over the floor.

Jack braced himself. They were in for a crash. Several crashes. Before and behind there were more islands of ice, many, like their own, bearing small groups of startled people.

It was impossible to keep a standing balance for a time, but soon the pitching floor settled to just a gentle rocking, this, in its way, more terrible. It meant that they were now moving freely toward the narrow arches of London Bridge.

"Oh, lor', no!" cried one of the lingering customers, who had managed to drape himself in a window. "We'll be dashed to death!"

In a deafening whoosh, three sides of the building burst into flame, and the shouts were now against the probability of being burned alive before the treacherous pilings could do their work.

Jack and his fellow passengers, eight men beside himself, were forced to the only wall not raging with fire, their arms raised to shield their faces against the blasting heat. Those nearest the window began to struggle out onto the rim of ice.

"Oh—eeh!" one called. "There's a lighter broke from its mooring and coming up beside. Jump for it lads and ride it to the bridge. Then it's off into the water and a grab at the arches for them as don't care to be pulverized. There'll be somebody to haul us out."

A fair assessment. A reasonable hope. Maybe the only hope

for bringing themselves off. But there'd been a scream. A hundred screams. But something was telling Jack that he had heard Madeleine.

Incredible, he supposed, to imagine he might have picked her voice from the din of a shrieking crowd. But what did it matter? She was out there somewhere, he hoped well on her way to the safety of the waterstairs. But he wasn't about to commit himself to the water, and the convenience of those who must fish him from it, while there remained the smallest chance she stood in need.

Only the center of the river was broken up, carrying with it dozens upon dozens of colorful tents and stalls, all bobbing helplessly, like tiny boats amid the rushing debris and vast flats of ice. To the right and left there was still a good expanse of frozen bank.

While the other men scrambled to the corner where the lighter was inching closer, Jack skirted the burning wall to the opposite edge. More and more of the fair was breaking away, but there, amid the pandemonium, he saw her, white fur clearly outlining the scarlet velvet of her cloak.

She was half running, half stumbling against the panic-charged efforts of the crowds. Foolishly, uselessly, valiantly managing to keep abreast of his flaming raft and heading straight for disaster.

She could only have been within seconds of following him into the booth. It must have broken away and burst into flames almost under her feet. A miraculous escape. But she was sorely tempting a fate that had saved her once. The bank was crumbling away. At any second she could be hopelessly lost in the water.

Jack shouted and waved, trying to direct her back from the edge. Her arms flew out in a helpless gesture, and he could almost see her lips form his name. But she kept coming, unable or unwilling to grasp his order to turn toward land.

Jack tore off his hat, his sword, his heavy cloak, his gaze all the while calculating the distance to the bank. An impossible jump. The other men were calling hoarsely, trying to make him understand that his last chance to save himself had come. When they saw what he was planning, they shouted all the more frantically.

But Jack had seen the dangers himself, or he'd have already made his move. What use would he be to Madeleine if he ended up under the ice and unable to surface? Or in the water, only to be knocked senseless by one of a score of undulating hazards?

Yet at times it seemed he might get his chance. They were continually colliding with ice floes and debris. Sometimes the impact thrust them nearer the bank. But never near enough. And he could wait no longer. The ice was melting, the congestion clearing, his rate of travel increasing.

At least the fire was burning more selectively now. Jack swung himself agilely onto the roof. It was just possible that the added height would lend him impetus to dive clean across the breech and into one of the soft mounds of snow. It would require split-second timing and a degree of balance that was not easily achieved, but it offered the only hope of reaching Madeleine in a state of usefulness.

He stood on a jutting beam, amid lapping flames, and watched it happen. A section of bank snapped away and Madeleine flashed downward and out of sight.

Jack pushed off, forgetting the snow heap. Forgetting everything but the stabbing agony that had come with the vision.

He cleared the water and fishtailed his body in an effort to meet the impact with the heels of his boots. A thin covering of water helped a little with the terrific slide he took along one leg and hip, but the floor of ice had been hewn by a churning river and was heavily serrated and pocked.

He bounded to his feet, unaware of the dozen scrapes and bruises he had sustained, and ran like a madman to the place where Madeleine had vanished.

Only seconds had elapsed. If he could just reach her . . .

Then with the miracle his heart demanded, she reappeared, forced to the surface by the same sheet of ice that had taken her down.

Jack plunged into the water. Madeleine caught at the edge of her ice floe but hadn't the strength to fight the rapid current or the weight of her sodden cloak. Her grip gave way almost immediately, and she began to sink just as he caught her arm.

Jack's own strength was considerable, his body well trained. Yet only by a monumental will did he manage to hold them fast to the bank with one hand while he raised Madeleine onto it with the other.

But he could do no more. The shifting ice had caught him a thudding blow across one shoulder. His boots were like the hands of a giant enemy, pulling, pulling. He hung there, unable to rally the strength to drag himself from the water.

"Away, Mady! Away from the edge," he panted. "Crawl if you must. But get back!"

She was beyond speech but continued tugging frantically at the fabric of his coat.

Jack tried again in concert with her but shook his head and let himself sink back in exhaustion.

"It's no use," he said hoarsely. "Get back, Mady. Run for the stairs. It's going to go at any minute."

"Then come out of there, damn you," she sobbed. "For I shan't. I shan't budge from here until you do."

He looked at her in desperation, then heaved, strained, held, heaved again, and finally caught one leg over the edge. Madeleine snatched at the leg, pulling it farther onto the surface, and he gave a mighty thrust, contriving at last to lift himself from the water.

With a startling new burst of energy, he sprang to his feet, taking hold of Madeleine's cloak and dragging her bumping over the rough ice. And without a second to spare. The very spot where they had been struggling gave a resounding snap and rushed away with the current.

He'd felt it beginning to go but had had no breath to say so. Nor was there time now for apology. The ice was spider-webbing all around them. He pulled Madeleine onto his good shoulder and ran toward the waterstairs.

An enormous breadth of ice broke free under them, the

spreading crack just a few feet ahead. Jack slowed only to adjust his balance. It was like the deck of a great ship in rough
seas. Then he charged forward, clearing the widening span
with little more than a foot. He continued without a check over
the final yards to solid ground and dropped to his knees. His
breath came in deep rasping gasps.

Madeleine was safe but not for long. Not if she remained in
those dripping, frigid clothes. The exposed portions of his own
weather-toughened skin felt raw and cut away. Pain of inde-
scribable intensity shot through the areas trapped beneath his
wet, clinging garments. He could only imagine what she was
suffering. But there was no need to imagine the fatal chill, if
she weren't got warm and dry.

When Madeleine saw that he meant to lift her again, she
begged him to spare himself. To wait until she could walk. Just
a minute or two, she was sure. But Jack knew from experience
that minutes could mean the difference. He hoisted her, protesting, onto his shoulder again.

He took the short distance to the Queen's Arms at a run,
pounded up the outside staircase, and wrenched open the door
to his chamber.

There was a small coal fire burning in the grate. Just enough
to keep the deep chill off the room and light his way. He
dragged Madeleine's sodden cloak from her and threw it to the
floor, then pulled off his gloves and hers. Her hat was long
gone, and he thanked God for a fashion that had kept her hair
to a length that could be quickly dried. He snatched up a towel
and thrust it into her hands with orders to begin the process.

Madeleine found herself pushed unceremoniously onto a
chair near the fire. She pressed the softness of the towel gratefully to the burning skin of her face.

Jack, already on one knee, was unfastening her boots. He
slipped them from her feet, tossing them aside. Before she
could even realize the relief, she became aware of his hands
running up her legs, seeking out her garters.

Her startled protest was no more heeded than the soaked
woolen knots. He cut the garters from her, sliding her silk

stockings down and away. A second towel was produced and wrapped in their place. Then he was standing, pulling her upright beside him while the fingers of his free hand probed for the hooks on her gown.

"Jack, Jack," she gasped through chattering teeth. "In the name of God, do you mean to strip me bare? No, no, pray."

"Mady, you've got to come out of those wet things. Now! Nothing else matters."

"Yes, but—Jack, see to yourself. I shall manage my own undressing. And—and could you turn?"

He quite audibly ground his teeth. "There is too much to be done to stand idly . . ." He broke off to stare threateningly at a wardrobe, a huge affair, half the width of the room and nearly as tall as Madeleine. Lunging forward, he tore it from the wall in one violent jerk, then drove her none too gently behind.

"Then do it. And with no more fuss!" he ordered.

"Yes—no. But, Jack—Your own wet things . . ."

"I am attending to them now."

She could just see over the wardrobe, but he was nowhere in sight. While she worked with numb, sore fingers at the fastenings of her gown, she raised herself onto her toes. He was seated just the other side, wrenching off his boots with muttered indistinguishable oaths. He stood after two great thumps and had his coat and cravat off before she had undone half of her hooks. She turned away quickly. At the rate he was going, he would be without a stitch in an instant.

A blanket flew over the top of her makeshift screen along with instructions to wrap herself in it as soon as she was dry. Madeleine was still struggling with stay-laces when she heard a loud clanging and ventured another peep into the room. Jack, already in a dressing gown, had been scooping embers into a warming pan and was now busily at work on the bed.

"What the devil are you doing?" he demanded without looking back. "Get out here before you freeze where you stand."

Madeleine pulled her shift over her head and emerged, self-consciously clutching the blanket about her shivering form. Jack was heaping great mounds of coal onto the fire.

Her sense of awkwardness was short-lived and unnoticed. She was caught as quickly as she appeared and bundled between more blankets and the warm mattress.

Jack strode immediately away, found a bottle of brandy, splashed it at the top of a glass, and conveyed what contents he managed to catch over to where he had dropped her on the bed.

Slipping one arm behind her shoulders, he propped her up. "Drink it. Down, down. All of it!"

She did as she was bid, gasping and clinking her teeth on the glass. She couldn't control the violent shaking that had come over her. The heated bed seemed almost to burn where it touched her skin, but the warmth would not penetrate. She gave him a smile that seemed as if it might crack her face into bits, but at least the dreadful brandy had begun its work inside.

Jack, observing her trembling, told her to lie facedown. "Just do it!" he snapped irritably when she hesitated for only a second.

She turned onto her stomach without a word. She was in no state to pit herself against this slightly unfamiliar Jack who went about in a dressing gown, pushing and pulling and barking orders.

She was, however, all too familiar with the large hands that began working through the blanket over the entire length of her body. But she knew better than to object, even if she had had the will to do so. It was heavenly.

She moaned gently as the warmth returned to her limbs, and the hands became more gentle and caressing.

Jack shot to his feet. "I've got to get out of here!" he snarled.

It was like the physical loss of those limbs to have his hands jerked from them so suddenly. But worse, he was angry again. In her shock, she could only think that he was still planning to go out of her life now that she was safe.

She spun round and into a half-sitting position. One arm flying out to him, the blanket dropping away and exposing both firm, white breasts. "No, oh God, not now, Jack. Don't leave me. I beg of you," she pleaded, never thinking what response such words might bring.

By the time it was plain, it was too late.

One hand shot behind her back and she was drawn against him so tightly that she could barely take breath. The movement that took him under the blankets was so swift that she knew nothing of it until he was there, pinning her with his weight and as naked as herself.

His mouth found and invaded hers in rough, sensual imitation, leaving her screams to sound only within a shocked and horrified brain. No! Oh, God! Oh, dear God, no, no, no . . .

She pounded ineffectual fists against the hard muscles of his back, but Jack was no longer of this world. There was no response. No sound at all but her own muffled tones against a background of gently hissing coals and the rustling urgency of bedclothes.

She twisted and struggled with what strength she had. It would have been an insufficient strength at the best of times. Finally she collapsed helplessly beneath the driving determination of his passion.

Even when he had done with her and lay beside her, clasping her tightly in his arms, she was beyond the effort to free herself. Beyond caring. She felt nothing but misery and shock. Not just from the experience. Bad enough. But Jack. *Her* Jack. Suffocating her with those rough—What were they—kisses? They had seemed merely a violation along with the rest. Along with the bruising of her arms and legs. The searing pain. Oh, God, how abominably he had hurt her.

She squeezed her eyes tight. Was it only a month ago that she had been so relieved that their relationship wasn't to include this horror? Relieved and grateful, and she hadn't know the half. And if she had begun to wonder a little if it might, after all, be less disagreeable than Claudia had foretold, she wondered no more. Worse. It was worse. A hundred times worse.

For several minutes she lay in no doubt that, if Jack would only rise from the bed and wish to leave her now, she would see him go, and gladly. But he did not rise. He continued to hold her closely until the warmth of his skin became familiar enough to soothe away memories of bruising and pain. Until the strength and comfort of his arms banished most of her fury and disgust.

But first light began to creep through the window and comfort flew from her again. Whatever would she find to say? She didn't think she could even *look* at him. And what would *he* say? . . . What would he *do?*

Once more it began to seem that her Jack had disappeared at the fair. Someone very different had said cruel things to her there. And someone even more unfamiliar had returned to pull her from the river and then ravage her mercilessly.

He had taken her against her will once. Would he do it again? He had been brusquely impatient with her modesty. Would he now scoff at it altogether? Oh, God, would she be forced to parade herself before him or just lie in this bed forever?

These were the demons that invaded the room with the light and sounds of morning. Pinching at Madeleine's frayed nerves and filling her exhausted mind with irrational fears until she could no longer bear to wonder.

She stirred, saying tentatively, "I should like to get up now."

"Yes, of course," Jack returned, removing the arm that pinned her to him.

That much was encouraging. He sounded very like the Jack she used to know. "You—you were wearing a dressing gown," she ventured further. "What has become of it?"

"It's here—on the floor," he answered, but his mind seemed miles away.

She waited, then said firmly, "I shall have to have it. Everything of mine will be wet."

"Yes, certainly."

She breathed again as he leaned over the great distance and caught up the dressing gown from the floor.

He passed it to her without comment, apparently still too preoccupied to notice the edge of expectancy that hung in her silence. Or at least Madeleine was fervently praying that it was preoccupation and no more that made him go on staring in that curious way.

"Will you turn, pray?"

"Oh! Yes. Sorry."

But even as he made to roll over, Madeleine, grasping at a slowly returning confidence, spoke out hastily. "In truth, I should be better pleased if you would dress first. And—and could you go down to the coffee-room after? I should very much like to have the room to myself."

There was a slight pause before Jack replied. "Yes, very well. I must report in at the war office. It will take a little over an hour. But first there is something I must ask. It is too entirely incredible, but—"

Madeleine had wondered about that. Everyone said that men could tell. Yet, in view of his brutish persistence, she had reached the conclusion that it must be all a hum. But now his words put paid to that. He *had* known, damn his soul! A burst of fury exploded in her brain.

"Oh, incredible, indeed! To be sure, *I* am finding it so. To think that in spite of a perfectly odious husband and the dozen or so lecherous rogues with whom I've been forced to deal throughout my life, I have managed to avoid this hateful—*revolting*—experience, only to have it forced upon me by you. *You!*—"

NINE

Jack shut his eyes and brought the palm of one hand to rest on his forehead. After a long silence, he murmured, as much to himself as anything, "But how could I have *hoped* to guess? How the devil could it *be?*"

From this, Madeleine judged that it was something they could tell but not in time to be of the least use to anyone. She was, in any case, already regretting her outburst. Not for its injustice, but because it opened the very subject she wished most to avoid.

Jack had lowered his hand and was looking at her. She cut across his questions with a bravado she was very far from feeling. "I don't intend to discuss . . . *anything* with you."

There was another moment of silence while he seemed to waver on the edge of argument. In the end he only made a small gesture of defeat. "As you wish."

"Then will you go now?" she said, turning her back to him.

Jack had left the bed curtains flung open on the side near the fire. He slipped wordlessly out and drew them together.

Madeleine heard him pouring more coal onto the grate, then shuffling through his trunks. It seemed no time at all until he was back, dressed in a makeshift way and staring down at her again. She was lying on her back now and she opened her eyes, wishing to God he would just go away and let her collect herself.

"You may depend upon two hours of privacy," he said. "I'll be having a bath before I go. Not in here, of course."

"A bath," she repeated.

"I'll have one sent up for you, if you like. Don't fear to be found here. O'Hare's chamber adjoins this. I'll see he keeps out of the way, and you can slip in there once hot water's been carried up."

"Thank you."

Jack hesitated. "I could have O'Hare fetch you up a breakfast—if you wouldn't object to his knowing of your presence."

After weighing this, she nodded. "It will be impossible to keep him from knowing. I shall need him to fetch Beker with something for me to wear in the street. Just tea, however."

"Very well. I'll leave him at your disposal. He'll arrange for you tea, bath, messages . . . Anything else you may decide on. Admit him through the adjoining door. I'll take away the key to the other, so you needn't fear the maids coming in here."

He stayed, looking down at her for the longest time, making her shame so acute that it seemed she would strangle from the effort to keep control.

At last he dropped the curtain round her again. "Good-bye, Mady. I . . . I'm sorry."

She heard the door close and the key turn and sighed. A deep sigh of deep relief. She sat up, her head thrown back against the ornate headboard, her eyes once more squeezed tightly shut. She remained like that for a few minutes, then, shaking her thoughts away, struggled into the dressing gown and climbed down the short ladder attached to the bed. Her bare feet recoiled from the chilled floorboards.

Gathering up the surplus length of her borrowed wrapper, she headed instinctively toward the fire but stumbled. Glancing down, she saw that it was one of Jack's boots.

She picked it up mechanically and found herself examining it with an odd sense of wonder. Her eyes traveled to where its fellow lay, and beyond, to what had been once a pair of flawlessly white, leather-cuffed trousers. Near them, intermingled with her velvet cloak, her stockings, and her gloves, were a wide leather belt, a crimson sash, a pair of leather gauntlets, a shirt, and a scarlet coat—one sleeve dragged wrong-side-out. She stared at these things, affected she knew not how by the sight of all this male attire strewn about the bedchamber amongst her own.

She stepped backward a few paces and climbed up to sit on the tall bed, her bare feet resting on one rung of the ladder. Once again her gaze dropped to the wet boot still in her hands. Almost as though she were crystal-gazing, she could look back and see the hurt behind Jack's anger when he had believed her to have a partiality for Charles. His wild fear, not for himself, but for her, when he thought he hadn't the strength to drag himself from the river. The look of exhausted determination when he had lifted her again. She counted the myriad of emotions that must have jammed themselves into those few minutes for Jack. The drains on his strength and endurance.

All her love and respect came rushing back. Back, though never really gone. She knew that. Just driven from her consciousness by shock and embarrassment. Her poor love.

She had no real conception of the sort of sensuous passion

that could undermine judgment and threaten control. But she was very well aware that it lurked there, just beneath the surface, in almost all men.

With the calm that was returning, she was able to see how Jack's overwrought condition might easily have tumbled down the barriers for him. It even offered some justification for his act. He'd believed her (and not unreasonably) to be the mistress of at least one man and to be sharing the connubial bed of another. Naturally, he had supposed her to be experienced. And, if not willing, decidedly beyond shock.

Honesty prevailed—try as she might to ignore the rest, she was forced to own that he might even have supposed her willing. Her conduct, her words, must, at the very least, be described as incautious. Would she have expected anything less of another man, had she lain calmly naked beneath his caressing hands? And *then* crowned her folly by exposing half of that nakedness while begging him to remain?

Yet this morning she could see no fault but his and could think of nothing better to do than cringe and scold with the outraged modesty of a frightened schoolgirl.

She might have laughed were she not so ashamed. Properly ashamed this time for the unreasonable way she had behaved with Jack. She was looking back on the picture of herself now. She, Madeleine St. Cross de Beauvoir, who had been dealing quite deftly with men these many years, to have found herself so out of stride that she could scarcely gather up the courage to speak. And not because she was being held captive by some uncivilized brute. No, merely because Jack—her own, dear Jack, who loved her and who had almost given his life to save hers—had needed and taken the comfort of her body . . . Much as she had needed and taken the comfort of his arms.

She resolved to speak sensibly to him of these thoughts and to soothe away the guilt she had so foolishly tried to impose.

Climbing down again, she moved about, collecting Jack's discarded pieces of apparel. She carried them over to the wardrobe and arranged them there neatly—though she saw with a pang that they were mostly all ruined, the trousers with great jagged gashes up the whole of one leg, the boots savagely nicked and scuffed, and the dashing scarlet coat sadly out at the elbow.

It recalled her to the probable state of her own things, and she hurried over to her temporary dressing room behind the wardrobe. Along her route, she noticed the wild disarray of Jack's baggage, and her step faltered. But she moved on, deciding that she must get her own clothing hung near the fire before she did another thing.

She dashed about, shaking her head at the torrent of rain that suddenly burst from the heavens, then returned to see to Jack's unpacking. Just as she had refolded the last of his shirts and placed it in a drawer, a gentle tapping caused her to freeze where she stood. But O'Hare's familiar accent met her ear, and she realized it was coming from the adjoining door.

He smiled pleasantly when she opened it to him, as though it were the most natural thing in the world for her to greet him in his master's dressing gown in the early dawn. He held a small packet and was unwrapping it.

"A toothbrush!" she exclaimed, forgetting her embarrassment. Though, to be sure, she was feeling less with him than with his master.

"It was the colonel that was after thinking you'd be glad of having it, me lady."

"Oh, *glad?* I cannot tell you. But how did you manage to come by it at this hour?"

"There be ways to lay hands to most anything—supposing, of course, you know the right places," returned O'Hare, not troubling to mention that it was merely one of several he had purchased with the intention of reselling them, at a handsome profit, back at camp. He returned to his little chamber and picked up a tray. "I have your tea here, me lady, and I thought maybe you might be able to fancy just a bit of toast."

"Yes, perhaps," she smiled. "I expect you've already heard of the adventure that landed me here in this way."

"Aw, bedad! A shocking, shocking business that. And me not knowing aught was amiss 'til the master was ashaking me in the bed. Whist! But that's after reminding me," he said, hastening over to pull the door closed between the rooms. "The maid'll be up in a twinkling, fetching in the water for your bath," he explained. "After that, the colonel was mentioning something of a message." He paused and added reluctantly, "—And that you might find it conveenient if I was to be seeing you home afore he could get back."

There was a flash of anger in Madeleine's gray-green eyes. *So,* she thought furiously—simply because I didn't rise up rejoicing over having been raped, I am to be spirited away by his servant like an unsatisfactory harlot!

She glanced up and saw that O'Hare was watching her with a shadow of concern. "I haven't had time to think what is best to do, O'Hare," she said as calmly as she could. "Perhaps after tea and a bath my head will be a little clearer. Will you come back in—oh, an hour?"

"Right you are, me lady. Though I wouldn't doubt your ladyship will be thinking you'd like a few words with the colonel afore setting out."

"We shall see," she replied dismissively.

O'Hare saluted and said he would wait in the next room until it was safe for her to come in for her bath.

Madeleine paced about for a few minutes, sorely tempted to let O'Hare take her away. Leaving his master to do *without* the balm of her forgiveness!

But this was only the unthinking reaction of wounded feelings. A few minutes of cooler reflection convinced her that Jack had probably just been trying to spare her further distress. He could scarcely have failed to see how awkwardly she had acquitted herself.

Fortunately, she reached this thinking before the maids arrived. She rushed back to summon O'Hare, instructing him to procure fresh towels and sheets, extra coal, and a separate jug of hot water for her hair.

She took the teapot over and placed it near the fire but was forced, by the array of drying garments, to climb back onto the bed with her cup. She propped herself up and lay back, pondering matters as she sipped at the exquisite hot tea. Soon another possibility for Jack's suggestion to O'Hare crept into her mind. She was no less convinced that consideration had played its part in his thinking, yet she began to see how he might have wished also to lessen the strain on himself.

Well, she supposed she could understand that and began to wonder, in light of their very opposite feelings, if it might be kindest if she *did* just take herself off before he returned.

The matter continued to exercise her mind through a second cup of tea, but it wasn't until she sat soaking in the bath that she reached a decision.

She wondered next if she weren't guilty of trying to preserve their relationship unfairly. Wishing to hold on to Jack but only on her own terms. She was unable to marry him and unwilling to have an affair. It rather offered him very little, when one came to think of it.

This thought hammered at her brain while she luxuriated in the warm, soapy water. How much was truly a moral concern and how much simply that she didn't wish to submit herself to the unpleasantness of such a relationship?

It occurred to her that, if her despicable husband had wished it, she should have done her "disagreeable duty," like it or not. It was through no fault of Jack's that he was not her husband. In many ways he was more a husband to her than Menard would ever be. It always seemed to be Jack who was protecting her, advising her, worrying over her.

She wasted no more time caviling over the rights of it and began instead trying to prepare herself to face the prospect. She recalled her mother's saying that, although it never became less disagreeable, it was something every woman learned to endure.

Well, she bolstered herself, she was more fortunate than most—to have reached such an age without having to endure it at all. And much more than fortunate because her enduring was to be only with a man she adored.

She found further comfort in the recollection that, once she had stopped struggling and let Jack get on with it, there really hadn't been that much time involved. No, and likely that form of kissing wouldn't have been half so suffocating and unpleasant if she hadn't been trying to bandy words with him at the same time.

Squaring her shoulders as she rose from the tub, she thrust away a final qualm for the morality involved. She might as well be hung for a sheep as a lamb.

While she toweled herself vigorously, she gave her mind over to how she should go about the business. One thing was certain. She had no intention of making a formal announcement of this decision.

The next hour passed easily enough, for she was kept very busy. First, washing her hair and rubbing it back to its usual dark, gleaming luster. Next, reorganizing the room and seeing that everything about it was perfectly tidy. By the time she had made all her arrangements and climbed back into the freshly made bed, there was nothing except the wardrobe, still standing awry, to show that a desperate scene had taken place at all.

But then she was left to wait. And to wait. A prey to the most acute anxiety. First, because she expected Jack to enter at any minute, and then in the liveliest dread that he would not. After the third hour was well underway, it occurred to her horribly that he might have gone off to seek consolation elsewhere.

When finally he did let himself wearily into the room, there was at least some consolation for herself. The long period of strain and its resulting irritability made it easy to lend great realism to the first part of her plan. It was most essential to take Jack off his guard, in order to dispose of the more awkward preliminaries. She'd decided the incessant rains would provide an excellent means (in fact, she could think of no other!) to get him out of his apparel. She was betting on herself to get him into the bed.

"Oh, Jack," she exclaimed despairingly. "You are soaked clean through. *Again*. Hurry. Out of those wet things at once. There. There is your dressing gown on the foot of the bed."

"Didn't O'Hare offer to escort you home?" he demanded, his

mind already rehearsing the ragging he would pour over that damned, interfering Irish head.

"Jack, I don't intend to watch you develop an inflammation of the lung while we exchange commonplaces. We shall discuss these things when you are dry. Go, now. Quickly. There is a warm towel near the hearth."

Jack found his lips twitching in spite of himself. Whatever else might have occurred in his absence, Madeleine had apparently recovered her spirit in full. With that much off his mind, he was able to acknowledge the logic of her advice. He was chilled to the bone and miserably sodden again.

He collected the dressing gown and dropped the heavy bed curtain, wondering if there would ever be an end to the surprises she managed to provide him.

When he returned, once more clad in the dressing gown, Madeleine forestalled his attempt to speak with a look of deep reproach. "You are much, much later than you said you'd be."

"I thought you might appreciate the extra time to organize yourself," he said, arranging his arms across his chest.

"You mean in order to scamper away," she accused.

"It did strike me as rather what you were longing to do."

Madeleine hesitated, then sighed. "Yes, I expect so. I am sorry."

"I believe you have taken my line in error," he returned dryly. "Emphatically, it is for me to say that."

"Well, you have. We both have. Now don't you think we ought put it from our minds and get some sleep? It's been well over twenty hours since I've had any, and, I daresay, considerably longer for you."

He nodded. "I mean to do exactly that. I'll use the chair by the fire. But first I'd like—"

"No, Jack," she broke in. It was plain he was going to make things difficult. Of course, she could scarcely blame him for guarding against a second loss of control after she had been at pains to describe his lovemaking as hateful and revolting. She paused, recalling her well-intentioned resolve to speak sensibly of her subsequent views. Yes, but that had been while she was still imagining everything could be swept away and forgotten. Now, with what was to come, she felt she simply couldn't bear such a pointed discussion.

"No, Jack, really," she went on, "you mustn't think of anything so foolish. A chair, indeed. When you are so much in need of proper rest. And I—" she continued hurriedly, seeing him about to wave away this objection. "—I am so plagued with visions of those terrifying moments on the ice that I need you to hold me—or, I vow, I'll not be able to so much as shut my eyes!"

"Mady, Mady," he sighed with a pained smile. Dropping his arms, he used one hand to rake through his thick brown hair. "At times you are such a knowing one and at others—"

She'd been afraid of that. Now he was going to *explain*. She shook her head, cutting him off, wondering what to do next. Her experience with seduction was entirely wrapped up in defense. She thought rapidly and decided that what had worked to her disadvantage last night might serve her today.

She raised slightly from under the blankets and held out her arms to him. "Jack, pray?"

Nothing!

This time, of course, she was wearing her shift. She supposed that might be making the difference—but *really!*

In the end, she resorted to the method most natural to her frank nature and cut off his second attempt to explain by saying, "Jack, I am not a child—even if I may too often behave as one." She settled back onto the pillows, extending a hand to him. "Come now. I want to be as much to you as I can. You are everything to me."

Jack's expression softened. He sat down on the edge of the bed, cupping the side of her face in one hand. The sleeves of the dressing gown were rolled high as she had left them, and Madeleine's attention became fixed on his exposed forearm, the soft covering of golden hair, the strong, sculptured, rather beautiful shape that she had seen on various statues of Greeks or Romans or whatever they were.

She continued to stare, realizing that, apart from Jack's fine, large hands, she had never seen so much as an inch of him below his chin. Or of any gentleman. Not even her brothers. Was it any wonder that one was so unprepared?

She ducked her head and caressed her cheek against the long line of that arm, her eyes lifting to the v-shaped section of neck and chest. More hair. Crisper, darker, longer, and curled. Even the statues didn't prepare one for that. Yet somehow she had known it was a condition common to even the most refined of gentlemen. Her thoughts drifted, trying to recall *how* she had known. Or why, then, it should be so surprising to see it there.

She looked up into Jack's strong, male face and smiled, deciding that it suited him.

Whatever Jack himself had been deciding during this interval, he stood quietly, lifted a corner of the blanket, and slid in beside her.

As far as it was possible to feel triumph over having succeeded in bringing upon oneself a much dreaded experience, Madeleine felt it. But she began immediately to relive all her former agitation and to wish only for the unpleasant business to be quickly over and done. He would hold her then, as he had last night.

He was doing so now, but, at the moment, she felt frightfully small and vulnerable against that broad, bristling chest.

He kissed her, long and gently, then raised his face to look into hers, something—not quite a laugh—in his eyes. "My poor Mady. You really hate all this, don't you?"

She came close to a hasty denial, then said, earnestly, "Not all, Jack. You must know how much I love being close to you. To have your arms about me. For you to kiss me . . . like this."

"Then why don't we just settle on that for the time being?"

"Oh, no!" She tried to push herself back with no success. "Jack, don't make me sorry for being honest with you. I meant what I said earlier. Your happiness is important to me, too."

"And do you suppose that I am not happy, being close to you and kissing you? I promise you I am. Now just be easy and tell me what has become of my trunks and clothes."

"Are you thinking I may have flung them from the window in my temper?" Madeleine laughed, unaware that she was being handled by an expert.

TEN

"Your clothing is in the drawers and wardrobe," Madeleine told him, going on to explain that she had asked O'Hare to find a safe storage place for the trunks. While she detailed the unhappy condition of his uniform, she fell unconsciously into her usual ease with him, just barely noticing that Jack was showing a lamentable want of interest in a subject that he himself had opened.

He returned only monosyllabic responses as his lips moved from one ear to the other, covering most of her face, forcing her at times to close her eyes, and at others to reach out and catch his lips with her own, as he passed softly, swiftly over her mouth.

He moved downward onto her throat and neck. Each shoulder. When he began to trace the shape of each breast through the thin fabric of her shift, Madeleine's talk faded. She wondered over his promise for an instant. Yet, in all fairness, she supposed such behavior did fall loosely under the heading of just kissing.

In fact, she was conscious of a sense of loss when he moved on. A sense of loss that soon became mingled with a giddy kind of apprehension, when she felt those kisses pressed firmly into the hollow of her waist. All the while a hand seemed to be slowly, slowly inching her shift onto her hips.

She stirred a little nervously, and another hand returned to hold her in place, its long fingers caressing her cheek, the nape of her neck. A few minutes more and she found herself having to clutch that hand, to press it fiercely against her lips. And not long after that, she was writhing and tugging at Jack. Wanting him back. Wondering without interest where the dressing gown had gone again. Arms and legs entwining with his. Yearning, eager, and murmuring abandoned supplications between long, hard kisses that she returned with as much passion as his own. Then crying out with sharp impatience. For what she hardly knew, but arching violently to claim it with an instinct as old as life.

When the clocks began to tick again for Madeleine, and she looked back on that unexpected journey into rapture, she thought surely the gods must be laughing at her. She felt dreamy and weightless and wanted to laugh with them. Especially as her mind turned back to Claudia. So entirely convincing whenever she assured her daughters that, contrary to what might be suggested in the rubbishing novels they chose to read, such activities provided no pleasure whatsoever—except for men. And she was hard put to understand that.

Madeleine opened her eyes and found Jack smiling down at her. "Are you going to tell me what you find so amusing?" he asked.

"Certainly not," she said. Though, oddly, she wasn't in the least embarrassed anymore, and slid her arms about his neck, pulling him down to nuzzle against his face as she murmured in a slow, awed tone, "Oh, Jack. Oh, my splendid, splendid, Jack."

He kissed her, then rolled onto his back, pulling her along. Madeleine nestled happily against him, her head resting on his upper arm, her fingers spread wide through the thick patch of hair in the center of his chest. Somehow she just couldn't get over her fascination with it.

As she lay there, her only regret was for her own ignorance. She felt deprived that the pleasure should have come on her all in a surprise, and she found herself already thinking of the next time—when anticipation could play its natural part in perfecting this new and wonderful experience. In fact, analyzing the wholly unfamiliar sensation that was beginning to build within her now, it seemed that anticipation was already hard at work. She began to wonder more specifically when that next time would be.

It occurred to her, in the midst of this mounting desire, that Jack might be delaying the event out of consideration. She smiled to herself, thinking she must instantly disabuse him of so silly a notion, and rose onto her elbow, only to find him sound asleep.

She had to fight down a rather startling flash of irritation and remind herself of her own words regarding his urgent need for rest. Yes, she thought resignedly, naturally he would be exhausted, what with so much rescuing and ravaging on top of a long day of travel.

Sleep eventually drove itself through her frustration, but Madeleine woke with Jack's first stirring and with no less a sense of that same yearning. She kissed the arm and areas of his chest nearest her, then raised a happy, smiling face to be kissed in turn. She found him fully awake, a frown of concentration on his countenance.

He returned her smile and kissed her with satisfactory thoroughness, but then merely dropped another quick kiss onto her forehead, saying, "We must talk, of course. But I daresay you're hungry. And I've had nothing but those curst brandy balls and coffee since yesterday noon."

It was beyond Madeleine to discount this last. However much one might like to imagine it possible to live on love, she was able to see the impracticality. Brandy balls and coffee! No, no, of course he must be given something more substantial and at once. She was even able, after a few minutes of quiet reflection, to acknowledge her own appetite for the roast chicken that Jack told her was the house ordinary for the day. And hot soup. Warm bread and butter. Tea and pastry. Yes, she told herself firmly, it all sounded most divine.

She turned her head with automatic modesty as he jumped out into the room. Then struggled behind the bed curtain into the communal dressing gown while Jack dressed himself beyond.

When she stepped out to join him, she couldn't help laughing at the sight of the abandoned articles on the floor before the fire. "You aren't very neat for a military man," she remarked, as she set about gathering up his clothes for the second time that day.

Jack walked over, looking rather dashing in just his shirt-sleeves. "O'Hare generally sees to such things," he returned, reaching to take the sopping coat from her hand.

"No, let me," she begged, drawing it away. "O'Hare can be better employed in arranging some hot water for me. Besides, I find I like tending to your things. Go along, Jack, and see to our dinner while I tidy up here and have a quick bath."

He took her by the shoulders and kissed her briefly, then turned to go, but she called after him. "Oh, and Jack, do you think we could manage a bottle of champagne—just for tonight?"

"We could," he smiled back, "even if the government hadn't been so liberal about my expense money."

"Oh, that's right," Madeleine chuckled while she went about her task, "I forgot we are here on military business."

She was headed toward the wardrobe, a second pair of wet boots in her hand, but she stopped suddenly. "Oh, that reminds me. I must confess to another extravagance on your behalf. I desired O'Hare to find a different chamber for himself, so that I may have the adjoining one for a dressing room. Not that I shall have much dressing to do," she said wryly, giving a comic display of the dressing gown, a good ten inches too long. "From the looks of things, it will take some doing just to get my gown and cloak presentable enough to give away. Still, I shall want the room for baths and laundry and fussing with lotions—which you will have to procure for me tomorrow, if my skin is not to turn to horsehide."

Jack hesitated, turning back to her. "Then you've made plans to remain with me," he said.

"Of course. I'm afraid I was too tempted by the opportunity to do otherwise. I dispatched O'Hare with a message to Leicester Square, saying I'd been rescued by a kindly family and would remain with them until recovered from a severe chill. A great lusty lie, I fear, but it was that or leave them to imagine I'd been drowned in the Thames. Not," she said reflectively, "that I can believe anyone there should have cared greatly." She saw Jack's eyes narrow and added swiftly, "Did they say at the war office how long I may keep you?"

"There was scarcely anyone in a position to know at that hour. They'll send word to me here. I daresay as soon as they have contrived transportation. The weather," he added, glancing out at the still heavily falling rain, "is in our favor. I fancy there's flooding to be expected now."

He paused again but said, as if in answer to his own thoughts, "We shall want our dinner before going into anything."

Madeleine was still making last-minute touches to the room when Jack, having taken time to have himself shaved, returned. Only minutes later, the arrival of their meal was heralded by considerable rattling and chinking outside the door.

Madeleine started like a deer at the sounds, then nipped into her dressing room, thinking she was learning, and fast, just what it was to be one of society's notorious incognitas. When Jack gave the all-clear, she returned, struggling with a sturdy bench to serve as a second chair at table.

"Mady, Mady," he laughed, striding over to her. "Just tell me when you wish furniture to be moved."

"It isn't that it's heavy," she said, looking a little harassed, "but, with one hand always occupied by this long dressing gown of yours, *everything* has become a trifle awkward. I must send for needle and thread, or perhaps just a few pins for a temporary hem."

She watched him put the bench in place, then added with a twinkle, "Well—now that you have *volunteered*, I should be very grateful if you would restore that wardrobe. O'Hare and I could not budge it between us, and it gives a most disorderly appearance to our little nest."

Madeleine was rearranging a small branch of candles on the table when he rejoined her. He was in his shirt-sleeves again, his neck cloth removed, his collar open at the throat. "Ah, that's better," she approved. "I must say I've been thinking you a trifle overdressed for your company."

He held a chair for her, and she took her place, lifting heavy silver covers from the various dishes left by the waiters. "Umm, good, plain English food," she smiled across at him. "Nothing could be more welcome."

There were dozens of questions Jack would have preferred to delve into, but once again he summoned his patience. "I hadn't supposed you to be of such a housewifely inclination," he said, exploding the cork from their champagne.

Madeleine held out her glass, toasting him with a smile full of meaning, but replied in kind. "I hadn't, either. I am certainly lamentably unhandy in most areas." She sipped a little of her wine. "But I like to dabble about a house and to arrange things. Tables, parties, dinners. And—well, even the house itself, with an eye to making it more attractive or comfortable."

He glanced about him, smiling. "I can't even be sure what it is you have done here, but you've contrived to give it more the feel of a home than just a place to rack up for a few days."

Madeleine paused to sample the slice of chicken Jack had put on her plate, touched by his appreciation. He didn't realize, and probably it was best that he did not, but to her it had become a home. Her first. She merely laughed and said, "Mostly I've just cleared away the congestion."

Jack refilled their glasses, letting her direct the conversation until they had done with the main course. Afterward, while Madeleine fetched the kettle from the hob and made tea for them, he collected and stored the plates on trays outside the door.

He continued exercising his patience while she produced a small dish of pastries, but as they got on to a second cup of the hot, creamy tea, he said firmly, "We must talk now, Mady— seriously."

She smiled at his tone. Apparently, he was expecting her to hedge off again. But however much she might have wished that it weren't necessary to cloud the atmosphere with such a disagreeable subject, she was fully prepared for it. And willing. Even if she didn't feel he was owed a pretty thorough explanation, she had twice now suffered a far worse consequence from keeping Jack in the dark. She wasn't about to risk it again. She nodded.

"To begin with," he said, "you are owed an apology—not only for my accusations at the fair but for my conduct after. If I had had the least guess—"

"Yes?" Madeleine broke in to quiz him with a soft laugh. "I understand that it is not the thing to tamper with innocents, but, on the other hand, married ladies are considered fair game, are they not? I keep wondering how you should have reconciled this rather bizarre situation with your code of honor."

Jack shook his head in comic bemusement. "I can only assure you that I'd have gone about it in a less shocking way."

Her look was mischievous. "It's as well you hadn't the least guess, then. If you had attempted to go about it in a less shocking way, I shouldn't have permitted you to go about it at all."

Jack rose, scooping her up and into his arms. "I hope you know you're making it impossible for me to feel properly penitent," he said, conveying her to the large armchair by the fire and drawing her onto his lap.

She was slightly breathless, having supposed for a minute that it was to the bed that he was carrying her. She realized at once how foolish she had been and settled herself comfortably, bringing her racing pulses under control by wondering why she had so unnecessarily been envisioning *two* chairs beside the fire in their imaginary home.

"And now, by God," Jack said, capturing the finger she had been tracing along his freshly shaven jaw, "explain to me exactly how this 'bizarre situation' comes to be."

"Yes, I wish to, Jack, truly. So that we may have it over and be peaceful again."

She set right in, telling him briefly of the events leading up to her marriage and the various surprises awaiting her when she settled into her new house.

Jack's frown grew and grew throughout. When she trailed

off, he exclaimed, "Mady, for God's sake! What the devil have you got yourself into?"

"Hush, now, darling. Matters could be far worse. Besides I should think you'd be glad that my husband has no regard for me in that area."

"I should, if I thought he had regard for you in all others. How can I feel anything but sickened when I think of his damnable convenant with Morland?"

Madeleine, troubled by the harshness in his expression said, "I daresay you are despising me, as well, for accepting my amusements on such terms."

Jack shook his head angrily. "Anyone who knows you at all would have realized the near impossibility of your doing anything else."

She studied him in silence before saying, "Then if none of that frightening anger is for me, I must beg that you don't allow it to lead you into anything rash on my behalf. Menard is not of a physical habit. He wouldn't challenge you, if that's what you are hoping. He is far more apt to bring 'criminal connection' charges—exacting his satisfaction in a damage payment. One that would not only strip you of everything you possess, but put an end to your career—this career and any other you may be contemplating with the government. And all to no purpose, Jack. It might give him the *right* to divorce me, but I am almost certain he wouldn't do it. Good God, not that I could wish he would," she added in alarm, her mind flying to Claudia and her reception of such a thing.

"Come now," she said, gently kissing the lobe of his ear, "there is nothing to be done but make the best of things."

His reaction was so swift that she was startled to find herself first on her feet and next back in the chair, as Jack shot up to stand furiously, one hand gripping the mantle.

"That's your way, Mady, not mine. I don't want to make the best of things. I want to make them right. I've been wanting to right this one since our first talk at Eaton Socon. *Then*, simply because I want you to be mine." He turned to hurl coal savagely onto the fire. "And though I shouldn't have thought it possible, there is an even *more* urgent reason now. I want you out from under the power of that pair of devils. Out of that damnable situation altogether."

This time Madeleine found it necessary to leap to her own feet. He *was* thinking of divorce!

"Jack, oh, dear God, there can be no question of what you suggest!" she exclaimed. "And no need. I *am* yours in heart, body, and spirit and always shall be. As to the rest, I am in no *danger*. It is no more than the legal right of *any* husband to confine his wife. Menard exercises no other power over me and Charles has none. Not a scrap. Not, at least, if I will content myself to sit at home in the evenings. I expect, after what occurred last night, the choice is already out of my hands, but, if it will calm you, I shall promise to do just that."

Jack spun back to face her. "Of *course* you must promise that! And *try* to realize, as well, that there must always be danger in *any* involvement with such a thoroughgoing blackguard. The least of it has been to your reputation. By allowing yourself to be seen exclusively in his company, you'd all but convinced the world—*and* me—that you were his mistress."

Madeleine bit at her lip as she moved over to the table, reaching nervously for her abandoned cup. "I would have been more circumspect for your sake, Jack, except that I'd supposed you had already washed your hands of me."

"Yes—well, fortunately for us both, you've a deal more luck than sense," he said, thinking back darkly. "But I'm not insisting on this promise to spare my pride—or even your reputation. Whatever else Morland is capable of, as an escort he is fit for nothing but a dusthole. Not only did he cower on the ground when I might have taken you from him, but haven't you realized yet that he must have been aware of your peril last night? He could have reached you long before I was able to manage it."

Madeleine couldn't help a wry smile. "In truth, I haven't given it a thought. If I had, I should have known Charles would be thinking of nothing but his own skin at such a time." She continued to look across at Jack, a wave of affection lighting in her eyes as she said, "I expect you think there are a great many men like you."

"No man worthy of the name would leave a female that had been entrusted to his care in such a predicament," he retorted. "And I want your word that you will *never* entrust yourself to him again."

She gave it, and he lapsed back into silence, just standing there, almost as though he had forgot her presence.

Madeleine stood, too, watching him, but her bare feet on the floor were becoming chilled. The light evening slippers that she had stored in the pockets of her cloak, while wearing heavier footwear at the fair, were still damp. She moved over to the bed, climbed up, and slipped her legs beneath the blankets.

What Jack wished for them made a beautiful dream. A dream that could easily madden her with yearning. But it was nothing they dared contemplate seriously. She wished he wouldn't go on teasing himself with it at the cost of what little time they might have left to them now. She lay quietly for a moment more, glancing at the cup in her hands impatiently. The picture he made there, broad shoulders braced against the mantel, was combining with the atmosphere still lingering in the bed and rebuilding a need for which lukewarm tea was in no way an adequate substitute.

She set the cup on the bed table and ventured cautiously, "Jack, it was to avoid just this sort of pall over our reunion that I held off telling you any of this at Eaton Socon. Come now, we've lost so many days already over the weather. Do not draw away from me like this."

Jack looked up, stared for a moment, then came to her, settling himself on the bed in the place she made for him. He put an arm around her, but it was plain that his mind was still working over his thoughts.

Finally he said slowly, as though he were assembling the bits of a puzzle, "The fact that de Beauvoir made no attempt to confine you during the day—even after your Christmas escapade—all but convinces me that he, at least, has no wish to draw attention to the oddities of your arrangement."

He raised his knee, resting one booted foot on the ladder stairs. "That, combined with his physical indifference, makes me able to face returning you there. It will take a few months to extricate you from this miserable marriage without involving an all-out—"

"Jack," Madeleine interrupted urgently, "I will—I *do* promise about Charles. But as to extricating me from my marriage, I beg you will put that right out of your head. You are imagining matters worse than they are. It is your alternative that I am finding so frightening! Even if Menard could be provoked into applying to parliament for a divorce, it would be the ruin of us both. And my family into the bargain."

She saw that Jack was regarding her with exasperated impatience, and quickly rechanneled her argument. "Even if it is just of elopement that you are thinking," she said, "there are as many objections. It would be tantamount to stealing the money Menard paid out for me and will only make our ostracism more complete."

She stared at him with anguished eyes. Why couldn't he see all this for himself? "Jack, if I've given you the impression that I am thoroughly scandal-proof, let me assure you that it is a *false* impression. Idle speculation is one thing. Social exile something else again. A runaway wife, Jack! My family would suffer as much from a divorce. People would say that an apple doesn't fall far from the tree, and my sisters would be in worse case than ever they were without dowries."

In an endeavor to break through his implacable mood, she raised up, putting both arms round him as he lay there, burrowing her face at the side of his neck and pleading with him to put such thoughts from his mind, her lips feathering the words just above his collar.

He grasped both arms roughly and lifted her away. "It's nothing new for you to be trying to keep your cake and eat it, too—but it didn't take you long to learn how to play on my instincts to gain your end."

Madeleine gasped, then struggled like an untamed cat, freeing herself from his hold and hurling herself out of the bed. She caught her balance and turned on him. "Nor is it new to have *you* forever at work, trying to destroy every *minute* of our happiness. Always, *always* wanting more! More than can be. More than I can give you." She clenched and unclenched her hands, fury or flight her only defense.

"I—I was not even thinking of *your* instincts," she cried, realizing too late that she was succeeding only in making her mortification more complete. A sob escaped as she spun round to take urgent refuge in the other room. But the dressing gown, which had been threatening to throw her to the ground since morning, finally had its way, and she gained no more than a few feet.

ELEVEN

Madeleine didn't even attempt to rise. This inglorious end to her efforts to preserve something of her dignity drove almost the last scrap of spirit from her. She remained as she was, half sitting, the back of one hand doing little to muffle sobs that were coming steadily now.

Not even a second passed before Jack was lifting her, stripping the dressing gown from her body and dashing it almost vindictively to the floor.

She was only briefly conscious of standing in the inadequacy of her shift. He drew her quickly, protectively into his arms.

"Are you hurt?"

She moved her head against his chest in a negative response, her voice just barely audible. "Forgive me."

His kiss was bruising, breath-robbing, yet no less than she needed.

"Oh lord," he groaned, raising his head, "don't you know how much I want this, too? It's been taking everything in my power just to keep from you. And only because I *do* want you.

Not merely for a few hours at an inn, but completely and forever."

She forced herself to look up, to meet his gaze through glistening eyes. "Jack, Jack, how can you imagine that I want less?
But—"

"No. Stop right there. No more buts, Mady. It's time to discover if it's even possible for you to come out from behind that
wall we spoke of. I won't pursue anything to my ruin. I'd be no
use to you if I would. And I've been standing on the edge of
ruin these two days past. There was a moment when I might
have killed Morland. Another tonight when I could have done
the same to that husband of yours. The time has come to take
this thing all the way or untangle myself from it completely."

"Oh, God!" She drew back from him, raising both hands to
her burning face. "How can you even suggest such a thing?"

"Because I cannot go on allowing myself to feel for you as I
do, while the right to order your movements remains in the
hands of others. Your mother, your family, your husband . . .
society in general. And now, by God, it appears that, while de
Beauvoir continues as your husband, even *Morland!* No, Mady,
so long as any of them can make you set a limit on my rights
and happiness, I must put an end to your power over me. I will
not let you turn me into an ineffectual shell, hovering in the
shadows of your life. And I cannot let you turn me into a savage
product for the hangman's rope."

He took hold of the hands she had lowered, but she whipped
them free to enclose his face in a convulsive clasp. His words—
strangely, because there was nothing singular about them—had
unleashed a sudden burst of insight. All at once, it seemed
incredible that she had never been able to see it in that way
before. Evidently it had become a habit to defend against her
own desires on behalf of her family—against the temptation of
Jack's persuasions. He was right. It was time to break old habits. Time she began to put him first. He was the only person in
the world who had ever loved her this much. The only man she
would ever love at all.

She slid her hands behind his neck, but he held himself

aloof. "I want you to say,it, Mady. In just one word. Are you or are you not ready to do whatever is necessary to be mine and mine alone?"

"Oh, yes, Jack. Yes, yes, my dearest. Anything."

His smile was a little crooked as he bent to kiss her. "You never could count."

She would have said more. Promised to run off with him to a jungle, to a desert. To go anywhere, do anything. Anything but try to go on without him again. That empty, empty life.

But saying more was impossible. He swung her into his arms and carried her to the bed, kissing her hungrily all the way, a madness seeming to come over him. As if he were trying to fit all the passions of the last year into these hours. And she, to her shame, if she could care for shame, was reveling in it. Giving life to her own passions, buried and lost for so long. Responding wildly to his every demand. Abandoning herself completely to his strong, brown hands, his warm, searching mouth, his hard, muscled body.

The candles guttered in their sockets, and the world beyond their own little curtained one passed into day. They knew nothing of it. Cared nothing, until an imperious knock fell on the door, and Jack was drawing on the dressing gown and carrying her, naked and already weeping, into the lonely coldness of the adjoining room.

"Not even two full days," she sobbed, clinging to him when he returned to her.

It had, of course, been his orders.

"Not even two full days, Jack!"

Neither of them spoke as he hurried into his uniform. He wasn't to set out for the continent until the evening, but he was wanted immediately at the war office to receive instructions. Afterward, it would be necessary to visit his army agent and replace the things he had lost or ruined in the river.

Madeleine waited all day in their rooms, too unhappy to eat or sleep, praying all the while that there would be a little time left to them.

But it was dark when Jack returned, wearing a new cloak,

with an oilskin cover fitted to a new cocked hat to protect it from the relentless rain. There was no time.

He gave curt orders to O'Hare. His things were carried away, she hurried into her ruined clothes, and they were left with only a minute to murmur endearments between desperate kisses and then to hurry down the outside staircase to the hackney coach awaiting them below.

The driver was given instructions, paid an extra fee to ensure his discretion, and in seconds they were rumbling over the cobbles.

Madeleine had had plenty of time throughout the day to think of things she wanted to say, but again there was no chance to say them. Jack spoke urgently, gruffly—though he held her close against him and brushed her brow with his lips.

"You must listen, Mady," he insisted. "When we draw up before your gate, I must set you down and be off without hesitation. We daren't risk someone hurrying out to see who has escorted you home. But I've sent O'Hare ahead, and he will remain in the shadows to watch you safely admitted to the house."

Only a few minutes were left, enough for one last embrace, broken off reluctantly for a brief explanation and Jack's promise to write in greater detail as to what she must do to gain her freedom.

But a month passed, and still there was no word.

Madeleine sighed and moved from a window that gave onto the morning activities of Leicester Square. Her family was expected to arrive in London today. She must hurry over to the house and make certain that all was ready for their comfort.

At another time, she should have been atingle with excitement to think of pouring over patterns with Dorothea and Jane. Taking them about to the shops she had found. And later, joining them all for evening entertainments.

Charles, of course, was having his revenge, and had not been by since the night of the fair. But it was as she had anticipated. The baron saw the complete impossibility of denying her the escort of her brother.

Not that she could feel any triumph in that—or pleasure in any part of it now. With her promise to Jack echoing in her mind, she could only dread everything to do with the visit. Think only of the moment when she must face them all with the news that she was planning to wreak havoc with their lives. A hideous prospect at any time—but just now, with the sole object of their journey that she might help to establish them in society . . .

She nodded when her butler came to say that her carriage was awaiting her at the door and went down grimly. But by the time the coach bearing her family clattered up to the house she had chosen for them in Curzon Street, she had rehearsed herself into the appearance of great pleasure. She exchanged joyful hugs, smiled brightly, and spoke gaily.

A pretense that threatened to be useless. Concern, in its various expressions, registered in Claudia, Dorothea, and Patrick.

Madeleine guessed the reason. She hadn't been sleeping well for weeks. She tried to forestall anxious questions with talk of a recent cold, but she needn't have worried. The instant they stepped inside the house, that matter and all others were forgotten in the confusion of Claudia altering each and every arrangement Madeleine had made for them.

Madeleine smiled wryly but could only be grateful for the distraction. In the absence of Jack's letter, she was in no way prepared to make her confession just yet. He had spoken of a possibility—one that she could not begin to envision—but something that would lessen the afterclap of obtaining her freedom. Whatever it was—however little it might serve—she wanted the information ready to hand before plunging into the matter.

Thinking about it, she could have screamed with vexation. If only she hadn't been so determined to head off Jack's attempt to discuss it at the Queen's Arms, he would have explained it all calmly. Now, thanks to the scene she had chosen to cause, there'd been time enough only for him to say that she must on no account permit the baron to remove her to France. Unless their luck were in, it might mean their only chance for bringing the thing off at all.

For an entire month she'd been cudgeling her brain but couldn't yet hazard a guess as to what wondrous thing might make all right if their luck *were* in. As to what Jack might have in mind if it were not, she had only a guess and no more—By refusing to *go* with her husband, she could not be held to have run away from him. Not that such a refusal was likely to be applauded, but she supposed she could see how it might be viewed with a degree of tolerance among the anti-French.

Yet that was the merest conjecture and, true or false, it left her no better off when it came to knowing just what she should do. Without Jack's letter, she could easily make a mull of things by taking the wrong steps. Steps that might be necessary at any minute. The war was winding to a close. At what point was she to know if their luck were in? And what was she to do if it weren't? Was she to take sanctuary, or merely hide? And could her husband invoke the law to have her brought to France once she revealed herself again? Or was she to stay hidden *indefinitely*, for God's sake?

She daren't look into any of it. One thing she knew instinctively. The baron must in no circumstances be given the least cause to suspect her intentions.

Several more days passed, still without word from Jack. On the fourth, however, when calling in at Curzon Street, Madeleine was greeted by Jane, who informed her that a letter had arrived from Lambert with distressing news of Colonel Ashton.

Madeleine brushed past her wordlessly, her face ashen as she demanded the letter from her mother. Eyes shifted and met wonderingly when she snatched it rudely. And again when she tore the paper in her rush to unfold the large sheet filled with her younger brother's scrawl.

Madeleine's own eyes never lifted from the page but raced impatiently over news of camp life and skirmishes, until at last they rested on the piercing words, "Colonel Ashton is long overdue at headquarters, and it is feared he may have met with misadventure. Lord Wellington has been out of humor all the week, for our friend is a great favorite with him. I trust however . . ."

But Madeleine did not go on. The page slipped from her fingers and she stared down at it with such a stricken look that Dorothea was beside her in an instant, guiding her to a chair.

Madeleine allowed herself to be pushed gently onto the seat but rose almost immediately, a look of purpose returning to her benumbed features. "Patrick—Jane. One of you," she said, looking at neither, "find my coachman. I think he has gone down into the kitchen. There is a call I must make. Forgive me," she uttered vaguely in afterthought and walked out of the room.

She returned on the following morning and each morning after, always with a frightened look of expectancy. For she had obtained Lord Hanbart's promise to learn what he could and to send word of it to Curzon Street.

It was four days more before that word came, though not in a message, but from Lord Hanbart himself. "I bring encouraging news, baroness. Your friend," as he discreetly referred to Jack, "was merely captured."

Madeleine managed to say faintly, "But I have been inquiring, and they execute spies, do they not? Unless—" She looked up hopefully. "Was he wearing his uniform at the time?"

"Well, no, my dear. That should hardly have answered . . . Oh, I daresay there can be no harm in telling you at this juncture. He was taken across the Channel by smuggler's craft on the night he left London. His mission was to return to headquarters through France. Wellington was eager that information regarding current political leanings be brought to him by direct and trustworthy means. You see, it will have great bearing on—

"Well, well," he broke off, observing Madeleine's look of anguished impatience. "You are naturally not interested in these matters. The long and short of it, my dear, is that an important contact in France had been unmasked, and Ashton walked into a trap. However—er—the usual procedure has been postponed in his case, because of the peace conferences that are going forward. Nothing has been settled, of course. And they would be quite within their rights to deal with him as a spy. But, with things so uncertain, many of the Bonapartists are eager to curry favor with the allies. Some have already turned coat. Others are just showing themselves as willing to be helpful in matters that won't compromise them too seriously. And so it is, you see, with the officer in charge of Ashton's confinement. He sent a very civil message to Castlereagh, informing him of the capture. Explaining that, while he naturally cannot release the colonel—or even permit him to correspond—he will guarantee his safety and comfort, pending the outcome of negotiations with his government."

Madeleine's family trickled back when Lord Hanbart had taken his leave and found her turned away, plainly dabbing at tears with her handkerchief.

Claudia made immediately to warn of the impropriety in such openness of sentiment but was quickly stilled by the combined efforts of all the rest. Not that it was any less a relief to them to have a more cheerful Madeleine calling in Curzon Street in the days that followed.

Nor was there any pretense in Madeleine's return to a naturally happy disposition. Lord Hanbart had been confident of the peace conferences ending favorably. And she, while knowing nothing of the matter, was confident, too. Jack had said that Lord Wellington's army was certain to be in Paris by the spring.

As to Jack's imprisonment, she found it a matter for great contentment. He was safe and comfortable and would continue in that state throughout the remainder of the war. She smiled, thinking he would no doubt be out of reason cross to hear her say it, but, next to keeping him in London, she couldn't have hoped for a better arrangement.

Well, nearly none better. Naturally it was extremely vexing that he was not permitted to write. It left her now with no hope of his guidance with her own pressing affairs. But that had come to seem a small matter, compared to the agony of the last few days. Just knowing that Jack was alive and well left her feeling that she could deal with anything else.

It was a belief that was to be tested a few mornings later, when she found her family lingering over coffee. Claudia submitted her to a long scrutiny and then commented on the weight she had lost.

"I cannot say that it is unattractive, Madeleine, but you must take care to lose no more. You will naturally wish to be in your best looks. If there is to be a restoration of Bourbon rule, there will be no place on earth more lively than Paris this spring. I have been thinking we might do well to give London the go-by and join you there for the Season."

They could scarcely be left to make plans of that nature. Besides, there was no *reasonable* reason to delay telling them any longer. Madeleine took the cup her mother had filled for her and the bull by the horns. "I shall not be removing to Paris."

Claudia eyed her in alarm. "Madeleine, you can have no idea what you are saying. The baron has made his intentions perfectly plain."

"Yes, and now I must make mine plain. To all of you," she said, looking apologetically round the table.

"Oh, preserve us!" Claudia exclaimed. "What outrageous thing are you planning? You are married and may not *have* intentions that run contrary to your husband's."

"I find that I have them all the same, Mama," Madeleine returned quietly. "I do not intend to continue in my marriage. And remaining behind when Menard returns to France is the one way I can hope to achieve my freedom with the least amount of harm."

"The *least*—You stupid girl! You will ruin yourself and the rest of us along with you!"

"No, I don't think it shall come to ruin," Madeleine replied, only hoping she had unraveled Jack's reasoning with some degree of accuracy. "You see, that way I cannot be held to have run off. And—and there will be no *moral* issue. Not in the usual sense. Or much noise in the English papers, because the divorce will not take place here, but in—"

She broke off, adding with a burst of inspiration, "Why, to be sure, there need be no *divorce* at all! An annulment is quite in order. And it will supply the curious with a satisfactory reason for why I wish to end the alliance. Yes, don't you see?" she continued excitedly, certain now that she had hit on Jack's plan. How *marvelously* clever he was. "It is Menard who shall be held to have violated the contract and broken the vows. I have already told you that he has never—" She broke off again. This time with an embarrassed glance at her brother.

Patrick was certainly looking at her with fascination, but he rose instantly, mumbling an excuse to quit the room.

"Stay!" commanded Claudia with a surprising return of control. "Since your sister is apparently planning to publish these facts to the world, there is no reason she should be spared your presence now."

Having only been hit with this fresh idea, Madeleine's thinking hadn't carried her that far. She saw that it would, indeed, be an extremely humiliating experience.

"Moreover," continued Claudia, pointing Patrick back to his chair, "since it is you likely to be most effected, you have a right to hear. We may only pray that Madeleine has as yet failed to consider how she intends to prove such a claim. It is more than probable that, to avoid public ridicule, her husband shall deny the whole." Turning a scornful eye on Madeleine, she demanded, "*Are* you, in all truth, prepared to submit yourself to the indignity of proving such a thing?"

Madeleine, realizing that she was not only unprepared but quite unable, merely flushed in silent reply. She wondered, as she strove for composure, if Jack had given any consideration to *that*. But in a twinkling it came to her that her mother could have no certain knowledge of such things. She was probably only hoping to frighten her into abandoning this plan. Yes, and with quite excellent effect for a moment there! But surely matters were not conducted along such primitive lines. Or even in open court. Likely no more would be required of her than that she sign an affidavit in the privacy of her own house.

Claudia, noting the return of quiet resolution, fired her heavy ammunition. "And are you aware, if you are brazen enough to succeed with this abominable scheme, that the baron will be quite within his rights to demand that the whole of the settlement money be returned to him?"

Madeleine's first reaction was one of dismay, but a second's reflection brought her to a sense of relief. Doing the baron out of such a sum after not even a year of marriage was one of the points that had lingered on to trouble her.

"No," she said firmly, "I hadn't thought of it. But if he doesn't demand it, we must offer to give it back. Every last penny."

"Oh, God have mercy on us! I didn't—I *couldn't*—believe you capable of carrying this so far. I can only guess that it must have to do with your major—colonel. *Whatever* he is! But can you not see that you might bring this whole terrible business down on us only to discover that he is dead. I learned only yesterday that the talks are not proceeding as well as hoped. He may be killed at any moment! He may have *been* killed already!"

Madeleine leaped to her feet, gasping furiously. "It seems that you have suddenly lost faith in a Bourbon restoration. Or is it merely that you have lost the *desire* for it?"

Three other chairs had scraped back simultaneously, but Madeleine recovered herself. Taking her seat again, she addressed her mother, the only member of the party who had remained frozen in her place. "Forgive me. I realize you can have no understanding of what I feel. Try at least to believe me when I tell you that I am deeply in love with . . . my *colonel*, and that such a suggestion—any unkindness where he is concerned—is a source of extreme pain to me."

"Oh, naturally I do not wish the young man any misfortune," Claudia temporized irritably.

"I know, Mama," Madeleine agreed with as little conviction. "Nor did I mean to startle you about the settlement. From now on we shall both take more care. And once I explain, you shall see that my idea isn't really so alarming as it struck you."

"Well, I shan't. I find this—this *idea*, as you call it, more alarming with each second that passes. And if you try to make sense of it to me, I am sure I shall run mad! It is you who must

calm yourself and listen. Although it is beyond me to understand how your own experience has not shown you as much.
Men—even the best of them—are wholly governed by an ani-
mal-like quality in their attitudes toward females. You are going
to ruin yourself, and us, only to find that once this colonel of
yours has had the use of you for a while, he will be off, like a
beast in the forest, in search of another on which to practice his
lustful—"

"Mama, pray," Dorothea intervened, "you forget your company." She glanced apologetically at her brother.

But Patrick merely laughed. "No, no, I feel quite privileged
to be present at one of these lectures to young ladies. Although, I must say, it astonishes me that any of them can ever
be persuaded to marry at all."

"Levity is not in order here, Patrick," snapped his mother.
"You may be sure that none will be persuaded to marry *you* if
Madeleine goes forward with this plan to sweep your birthright
from under you again."

She eyed him thoughtfully, then added, "Of course, if you
were meaning to imply that my advice is not sound, perhaps
you would like to assure your sisters that you continued to
fancy yourself in love with that Smith woman after you succeeded in bedding her a few times. Or that you are intending
to marry the widow, of whom you are currently enjoying carnal
knowledge."

TWELVE

It was as well that Patrick had no thought of replying, for he
was given no opportunity.

"If you are honest," Claudia said to him, flicking a meaning
glance at Madeleine, "you will own that like all men, having

had your way with this female and that, you will eventually seek your wife from among the innocents just out of the school-room and spend the rest of your days humiliating her with your infidelities."

All eyes were on him, but he was unmoved. Rising, he shrugged. "Can't deny it. Who's to say?"

He walked round the table to Madeleine and rested an arm on her shoulder. "Can't say either what will come of this march you're planning up the cannon's mouth, old girl. But don't cry off on my account. You've a right to your life the same as the rest of us. I'll stand behind you whatever you decide."

While Claudia was glaring after his retreating figure, Dorothea seized the opportunity to speak. "Mady, none of us wish—have *ever* wished—to have our comfort at the price of your happiness."

Madeleine was so moved by now that she could manage no more than a grateful nod and was almost relieved to hear her mother's cold accents break in.

"Well, it seems we need only for Jane to assure us that she, too, is delighted by the prospect of disgrace and poverty."

"There need be no thought of poverty," Madeleine injected, nodding an affectionate response to Jane's wink. "We must give back the money, yes, but we cannot, if we would, give back what has been accomplished through the use of it. Lambert has his commission. Everyone is outfitted from head to toe. More important—the house, the land, and the buildings have all been restored. Because of it, a substantial income is now at our disposal. And it is from this income that we must repay Menard." She paused, then added, confident that Jack would agree, "I shall pledge the whole of my portion until the matter is settled. The rest of you could surely make do on a fourth of yours."

"And just how long do you imagine that will take, Madeleine?" her mother demanded hotly. "Never mind," she waved at her with a despairing look. "I shall tell you. It will take something over ten years if he does not demand the interest, and the remainder of our combined *lives*, if he does! And what sort of matches do you suppose your sisters will make with a mere hundred pounds a year to their portions?"

"A deal better than we should have done with nothing," Dorothea intervened. "And it is Mady we must thank that we shall have so much. Even you, Mama. You will have two hundred. Quite enough to manage—even when Patrick marries and you must remove to the dower house."

"We needn't consider my remove," Claudia snapped back. "Patrick is scarcely going to find anyone wishing to marry a man with only three hundred and fifty a year."

"Maybe the widow will have him," offered Jane with an irrepressible giggle that successfully caused her expulsion from the proceedings.

Only Madeleine and Dorothea forged on until their usually indefatigable mother wearied of the discussion and waved them to silence.

Yet, even in stalemate, the peace talks in Curzon Street were a greater success than those taking place at Chatillion, which on the nineteenth of March were declared abortive. The news reached Madeleine two days later and brought a chill to her heart.

Fortunately, a reassuring letter from Lord Hanbart was awaiting her at her mother's house.

"My dear baroness," he wrote. "Pray do not let the news cause alarm. Further word of your friend was received, and he has been granted a two month's stay of execution. The officer who has him in charge is both a clever and a cautious man. He is fully aware that our failure to achieve a diplomatic peace is of little moment when our military victory is almost assured. It is not known yet whether Bonaparte will try to defend Paris—but that is *all* that is not known! We have him in a hole. He will require a miracle to maintain power for more than sixty days."

Clutching the letter in her gloved hand, Madeleine ran up the stairs, the hem of her flounced skirt swirling gaily with her lightened mood. She found Dorothea alone in the drawing room.

"Oh, dear, is my mother still keeping her room?"

Dorothea flicked a hand. "She is. But do not let it sink you. I collect you've had favorable word of Jack."

Madeleine nodded with a dazzling smile. She clipped the letter between her teeth while she pulled off her gloves, then sifted through her reticule for a place to store it safely.

At length she found a small folder containing nothing but a bit of waterstained paper. It was one of the poems she had purchased from the great presses at the Frost Fair. It had merely struck her romantic fancy at the time, but it was now her most precious memento. She glanced down, smiling and unable to keep from reading it for the hundredth time.

> *I have a lover—Jacky Frost,*
>> *My dad the match condemns;*
> *I've run from home to meet my love,*
>> *Tonight upon the Thames.*

Folding Lord Hanbart's letter carefully inside it, she slipped them both into the folder, then sighed as she began to untie the wide ribbons of an extremely fetching bonnet. "Oh, lord, Dorothea, I wish she wouldn't take on so. Things are bad enough, but to see her sulking away the time that *might* be peacefully enjoyed here in London . . ."

"Yes, but say no more or she shall never adjust to the matter as final."

More or less in proof of this theory, Claudia returned to the society of her family that very afternoon, her first words a decree. Since the ball Madeleine was to have given for her sisters seemed destined never to be, she was to introduce them at the very next affair in Leicester Square.

The very next affair in Leicester Square was one that the baron had arranged some time ago. One of the "political dos" that Charles had scorned, and not at all suited to the purpose. But Madeleine agreed instantly and without comment.

If the baron thought it odd to find his wife's family scattered along the table amid his carefully selected guests, he, too, accepted the unsuitability in silence.

Madeleine felt a little guilty to be making use of him in this way, while plans to outwit him were tumbling in her brain. She would have liked to sit down and discuss the matter openly. To offer the terms of repayment she had worked out and to settle the arrangement civilly. But a stronger sense of caution warned against tipping her hand. She didn't trust him. Indeed, she didn't know him. And, if possible, he had become even more uncommunicative of late.

That, at least, she could understand. The outcome of the war would naturally have as much personal significance for him as it had come to have for her. And she was learning, to her cost, that to have matters drawing steadily to a close, yet seeming to hang forever on the edge of suspense, was excessively nettling to the nerves.

But, in spite of it all, she resolved on doing whatever she could for her family, while she might. It was still too early in the year for any really large balls, but she managed to have her mother and sisters invited to a small party got up by Lady Hanbart and to put together a few impromptu affairs of her own.

When, after a soiree and two dinner parties, her mother complimented her on her abilities as a hostess, Madeleine was touched almost to tears and took the opportunity to say with perfect truth, "You must know, Mama, even if I haven't adhered to all your views, any success I've had in society is owed entirely to you."

Claudia accepted the tribute graciously, then patted Madeleine's hand.

Peace in Europe reached its more spectacular conclusion at about the same time, with Napoleon abdicating on the sixth of April. Its aftermath began for Madeleine on the following day.

She had conveyed her mother and sisters to St. James in her carriage, and they were returning to Curzon Street in that pleasant state of fatigue that usually follows an orgy of spending.

The butler, who had been hired with the house, admitted them with the news that a message had been brought by hand for the baroness. Madeleine's heart leaped as she accepted the sealed letter directed in Lord Hanbart's now familiar fist.

Claudia, unable to show any interest in a young man who had turned her most practical daughter into an unseemly mixture of obstinacy and sensibility, retired to her private sitting room.

Dorothea and Jane, after a quick glance at the other cards and letters, followed their bandboxes and parcels up the stairs.

Madeleine, meanwhile, had fled into a small reception room to the left of the entrance lobby. The letter was brief but contained all she could wish to hear.

"I am off immediately to the dominions, my dear baroness, but I could not go without scribbling these happy tidings. You will read in tonight's paper that Boney has thrown in the sponge. Your friend will be released, and you need fear for him no longer. He is naturally expected to report to his headquarters, which we believe to be presently near Toulouse, but I have no doubt of his ability to obtain immediate leave. I'll warrant you may safely depend upon having him on your doorstep in little more than a fortnight."

Madeleine's joy was too much to contain. She sailed up the two flights of stairs to share the news with her sisters. It was received to her complete satisfaction by an unladylike huzzah from Jane and a spring of tears from Dorothea.

Madeleine was forced to dash at her own eyes once or twice, but her mood was buoyant as she dropped onto the edge of Dorothea's bed. "Oh," she sighed, "not only is he safely out of this scrape, but he will shortly be out of the wretched army altogether."

She found herself having to fight an inclination to expand on her feelings. But, recalling the tedium she had often endured having to listen to other young ladies boring on about their romantic attachments, she resolutely turned the subject from Jack to the gentleman who had been causing Dorothea to take such unusual interest in the visiting cards.

Her sister smiled as she tested the set of a new hat in the mirror. "I hesitate to speak of him before Jane. She has said so often how boring everyone was that night."

"Truly, Dorothea?" Jane asked. "Have you a *tendre* for that oldish gentleman you met at Mady's dinner?"

"I doubt he can give your 'oldish' sister a full ten years," returned Dorothea. "Should you find it more acceptable if I made a dead set at that coronet of dragoons you seem to favor?"

With Jane effectively stilled, Dorothea placed the hat on her dressing table and came over to sit beside Madeleine. "He has called again today," she confided. "It is too soon to be making plans, but it begins to look hopeful."

Madeleine agreed that it did, and Dorothea went on with a chuckle, "Happily, Mama has become less and less particular these days—in light of what she describes as 'the desperate necessity to make haste.' I might have brought her about with a minimum of fuss, except for Lord Glynn's third son. Naturally, she favors him as 'having at least the *hope* of a title.' If he had the hope of a chin, I should be more impressed."

Rising, Madeleine laughed and promised to add her mite toward convincing Claudia that Mr. Hunter, though a mere MP, possessed the more solid future.

She kissed them both and returned home, to be admitted by a complete stranger. Amazed that her butler should have left such an individual in charge of the hall, she could only stare, brows raised with wonder.

"Would you be the Baroness de Beauvoir?" he asked.

"I am. May I know whom you are, pray?"

"'Tis yor right. I am 'Is Majesty's servant, 'ere to place you under arrest. This way, if you please, yor la'ship," he said, clapping her first on the shoulder, then catching her above the elbow in a crushing grip when she faltered backward.

Madeleine knew it all had to be some sort of mad hoax or frightful error. She was furious with herself for having given way to such a sinking feeling of terror. "My dear sir," she said, trying to bring an unaccustomed note of hauteur into her tone. "Plainly there has been a mistake. It is absurd to imply that anything I may have done could warrant arrest."

"That's as may be seen," replied her captor, leading her inexorably toward a large saloon off the entrance hall.

"Then I demand you tell me what it is you imagine I am guilty of. *Why* am I being arrested?"

"That be yor right," he said equitably. "You stand charged with treason to yor King and Country."

Madeleine could again only stare, her eyes wide with disbelief. But she was no longer able to persuade herself that the situation was anything but very real and extremely grave. She mustered her dignity, and, though her legs had begun to tremble violently, insisted that she be allowed to walk freely into the room.

A sudden chill sent her gratefully toward the small fire burning in the grate. She seated herself before it, but made no effort to remove her gloves. The palms of her hands were already damp. Somehow it was important to her that he didn't realize how frightened she was becoming. Her senses seemed wholly disordered, but she worked to calm herself by concentrating on the tranquil picture of the tiny flames licking up from the coals.

Treason! She tried to think what it was one did to be charged with treason. It stirred in her memory that someone had once been jailed for criticizing the Regent. Oh, but she had said nothing of him that wasn't laughed about in such a general way that he would be forced to imprison the half of London. Besides, criticism of His Highness's personal follies must, more properly, come under the heading of slander. Oh, yes, surely, she reasoned numbly, one must be involved in no less than a plot to usurp his throne for it to be *treason*.

Oh, Jack. Jack, her mind called out. She was insensibly certain that, if he were by, none of this would be happening. Or, at least, he would know how to make everything come right. But her poor Jack was miles away and in prison himself.

There was a click in her brain, a vague sense that something of importance was to be drawn from this thought, but it was instantly flooded over by the near panic that arose from the word prison. Yes, good *God*. After arrest came prison!

Her fright again mounted to terror, and the pounding of her heart made her feel ill. Prison! All the hideous things she had ever heard of the London prisons leaped into her mind. Filth, disease, bone-chilling dampness. A mob of violent, demoralized creatures all cast in together and preying upon one another. Yes, and it was said that only a small minority ever lived long enough to be released. . . .

Oh, dear God!—But, of course, one *wasn't* released when it was treason. One was hanged! Or was it shot? She began to pray feverishly that they would shoot her and quickly. Oh, *Jack*.

An urge to scream hysterically had been building steadily. She felt on the brink of claiming the relief it seemed to promise but pinched hard at her gloved hand, vowing she would let her hammering heart suffocate her before giving way to such craven behavior.

Her eyes darted left and right with the effort of thought, and it occurred to her to wonder why she was being kept just sitting in this room. Where *was* everyone? One *ought*, she thought bitterly, to be able to rely upon one's husband at such a time. Where was *he?* He had a degree of influence. Why was he permitting great, brutish strangers to terrorize his wife? She mightn't mean anything to him personally, but she was, after all, a possession. Just as a matter of *pride* . . .

"Where is my husband?" she demanded, her mouth so dry her voice sounded foreign in her ears.

"Ay, and wouldn't we all be glad of knowing the answer to that. Sherried off, that's what. Gave you the bag good and proper. And *that*, little lady, is what yor owed for tying up with a ferriner."

"He—he has run away, are you saying?" She tried to absorb this. "Can you possibly mean that you intended to arrest him for treason, too?" she asked stupidly, her mind more of a burden than a help to her.

"Nay, nay. Now whatever would we be at—arresting a ferriner for treason?" he asked, making it sound something of an honor.

He shifted his bulk and went on reflectively, "Ay, mizzled off as clean as you please. And what I say is, it's something wonderful that we've had the best of this war, when a ferriner has quicker means of being tipped the wink than us. And in our own country!" he added illogically.

"My husband has been working with the government," Madeleine said vaguely. Then enlightenment seeped through her fear and confusion. "Oh, my *God!* He is a Bonapartist! A Bonapartist," she repeated, as though to make it seem more possible. "You are saying he has only been pretending to be Royalist! That he has been here *spying!* Is *that* it?" she demanded, but went right on in furious accusation. "And you think *I* have been helping him to do it! Oh, the contemptible, stiff-rumped, odious fiend! May he burn in hell through all eternity! To—to *use* me like this!"

Her jailer was momentarily taken aback but thoroughly impressed. Not only with what he considered a highly proper attitude, but with the little lady's exquisite temper.

"Well, now," he soothed, "it ain't for certain nobody's saying you actually went so far as to '*elp* the blighter. But it be treason all the same to turn a blind eye to the enemies of yor King and Country. And it ain't likely you wouldn't know what was going forward right under yor own roof, now is it?"

"Well, I didn't know!" Madeleine snapped back. "How could I be expected to know anything, when he scarcely came near me unless the house was full of company?"

"Ah, now." He shook his head. "Just when I was beginning to think it *might* just be possible that he went and sold you a bargain, little lady. No, that's coming it too rare and too thick, that is. Even a ferriner ain't likely to be so smokey as to beat a wide path round so fine a white ewe as my eyes tells me is sitting before me now."

Madeleine suddenly realized the foolishness of wasting her time in conversation with someone who had obviously been set only to guard her.

She was no less alive to the danger of her predicament, but possessing an understanding of how she came to be in it—having something solid to combat—brought immediate relief to her nerves and went far in restoring her courage.

Her mind began to run back over the information to hand. There could be no doubting that the baron was, as they said, a Bonapartist agent. His flight was as good as a confession. Yet there couldn't be anything of a concrete nature to implicate her. He had never involved her in his work, whatever it had been. She was suspected, merely. Suspected for no better reason than that she was married to him. But suspected of what? The answer came in the same breath as the question. Wheedling secrets from men, of course.

Yes, she thought, and they are looking for evidence to substantiate that now. Documents that might reveal which men. Her mind ran over the contents of her writing room and bedchamber. There was nothing to link her with men in a position to tell her war secrets, unless it would be in guest lists from former entertainments. Surely there could be no danger there.

Suddenly she drained white. Lord Hanbart! Lord Hanbart of the *War Office!* He wouldn't appear on the lists, but she had two letters from him at this very moment. Letters proving that he had been engaged in securing information for her.

She scolded herself into cooler reflection. To be sure, it would scarcely look well for it to be known that she had asked and received the favor of special information from an official at the war office, but there was nothing, after all, in the letters that could be conceived as remotely useful to the enemy.

Still, she decided that she ought really to make a push to spare poor Lord Hanbart the embarrassment of his messages being found and suspicion falling upon him even temporarily.

She glanced up at the rugged man who had been eyeing her watchfully through her silence. She must find a way to be rid of him long enough to burn those letters. While seeking an excuse to ask him to step from the room, she wondered inconsequentially if she dared risk the time to separate the little poem she had kept in remembrance of the part the Frost Fair had played in her new relationship with Jack. Oh, dear God in heaven. *Jack!*

Panic returned in leaps and bounds. Jack! Who, in the name of all that was wonderful, could be in a better position to provide her with the very things the baron would wish to know than an intelligence officer fresh from Lord Wellington's headquarters? Her mind raced frantically. And Jack's last visit to London had involved something so secret that even Lord Hanbart had been unable to learn of it.

It was no longer a matter of thoughtfulness for his lordship but one of desperate urgency for herself and Jack. If those letters were found, Lord Hanbart would be required to identify the "friend" he was discussing. They would learn that she was on intimate terms with an intelligence officer. And then imagine, surely, that she had been corresponding with him throughout.

They would never believe that Jack hadn't told her things. He could be released from the French prison only to find himself clapped into an English one. They might even suspect that it was the baron's influence that had kept him from being executed in France!

THIRTEEN

Again Madeleine forced herself to think calmly—carefully. There was nothing beyond the letters to cause them to question Lord Hanbart. He didn't figure in any of the lists of guests. From one cause or another—probably a healthy dislike—he had never accepted an invitation to the baron's house. It would appear that her friendship had been centered completely on Lady Hanbart.

Moreover, Madeleine recalled triumphantly, his lordship had gone out of the country early in the day. There wasn't even the danger that he would involve himself voluntarily. In a way, it was a pity. He was the one person of importance who might have spoken in her behalf. But no—such help would be as nothing to the harm. He'd have felt obliged to reveal her involvement with Jack and only made the case against her worse—besides bringing all manner of trouble upon himself.

She went on, exploring other means of tracing her relationship with Jack. Thank God, there had been no letters. Only one written message and it sent to Hans Place. Nor was there anyone in Leicester Square to associate her with Jack . . . except Beker!

But even before alarm had come fully home, Madeleine found herself wanting to shout with exultation. Beker knew Jack only by the foolish name they had concocted for him.

No, there was nothing. Nothing but those damning letters of Lord Hanbart's. If only she could contrive to rid herself of them, Jack might yet be kept safely out of it all.

She fixed a speculative gaze on her jailer. "Why am I being kept sitting here like this?"

"Well, it's as 'ow Sir Lloyd thought you'd rather do yor talking 'ere than at the orfice. You being quality and all."

Relief cascaded over her. It would be a gentleman conducting her interrogation. A gentleman who had already shown consideration for her sensibilities. Well, she must think what to say to this Sir Lloyd. Perhaps she could convince him of her innocence. It seemed at least hopeful. And while there was the least doubt of her guilt, surely any gentleman must recoil from casting her into Newgate.

It came to her then, out of the haze of sketchy memory, that political prisoners weren't sent to Newgate, but to the Tower. And beheaded! No, no. Not for some time now, surely. No, she ended weakly, for suddenly she remembered hearing that they had gone on to burning female traitors alive! In the name of God! Surely they didn't do that any longer either!

But whatever they did—all too hideous to contemplate— there wasn't time to be dwelling on such as that now. She must see to those wretched letters!

She spoke with polite authority, much as she might to a butler. "Kindly discover how much longer Sir Lloyd will be."

It had its desired effect. The man was accustomed to receiving orders and far from accustomed to dealing with prisoners who issued them. He moved without thinking. But then his steps began to slow, finally coming to a complete halt at the door.

Madeleine was gripping her reticule tensely when he looked back to run his eyes over a long row of windows built high from the floor to avoid the curious stares of passersby. He dropped his gaze and let it rest on fragile wrists gloved in lemon yellow, then again to small, shapely feet shod neatly in matching kid.

Comforting himself that surely such a dainty little lady wouldn't be capable of vaulting up and throwing a leg over the high sill, he was, nevertheless, moved to say mendaciously, "I ought to advise you of the cove on guard just outside."

Madeleine flicked a disdainful glance at the windows. "Don't be absurd."

"Er—no. Not—Well, I jest thought I ought to advise you," he muttered defensively as he pushed out of the room.

Like lightning, the strings of Madeleine's reticule were drawn back and the folder dipped out and flung to the rear of the fire. She watched the telltale, shooting flames, praying that he wouldn't return until they had died down.

He didn't return at all. A short while later, a tall, lean gentleman of middle years entered the room. The fire was burning more evenly now, but Madeleine was still uncomfortably conscious of the thin black crusts of ash lying on top of the coals. She rose, as if to greet the newcomer, placing herself between him and the grate. There was no longer the least danger that the sheets could be retrieved and the writing on them discerned, but she felt it could do her no good for it to be known that she had made immediate use of an opportunity to burn papers. As it was, the timing had been so precarious that she was thanking God that she had made no effort to rescue her little poem from the lot.

Her new captor bowed politely and invited her to be seated.

"Are you Sir Lloyd?" she asked, bidding for a little extra time. He said that he was, and she went on. "Then I do pray you will be able to give me a better notion of what is going forward. I take it my husband has been discovered to be other than I had supposed, but am *I* truly suspected of being a part of his outrageous activities?"

"I fear, baroness, as a resident of this house, you must undergo an investigation into that possibility." He spoke courteously, but he possessed none of the exaggerated gallantry Madeleine had been hoping to encounter. Instead, she judged him to be a man who undertook his responsibilities with extreme seriousness and performed his duties with painstaking care.

Again he suggested she might be more comfortable seated. Fearing to raise his suspicion, Madeleine complied, careful, however, to select a chair that would draw his attention away from the fire. Yet, to her horror, he walked directly to it.

She could tell nothing from his expression when, after a perfunctory glance at the coals, he turned to face her. He explained, with unfailing civility, that he was not yet prepared to go deeply into the matter with her, but there were a few areas, if she would be so kind, in which she could be of help.

At last he came away from the fire and seated himself in the chair she had indicated, removing from his pocket what she had no difficulty in recognizing as a collection of guest lists from former parties. Selecting only names denoting high military or naval rank or men with government positions, he asked, after each, if they had ever spoken to her of their work.

She replied openly that they had, adding that she had never known a gentleman, whatever his profession, who didn't hold forth about it at length. As to whether these particular men had told her things they ought not . . . on what basis could she possibly judge?

"To own the truth, Sir Lloyd, I have a tendency to listen to such talk with polite inattention and then forget, if I ever knew, all that was said. I can assure you, however—if they *did* tell me secrets, I did not pass them on."

Despite this assurance, Sir Lloyd continued down the list until the door opened long enough for a face to appear briefly.

At this point, he explained that he felt it would be best if he gathered together his facts before taking up any more of her time and suggested that she might like to go up to her bedchamber. Which Madeleine interpreted correctly to mean that they were now finished searching it. She thanked him and rose.

As he held the door for her to pass out of the saloon, he said, in the same politely calm tone, that he would not trouble her again until morning but regretted that it would be necessary to confine her to the house until the investigation was complete.

Madeleine was so relieved that she wasn't to be carted off to a filthy prison that she insensibly thanked him, then airily waved away his further regrets that she would doubtless have to make do with a cold dinner, since the servants were in so high a state of agitation that it seemed unlikely much more could be expected of them.

As she started up the steps to her bedchamber, a woman, obviously a servant, made as if to accompany her.

"I'm to come and see you undressed," she said in response to Madeleine's look of inquiry.

Hearing the remark, Sir Lloyd, who had been conversing with one of his men, turned and addressed Madeleine. "It is our custom, in such cases, baroness, to impound the clothing of all persons involved."

Speaking then to the woman servant, he added, "However, Wheeler, we may forgo that in this instance. It seems Catleugh allowed himself to be persuaded to leave the baroness unattended for several minutes. We may take it that, if she had anything of interest concealed about her person, it has already been disposed of . . . most likely at the rear of the fire."

Madeleine, unreasonably nettled by the veiled accusation, consoled herself as she continued up the stairs. If she hadn't exactly taken *all* the tricks, at least no one could accuse her of having played her cards foolishly. Knowing that she had thrown something on the rear of the fire was a deal less valuable than possessing her letters.

The investigation wore on for several days, with Madeleine very little involved but unable to go from the house or receive callers into it. The idleness, the not knowing what was happening, pinched at her nerves and left her prey to the darkest imaginings. Her thoughts dwelled heavily on her family, knowing they must be frantic. They would naturally have tried to call when she failed to appear in Curzon Street. She envisioned her mother, doubly anguished by the horror of this unlooked for scandal, which, innocent though Madeleine might be, would nevertheless make her a byword among the gossips. And poor Dorothea. What would become of her hopes where Mr. Hunter was concerned?

But far more fearful things were soon occupying Madeleine's mind, when at last Sir Lloyd settled himself to deal with her. The first was his alarming request to be told more about the colonel who had joined her during the Christmas season at an inn on the Great North Road. It seemed that Beker had indeed been busy, for she had assured him that the colonel in question, although dressed in a British uniform, was unquestionably a Frenchman. Which she, Beker, felt herself most qualified to judge. He had been too dashing, too brave, too altogether romantic. And, besides, his accent had been quite flawless.

While Sir Lloyd was not ready to accept the first three qualities as being unequivocally Gallic, his interest in an accent that could deceive two natives of France was pronounced. For his investigation had also unearthed a page who admitted to being approached by the same officer, reportedly "lurking outside the house on the night the disaster had occurred on the Thames."

A new panic began to assail Madeleine, for Beker had seen Jack that night, as well. It had been she who had sent him on to the Frost Fair. If asked, she could supply the name of her mistress's escort on the occasion, and Charles would be easily able to identify Jack by his real name.

Madeleine saw now why her summons for a maid invariably produced the woman Wheeler, with an explanation that Beker was not available to attend her. They had guessed that Beker would be in the best position to tell them what they wished to know of her mistress's activities. They were taking no risk of her being intimidated or bribed into holding her tongue.

Madeleine could do nothing but attempt to brazen it out. She laughed at the story of a Frenchman in a British uniform. She knew of no such person. Besides, Frenchmen went about freely in their own wardrobe. What would be the use of such a disguise?

Sir Lloyd countered that the man in question might have made use of the uniform as a means of escaping from one of the prisoner-of-war camps in England. "Of course," he went on coolly, "his turning up at your gate over a month later does not lend credit to such a hypothesis. It does, however, fit neatly with the possibility that it was not a disguise at all. This person could very well be a Bonapartist agent that has succeeded in actually entering our army."

Madeleine could have sworn at the perversity of circumstance that now made the matter of Jack's identity of such supreme interest to the authorities.

Evidently sensing her vexation, Sir Lloyd added quickly, "I do not mean to imply that we believe this to be the case, baroness. But you must see that we cannot permit such a question to go unanswered. Naturally, you did not present him to your maid. She knows only that you referred to him as 'the colonel' and addressed him as 'Edelmar.' You could save us much time if you will simply supply us with more details."

But Madeleine was determined to supply them with nothing that would lead them to Jack. If anything, she hoped desperately to lead them as far away as possible. "But how can you know that this person 'lurking outside the house' was the same man who joined me at Christmastide?" she fenced, hoping to learn if Beker had even thought to mention the night of the Frost Fair. Perhaps they were being guided solely by a matching description.

Although dismayed, she couldn't help a slight smile when Sir Lloyd presented her with a note that Jack had jokingly signed 'Edelmar.' But there was still a chance, and she decided to take it. When Sir Lloyd asked if he might be told what she found amusing, she replied, "Why, two things, really. I wondered how anyone could suspect a Frenchman of having such a name.

And then I found myself envisioning Colonel Croft's annoyance as he awaited me in the park the next day. Obviously, he paid the page to deliver this note, not to keep it as a memento."

"I see," said Sir Lloyd, noting down the name in his pocket-book. "Well, the boy ought, of course, to have given it to you eventually, but he cannot be blamed for your failure to keep the assignation in the park. You are forgetting your plunge into the river, madame, and the chill that kept you in a kindly stranger's bed throughout the night and following day."

Madeleine blushed, remembering her own note, sent from the Queen's Arms to explain her absence. She could see that she wouldn't have a shred of reputation left when all this was done. Sir Lloyd might be in some doubt as to whether she was a spy, but nothing would ever convince him that she wasn't engaged in so many clandestine affairs as to be unable to keep them straight in her head.

It was unfortunately while her mind was occupied with this embarrassment that Madeleine committed a tactical error. When asked by Sir Lloyd if she were sufficiently familiar with Colonel Croft to be able to vouch for his being an Englishman, she snapped, "Of course!" Adding that naturally she had known him for some time.

It had been a foolish wish for it not to appear that she indulged in affairs with near-strangers. But no sooner had she spoken than she realized her mistake. She had been planning, when it was discovered that there was no such person as Edelmar Croft, to say that it was the name he had given her and all she knew about him.

Still smarting with vexation over her folly, she replied irritably, when asked to name Croft's regiment, that she knew nothing of military matters. And, no, she hadn't a guess where he was serving or whether he was with the cavalry, infantry, or artillery.

Well, could she at least describe his uniform? "Why, yes," she replied unhelpfully, "he wore a scarlet coat."

"What else do you recall about it?" inquired Sir Lloyd, struggling to overcome his exasperation.

"Nothing," replied Madeleine, not troubling to struggle with hers.

The facings on his coat? Silver or gold lace? Whether he wore his pantaloons inside or outside of his boots? The *color* of his pantaloons? Or perhaps he was not wearing pantaloons. Had they been trousers instead? Sir Lloyd persevered, becoming redder each time she shook her head.

"Thank you, baroness," he said, rising. "You have at least been helpful to the extent of eliminating the artillery, a few rifle companies, and a cavalry regiment or two. I daresay we need only address ourselves to five score others to end our suspense."

Sir Lloyd attempted to take his leave as graciously as possible after this biting sarcasm, but Madeleine detained him. Only this morning she had discovered that there was no money in the house except the few shillings she carried in her reticule. The baron had made off with every last farthing piece.

She requested Sir Lloyd to have someone contact the baron's man of business about funds to buy in supplies and pay the first quarter's wages. But she learned, to her further chagrin, that the baron's supposed wealth was nothing but a fudge. Investigation disclosed that he had managed to escape the Terror with only a small portion of his original wealth. He had then speculated rashly, hoping to repair his fortune, but ended by loosing everything instead.

Bonaparte had been promising to restore members of the old nobility to their former prominence if they would consent to return to France under his regime. The baron, in desperation, had applied to him. In his case, however, Bonaparte's government had had a different proposition to make. They had promised to restore his estates in France, but only after the emperor had won the war against England. In the meantime, the baron was to put it about that his investments had flourished and remain in London as one of their agents.

They had provided for him handsomely, so that his circumstances would appear to be in keeping with the lavish entertainments he must give. Yet he had been ordered to circulate as little gold into the English economy as could be contrived. Consequently, he had paid only those bills that could not possibly be put off. With the inevitable result that there was a mountain of debt owing to various merchants and venders, who had seen no reason to press someone so obviously swimming in wealth.

They had discovered their mistake by now, of course, and Madeleine was told wryly that, in this respect at least, she might consider herself fortunate to have the government acting as porter at her door. The duns were swarming in ever increasing numbers all about the house.

She was indeed grateful, for she felt she could bear no more. During Sir Lloyd's disclosure—alarming enough in itself—she had realized that the large sum paid to her as a marriage settlement could only have come directly from enemy funds. If he didn't know it already, she held no hope that he would remain long in ignorance. And she could think of little else to make the case against her more hopelessly black.

She didn't see or hear from Sir Lloyd for another four days. But when at last she was summoned before him in the library, his greeting, his entire aspect, was extremely grave. She'd been expecting no less and tried to gather the fragments of her courage and dignity, for she felt certain that this interview must end in her being removed to a prison.

"Be seated, baroness. I have tried to spare you the discomfort of an official interrogation, thinking that perhaps investigation might render such a course unnecessary. Even knowing that your first act was to bamboozle one of my men, with the object of burning papers that were in your possession, I have tried to allow for the possibility that you were no more than a dupe in the baron's deep game. Used merely as a social front— an attraction to lure susceptible men to his gatherings."

Madeleine sat perfectly still, waiting for the whip to fall. It came with Sir Lloyd's next words. "However, the facts, madame, combined with your own conduct, indicate a far more profound involvement. Unless you are able to answer to my complete satisfaction, you would do well to prepare yourself to face the consequences."

Madeleine felt a desperate need to clear her throat, yet was, at the same time, insensibly convinced it would make her appear foolish. She remained silent, her eyes alertly fixed on Sir Lloyd's grim countenance, feeling all the discomfort of agonized fright yet, except for a not unattractive pallor, looking perfectly calm and self-possessed.

"Very well," he said after an appraising pause. "I shall begin with what you must yourself know to be the most condemning evidence. We have looked carefully into your background, baroness. And while I do not imply that it is not perfectly respectable and genteel, it is by no means such that would command the settlement that was made on you at the time of your marriage. Your extreme beauty and charm might have served to explain this, if—*if*—the baron had had considerable funds at his disposal, to use as he wished. And *if* there were evidence of his own susceptibility where your attractions are concerned. Unfortunately, such conjecture becomes absurd when, as we know, the baron had no such funds—and your maid offers the statement that he has never, from the day of the ceremony, shared your bed!"

Both Sir Lloyd's tone and expression joined to indicate that this was an incredulity that no circumstance could render more conceivable. He added, seemingly more to convince himself than to inform Madeleine, "This statement was supported by the testimony of two other servants and corroborated, to our complete satisfaction, by the woman whose bed he did share!"

Madeleine's eyes flew to his questioningly, and he replied abruptly, "No more should I reveal *your* personal activities outside official circles, madame."

"It—it was not curiosity as to who she might be. I was just surprised. I hadn't realized that my husband was in the habit of going from the house at night."

Sir Lloyd coughed slightly and said, "Yes, well, we stray from the point. Which, baroness, is that we are left with the only conclusion *possible*—The money was transferred to you directly from the Bonapartist government to assure your cooperation. Unless you can offer a reason, beyond the obvious, why they should have been willing to do this."

"I—There must *be* one! I have thought on it for days. Ever since you told me how my husband's finances stood. I can only suppose that it is as you said at the start—that they wished him to have a wife as a—a social front."

"My *dear* lady! If that were *all* that had been wanted, I'll venture any of a dozen *innocent* ladies could have been had for a tithe the amount handed over to you. And, if your modesty prevents you from pointing out your quite exceptional value as an inducement to men, I shall allow it to be worth perhaps a *fifth* part of the sum actually expended. No, baroness, I fear you'll catch cold if you plan to offer no better to the court that will try you."

Madeleine knew him to be speaking the truth. But her hands twisted together in her lap as uselessly as her brain sought for an answer. She was confounded almost to the point of mental dullness. Sir Lloyd had at least been able to content himself with an answer. But she was left in the nightmarish fog of knowing that *the only conclusion possible* was not true!

FOURTEEN

Sir Lloyd's voice, cold and implacable, broke in on Madeleine's distraught thinking. "We shall leave that for the moment, baroness. And turn instead to the matter of the colonel, about whose identity you were so helpful. It is, of course, unnecessary to advise you that there is no one serving in our army by the name of Edelmar Croft."

"Sir Lloyd!" Madeleine countered sharply, "it is equally unnecessary to advise *you* that my marriage was one of arrangement. *Not* the arrangement you suspect, but one without even mutual affection to make it tolerable. The man we shall call Croft is not a Frenchman in disguise! Not an escaped prisoner. And *not* a Bonapartist spy. He is simply the only man with whom I do share that form of affection. The false name came about purely in the interest of discretion. I persisted in it because I will not have his career compromised by this—this *abominable* scrape into which I have fallen."

"Again, baroness, I can only stare to think of the stupidity with which you credit me. If he were really no more than a lover—or, if you truly prefer, we shall speak of him as an affectionate friend—in what way could he be so seriously compromised? His correct name and regiment—a quick look into his background and record! No, I think when we find him—and make no mistake we *shall* find him—we shall learn that he has been every bit as involved as yourself. You see, madame, we *know* the baron was receiving highly secret intelligence on a regular basis. Intelligence that could only have come from a person or persons in a position of trust. I can scarcely expect you to enter into my sentiments, but somewhere there are Englishmen with access to secrets involving national security. Englishmen who have been persuaded to betray this country for money—or," he amended bitterly, "let us say rather for a *consideration*. Having done so once, they will not hesitate to do so again. And I promise you, I shall leave no stone unturned until every last man-Jack of them has been run to earth."

Madeleine winced as he spoke the name that never ceased to drum in her thoughts.

Sir Lloyd, mistaking this for a sign of capitulation, leaned forward to press home his advice that she aid her own case by naming her accomplices and giving the true identity of the traitor called Croft.

He badgered her for hours, cross-questioning her until her head ached, but all she could do was repeat endlessly that she had no accomplices and that she had spoken only truth of the man called Croft.

Sir Lloyd's comments about the baron's source of supply had

served only to make her more determined than ever to shelter Jack from the sort of persecution she was enduring. And, whatever Sir Lloyd might say, she was persuaded that nothing could aid her case. Not so long as the authorities remained convinced that she had been paid by the Bonapartists to keep them provided with secrets.

She stayed in the library for several minutes after Sir Lloyd took his leave, stunned to helplessness that he had not summoned some great, rough creature to drag her off to prison.

She continued in dreaded expectation of this each time he called, but he merely went on, submitting her to the same exhausting and inconclusive routine, day after day.

It was a full week before he varied it, greeting her with news instead of the familiar round of questions.

"Your frankness, baroness, as to the absence of attachment between yourself and the baron renders it unnecessary to deliver this intelligence in less than precise terms. We have just received word that your husband is dead."

He allowed his statement to register and went on to explain the circumstances. "He was traced to Bristol, where he was attempting to have himself rowed to a merchantman waiting off shore. When his boat failed to respond to signals, it was fired upon and lost. Together, I expect, with whatever funds the baron had about him at the time. The body was recovered but nothing more."

Sir Lloyd paused before adding, "And yet, even allowing your relationship, madame, I feel condolences may be in order. If there is a shred of truth in your preposterous assertions, I fancy you are now bereft of the only person in a position to attest to it. I was awaiting the baron's arrest before making a final decision in your case."

"You mean now to send me to prison," Madeleine said dully, almost glad to have the strain of anticipation over and done.

"I expect my investigation regarding this house and those in it to be concluded sometime tomorrow. You may enjoy its comfort as long as it is necessary to keep it guarded."

He bowed and took his leave, not even troubling her with

further questions—though it had plainly become something of an obsession to learn the identity of the man called Croft.

Madeleine remained there as before, this time in a state of listless despondency. With so much else on her mind, she hadn't thought that they might have captured the baron. She saw now that there had been a hope she hadn't even considered. The last hope, as Sir Lloyd had so grimly pointed out.

For the moment she could think of nothing but that she would never know the comfort of Jack's arms again. Couldn't even wish it. Not if it meant he must see her in the degrading state to which prison life would soon reduce her. Tears formed in her eyes, already painfully reddened from lack of sleep, and she sank back in a chair that seemed to swallow her.

In a few minutes the door opened quietly, and the baron's cousin, Marie, came to stand before her. She, too, had plainly been crying, and Madeleine braced herself for an incomprehensible outpouring. Yet to her astonishment, she was addressed calmly and in her own language.

"But, Marie!" she exclaimed, forgetting everything else in her surprise. "All this time! I hadn't a notion you could speak English."

"You weren't intended to know, madame."

Marie went on, explaining in an expressionless voice that it was thought if the gentlemen who flirted with Madeleine believed her companion to have no command of the language, they would speak more freely. Her business had been to listen, hoping that, when wine loosened the tongues of these gentlemen, and their interest in Madeleine caused them to become boastful, useful bits of information might be collected about troop movements or other matters under consideration in various government offices.

She'd reported anything of this nature to the baron, who sifted and sorted through it for items of sufficient interest to forward on to France. Often these scraps served no more than to support facts already gathered by other means. But there were times when the accumulation of several minor points formed an amazingly complete picture of the whole.

Madeleine sat forward in her chair, a spark of excitement lighting behind her glistening eyes. It was something! Some explanation of the value they had received for their money. But was it enough? Sir Lloyd seemed to possess a tradesman's sense of worth in such matters. She could almost hear him saying that it merely advanced her value from a fifth to a fourth part of what they had paid.

Nevertheless, the woman knew things and was in a mood to confide them. And, by God, Madeleine meant, if she could, to do a little sifting and sorting of her own.

She roused Marie from a melancholy trance with a murmur of encouragement, and the unhappy woman continued. "This room, madame—in which the Englishman Sir Lloyd speaks to you. It is, as you know, the one Menard used to receive his important callers. He would then step out and listen to what they might say amongst themselves when they believed him to have gone out of hearing. But there is a place," she pointed to the grillwork beside the mantel, "where one may hear everything from the room beyond. I have heard everything, madame, of what this Sir Lloyd has said to you. It was a matter of concern to me, you understand, to learn what had become of Menard."

She went on to explain that, although she was, in truth, a distant cousin, she had been Menard's mistress for many years and that it had been their plan to marry once the emperor no longer required his services in England.

Madeleine didn't trouble to ask how the baron had planned to dispose of her. She guessed it would have been a quite simple matter once Bonaparte "no longer required his services in England."

"Ah," Marie sighed, "but now all is lost. Napoleon, they say, has abdicated. Our friends in Paris have betrayed us. And Menard . . ."

Madeleine offered her sympathy, although she couldn't help being struck by the incongruity of the situation. "Why do you confide this to me, Marie?"

Marie shrugged her reply. "All is lost to me, but I can help you, madame. And why should I not? I have heard you being questioned. You have a lover that you wish to protect. In this we have been alike. So I shall tell them that they are foolish to plague you about your English colonel. And I shall tell them about the settlement money that is of so much interest to your Sir Lloyd."

"*Can* you?" Madeleine asked, astonished. "It has become of great interest to me, as well. Sir Lloyd has made me realize that I must have been extremely conceited never to have wondered about it before."

"Ah, *mais non*, madame! Were you not offered the same by another gentleman?"

"Yes," Madeleine sighed wearily. "But Sir Lloyd feels that there is no mystery as to why *he* was willing to expend such a sum. But do tell me, pray."

"*Oui*. It is something your Sir Lloyd will be happy to understand, because it was for quite the *same* reason as the other gentleman. You see, it was the wish of your other lover."

"My—? Marie! You will have to tell me whom you mean."

Marie, accepting equitably that Madeleine must, of course, have more than two, explained that it was of *M'sieur Morland* that she spoke.

"*Charles?* Oh, I do not understand this at all."

"I shall make all clear," Marie soothed. "It is because he is the relative of *M'sieur le Baron de Hanbart* and was able to keep Menard supplied with many useful documents. They were brought here to be verified and copied and were then returned, with the English baron none the wiser."

Madeleine gasped, and Marie nodded. "*Oui*. Your Morland was our best source, madame. And he knew that Menard had been ordered to take a beautiful English wife so that his entertainments could be grander. He knew, too, that Menard would not wish to make a real marriage—I have already told you that Menard and I made plans to marry together. Our religion, madame, does not permit of divorce."

Madeleine nodded without really thinking about it. She was now on the extreme edge of her chair and wild to know more.

"Your Morland," Marie hurried on, seeing Madeleine's impatience, "wished very much to have you for his mistress. But of course this was not possible until you could be married. So it struck him that nothing should suit him better than that you be the one to make the arrangement with Menard. You see, he was very much pleased that, in this way, he should be the one to have you for the first time. He tells Menard this, and Menard has no objection, if you are as described. But then he learns of the settlement you require and says it is too much. Our government would not permit."

"Oh, my God, my *God!*" Madeleine exclaimed, sinking back in the chair again.

Marie went on as calmly as before. "It was decided to wait, in the hope that you will not be offered so much as you wish. Your Morland makes efforts to see to this, but one man persists regardless. He tells Menard that he must meet the offer of this man, or he will no longer sell him intelligence. Ah! This we cannot permit. So Menard sends word to Paris, telling of the difficulty. They agree that your Morland's contribution is of sufficient value and send the funds. But he is very jealous, your Morland, and makes it part of the agreement that Menard must manage so that you cannot have other gentlemen. Not even cicisbeos, *mon Dieu!* Menard promises and does his best. But we learn from Beker of your Officer Croft. *We* had no objection, you understand. Not so long as your other lover does not learn of it and become difficult about the documents."

Madeleine could only stare, aghast at the way her life had been manipulated. More aghast at the predicament in which she now found herself. She had her answer, but she daren't make use of it. Charles was not only jealous, he was childishly vindictive. Upon learning he had been exposed for no better reason than to remove suspicion from herself, he was more than capable of swearing she had been a willing party to the whole.

She would stand in worse case. If there had been no one to speak in her behalf, there had at least been no one to testify against her. And of no less concern—Charles remained the only person both willing and able to supply them with Jack's true name. The authorities would certainly question him as to others whom the baron might have employed, laying emphasis on the colonel whose name she had withheld so tenaciously.

Then, apart from these personal dangers, there was Lord Hanbart to consider. How mortifying for *him*. And how perfectly dreadful for Lady Hanbart. With both the misery of her husband's disgrace and the anguish of seeing her adored brother pay the supreme penalty for his crime.

She reached a rapid decision that the only good use to be made of this information about Charles was to warn him. He had probably escaped the rigors of "official interrogation" so far, because he held no position of interest to the authorities. But they knew very well that he had been a frequent visitor to the house, and, until recently, her "favorite escort." When more promising suspects wore thin, they might, indeed, focus their attention on him.

Madeleine took hold of the Frenchwoman's wrist imploringly. "Marie, you must promise me not to reveal Charles's part in this."

She went on, carefully communicating her reasons, until at last Marie nodded wisely and gave her word.

"But you, madame?" she said.

"Well—Marie, have you thought of that? Of yourself? In order to tell anything, you must expose yourself."

"It is of little moment," Marie replied with another shrug. "The English are already planning to hand me over to the new government in France. But I am guilty of very little, after all. I have repeated conversations to my lover and refused to betray him because he supported the emperor. To punish everyone in France who did no more would be an awesome task, madame."

"Very well," Madeleine smiled gratefully, "I must content myself with half a loaf. You will tell them that Menard informed you of the arrangement he made concerning me (it is natural that he should) but *not* the name of the man in question. And you mustn't mention the part about restricting the company of other men. In fact, it would be helpful to suggest that I was *encouraged* to see other gentlemen in order to draw attention away from the one who struck the bargain with Menard."

She paused thoughtfully, her spirits stimulated by this new hope. "They will naturally ask me whom this man might be . . . Well, I shall just have to supply a list of everyone who has ever shown an inclination to want me for his mistress. Dear me, if we are to speak of awesome tasks . . . Well, fiddle, I cannot be blamed for preferring that they spend their time on this April fool's project rather than in building a fire under me."

She hesitated as another thought occurred. "It is a pity, but it would only make Charles more conspicuous if I failed to include him on this list." She sighed. "Yes, yes, I must, of course. I shall just have to rely on being able to warn him in time."

Sir Lloyd was summoned back and remained closeted with Marie for several hours, finally taking her away with him. Madeleine did not see him again until the following morning, but it was to learn that Marie's intervention had succeeded beyond her greatest hopes.

He kept her only long enough to probe into the question of which man might be the one to have influenced the baron in the matter of her settlement.

Madeleine feigned deep curiosity and every desire to cooperate, and after supplying him with a list of possible candidates, was rewarded with the news that the guards had been removed from her house an hour since. She was free to come and go as she wished.

She was too exultant to wonder at the swift turn of events. The threat of prison was miraculously swept from her horizon. There would be ample time to warn Charles. Jack would be safe when he arrived back in England.

Before taking his leave, Sir Lloyd presented her with a packet of letters and a small stack of visiting cards, all of which had been left during the time his men had guarded her door.

She scanned through the cards briefly, eager to be away. First to Curzon Street to let her family know she had come off safely. Then to Hans Place, with the same news for Cousin Fanny and a note of welcome for Jack.

Most of the cards represented repeated visits by members of her own family, but she raised a brow to see that the baron's relations had been among others who had called. They had never come before, not even to the wedding. In fact, she only knew of their existence from Sir Lloyd. They were, he'd said, a respectable Royalist family, quite above suspicion, who were passing their exile quietly in a rural district of England.

Madeleine tapped her cheek thoughtfully with their card as she riffled through the rest, noting wryly that they were nearly all from friends made through her cousin. The more fashionable of her London acquaintance had evidently dropped her during this spell of notoriety. Even, she thought, nodding slowly at the irony, Lady Hanbart.

Before turning to her letters, Madeleine walked over to the bellpull to summon her butler and to order her horses put to. Then, as she began to leaf through them, she saw that the seals on everything, including the bills, ' had been broken. She shrugged. Jack would not have written to her here, and that was all that signified.

She was becoming so accustomed to having one more disagreeable fact tumble in on top of the rest that she was equally unmoved by the news that the house in which she stood was not, as she had been led to suppose, owned by the baron, but merely leased.

She tossed down a notice to quit the premises with no more than a mental note that Jack must be told to find her in Curzon Street. Gave only a gesture of "what next?" as she read another, stating that a distraint against the carriages, furniture, and all possessions of value had been obtained. All were to be sold at auction on the site, the proceeds to be distributed among the baron's creditors.

She sighed and glanced curiously at the large double doors, for no one had come in response to her ring. She gave the embroidered velvet pull another tug, then made a quick perusal of a letter from a former friend of Jane's at Harrogate. It announced that Miss Carver would be arriving in London for the Season and hoped she might have the honor of waiting upon her dear friend's sister in Leicester Square.

Madeleine cast it aside, sure that the writer was by now making plans to cut her dead should they pass in the street. She frowned again at the doors and finally stepped out into the hall. The house seemed oddly quiet after so many days when one could scarcely move in any direction without coming upon a total stranger or a distraught servant.

In a moment, her straining ears were rewarded by the sound of footfalls hurrying up from the nether regions of the kitchen. Her eyes widened slightly when she saw that it was the younger of the footmen who had been assigned to her carriage.

"Your pardon *madame la baronne*," he panted, "but I could not come while Cook was attempting to take away the last of the beef and cheeses."

"Have the others all run off, then?" she asked.

"*Oui, madame*. All have fled with the first opportunity."

"And you, Roget?"

"I shall remain until you require me no longer, madame," he replied shyly.

Madeleine thanked him and labored on in a mixture of English and ungrammatical French. "I have a little money of my own, which I am going now to see about. I should have paid all the wages before closing the house but, since the others have scurried away, they may fall in line with the rest of the creditors."

A knock sounded on the door, and she smiled. "Well, my faithful Roget, I wish you to carry a message to a gentleman in Bury Street. But in the meantime it appears you have been elevated to the post of butler. Will you see who is at the door and be very brave and fierce if it is someone demanding payment of a bill?"

"*Oui, madame!*" he returned, delighting, as always, in his beautiful mistress's amusing accent and alarming choice of words.

Madeleine hurried up the stairs to change from her morning

gown into something suitable for streetwear. While she was hunting through her wardrobe to begin the now unaccustomed project of dressing herself, she suddenly recalled that she was a widow.

She moved away and sat down on her bed to review this knotty problem. Was it likely to raise more of a breeze if she wore colors with a husband only two days in his grave? Or for her to go through the motions of mourning the death of a proven enemy of her country? She arrived at the unsatisfactory conclusion that, if she knew her world at all, she would be equally censured whichever course she followed.

She rose again. Since she possessed no widow's weeds in any event, she could do no better than strike a compromise.

She had taken only a few steps when there was a light tapping on her bedchamber door. Supposing it must be Roget, she didn't call out but went over in reply. Much to her surprise, she found the young maid with whom she had become friendly at Hans Place.

FIFTEEN

"Why, Atty!" Madeleine exclaimed.

"My mistress thought you might be glad not to be left with only foreigners, now that he is dead," the girl explained, referring to the baron, who had refused Madeleine's request to employ at least one English servant. "She sent me along yesterday, after seeing about him in the papers. But they wouldn't let me pass. Not front door nor rear. Nor even promise to tell you I was by."

Madeleine smiled gratefully, stepping back so that she might come into the room. "But surely my cousin cannot spare you, Atty."

"Well, as to that, my lady," the girl began slowly, with carefully schooled speech. But then her nerves got the better of her, and she continued all in a rush. "Well, as to that, she knows of my hankering to become an all-time lady's maid. And she thought you might be willing to take me on probation. Owing that we'd seemed to get on and all. And she can find another maid-of-all-work to take my place. And I've been learning, off and on, for years, you see. And I reckon I know to a cow's thumb just how to serve a lady of quality in all matters of hair and dress."

"Do you now?" Madeleine laughed. "Then your first task shall be to turn me out as a respectable, but not too sorrowful, widow."

Madeleine arrived in Curzon Street in a hackney coach, but, having some days ago exchanged the contents of her purse for "the last of the beef and cheeses," she was obliged to ask her mother's butler to advance funds for the driver.

"I haven't a guess how much he will charge, Flint," she apologized.

"If he asks more than a shilling from Leicester Square, my lady, he'll be subject to a fine for exceeding the legal rates. And so I shall tell him," added Flint, advancing on the jarvy whose only divergence, in an otherwise blameless career, was in once failing to notify the Hackney Office of an "almost empty" bottle found on the seat.

Madeleine hurried upstairs, unclasping a dark blue pelisse, divested of its more attractive trimming and far too heavy for the fine April day.

She was greeted at the head of the stairs with tearful hugs from both sisters and several bracing claps on the back from her overwrought brother.

"Yes, yes! I've been freed at last. Did you think I'd escaped down a knotted sheet?" she asked, laughing at the bombardment of questions. "No, I haven't a cold. This pelisse is just the least frivolous thing I possess. Patrick, darling, would it be possible to express your affection in a less brutal way?" she laughed again, turning from her sisters to embrace him warmly.

Claudia, though less demonstrative, was relieved to the point of fatigue. Madeleine was made to come in and sit down and to relate even the smallest detail of all that had occurred. When it was learned how meager and uninspiring had been her diet, a tray of delicious sandwiches was sent for immediately.

Madeleine, in turn, was relieved to learn that, although Dorothea's Mr. Hunter had not yet come up to scratch, neither had he deserted her. He had continued to call and had three times taken her for a drive in the park. An excessive show of courage for an MP, and one that left little doubt as to his intentions.

Madeleine was surprised, however, to find her mother—usually so ready with an opinion—was as much at a loss as herself over the matter of her mourning.

But Claudia recovered her reputation promptly by adding, "I am, nevertheless, in no doubt whatsoever that it would be less than prudent to remain in Town while this vexed question exists."

Madeleine could only agree. But she would naturally await Jack's return. Surely only a matter of days now. Then, provided he wasn't required to take up his new position with the government quite immediately . . .

She wondered, with a twinge of impatience, if she would be expected to wait a year to remarry, but made no attempt to raise this subject with her mother. On that head, she would be guided only by Jack.

Patrick, who had been pacing about the room, still afflicted by a bitter regret that the baron should have died at hands other than his own, suddenly broke into her thoughts.

"Mady—didn't you say they were perfectly satisfied as to your innocence?"

She glanced up, a feeling of foreboding already coursing through her. "What is it?"

"It's just that I have this minute recognized that muffin-faced cove who was on duty outside your house every time I went by."

Madeleine hurried to the window, but the face was not familiar.

"Yes, but don't you see," said Patrick, "if they are having you dogged, they would have chosen him for that very reason. I'll go bail he's the one."

"Oh, yes," Madeleine replied, returning to her seat, a rapid retrogression of mood sweeping over her. "Yes," she finally said, "naturally you are right. They don't believe I am innocent at all. They released me merely in the hope I shall lead them to my accomplices."

Madeleine had lost a telling degree of weight. There were dark areas beneath her red-rimmed eyes, and now, suddenly, her smooth countenance seemed terribly drawn.

"Madeleine," Claudia said, in concern, "it is disagreeable in the extreme to be teased this way. But, my dear—since you *have* no accomplices . . ."

"What does that signify?" Madeleine exploded. She covered her lips with the back of her fingers immediately, then said, in an altered tone, "Forgive me, but don't you see? They are going to force me to avoid Jack." She went on, her voice breaking on the words, "And I need him so desperately just now. Patrick!" she gasped at the swift movement toward the door. "Where are you going?"

"I'll *kill* the damned fellow!"

"Patrick," she repeated softly, holding out her hand to him. He took it, and she pulled him down beside her on the sofa. "I fear the government can hire far more men than you can kill." She smiled with an effort and laid her head on his shoulder, keeping tight hold of his hand.

She was recovered from her momentary loss of control, but the frustration that had caused it was fast turning to fear. Just before coming away to Curzon Street, she had sent Roget to Charles's lodgings. Charles, thank God, was out of town, but the government men had undoubtedly followed her footman there.

Now with Charles expected back tomorrow, and she having so foolishly drawn attention to him, she must, *must*, contrive to see him before Sir Lloyd could get on to him from that list of suspects she had supplied.

But that was far from the only problem that had flown up in her face. She saw at once that she daren't go on to Hans Place and turn their attention to it, as well. They were all too apt to set a guard on Cousin Fanny's house, as they had apparently done here, and would need wait only a short time until Jack appeared, resplendent in his colonel's uniform. But, how, if she did not go, was she to get a warning—or word of *any* kind—to Jack? It was her only means of communicating with him.

"Mady," said Dorothea, speaking for the first time, her calm, sensible tone just thinly covering her own sense of grief and vexation. "Perhaps it will not be so detrimental as you suppose—if they were to learn of your relationship with Jack. They must eventually, you know."

"Yes, but—oh, I don't know," Madeleine said, sitting up and releasing her brother's hand with a grateful pat. "Perhaps if I had given his name at the outset. But I was so terrified then. So in the dark as to what had actually taken place. Just what sort of information Menard had passed on to France. How much proof they require before clapping one into prison. It seemed—and so it does still—that so long as they suspect me, Jack must be in the gravest danger. There has been no time when he mightn't have told me extremely damaging secrets. Imagine! If just *one* of the things to which he has been privy chanced to coincide with something Menard got wind of in another way."

She sagged under the weight of her own thoughts. "At all events, it cannot signify now. I didn't tell them, and my very refusal has increased their suspicion to a point where they may never be convinced of his innocence. All that matters is what am I to do for the best now. I must find a way to warn Jack, but—Oh! *Pray* do not any of you go near Hans Place! It is possible they are keeping watch over all of you, as well."

She rose, her mind now craving solitude so that she might think—find a way of getting a message to Jack. But recalling the state of her finances, she dropped back onto the sofa and said with a wintry smile, "Well, this abominable situation has brought one advantage. There is no longer a need to repay the marriage settlement. Unfortunately, Patrick, dear," she added, turning to her brother, "owing that my pockets are now wholly to let, I fear I must lay claim to my portion."

"Of *course!*" he exclaimed, leaping to his feet. "I—but, how should you like it? The entire four hundred at once, or shall you prefer I arrange quarterly payments?"

"You will need to consult with Jack as to permanent arrangements. Just now, I think a quarterly payment will serve to keep me beforehand with the world. And will you send someone to fetch me a hackney? I think I must be going."

"Your beautiful carriage," sighed her mother.

"Jack wouldn't wish me to keep that, were it possible," Madeleine returned tensely.

Patrick, trying to lighten his sister's mood, injected that, at any rate, it wouldn't look so natty by half with the arms laid out on a dowager's lozenge.

Madeleine produced an obliging smile, accepted what funds her brother could spare until a visit to his banker, and became lost in her own plans while awaiting the arrival of her hackney.

Only minutes after she was set down in Leicester Square she dashed out a letter to the young lady who had written from Harrogate. She planned to use this innocent missive, set out on a distinctive black-edged paper, to see just how thorough her watchdogs intended to be.

She rang for Roget and gave a twenty-pound note into his hand, bidding him enjoy a hot dinner at a tavern before fetching back food for the house. Passing him the letter, she explained its purpose and told him what she wished him to do.

He returned in less than two hours with the change from the twenty-pound note and a good selection of things from which Madeleine and Atty could make a cold meal. But the news as to the fate of her letter was rendered no less depressing for having been anticipated.

Roget had waited in a nearby shop from where he observed a man slip into the post office, present a document, and come away with what he was ready to vow was the very letter he had posted only moments before.

Madeleine nodded grimly and put from her mind all hope of getting her message to Hans Place through the penny post. After bringing her footman's wages up to date, she sent him back to the card game that had somehow surmounted the stumbling block of language for him and Atty.

Madeleine remained, staring down at her idle writing materials, her mind in a hopeless quandary as to what to do. Where was she to suggest Jack come to her? Since she had been followed to Curzon Street, there was no reason to suppose they wouldn't track her into Yorkshire and watch her brother's estate, as well. Even if she could find the means of getting a letter safely delivered to Jack, it seemed that there was nothing but to warn him to keep away for months and months.

Just the thought of framing such words brought a now familiar constriction to her throat. If ever she had needed the support of his calm good sense and the comfort of his love, it was now. Yet it seemed they meant to deprive her of both her peace and her palliative until she should be grateful to confess to a crime she had not committed.

Happily, she was not left to languish in this fit of depression for long. In little over twenty minutes there was a knocking on the front door that heralded the solution to both problems.

Madeleine was already looking up expectantly when Roget came in to advise her that he had placed the baron's relations in the large reception room on the ground floor. Madeleine bid him show them to the drawing room and gave him the key to the wine cellar.

"Choose a few bottles of the best to be had. And while you are about it, Roget, take one for your own supper. We may as well drink what we like while we are here. It will be auctioned from under us soon enough."

She replaced the cover on her inkpot and went to greet her guests. They were a pleasant party of four, consisting of the baron's sister, her husband, and their two daughters—both of whom Madeleine judged to be in their early thirties.

Fortunately for the advancement of their relationship, Madame Montefiore was able to comprehend most of the English that threaded through Madeleine's conversation and to supply some in return.

Madeleine learned that her guests were just a small delegation of a family linked by such a complex tangle of relationship that she soon gave over trying to keep abreast of the names. But she followed their story with interest.

They had all drifted into England at different stages during the Terror and then, except for the baron, banded together on a rented farm in Somerset, sharing the work and waiting out the years until they could return to their homes in France.

News of the baron's perfidy had made it difficult, however—and in one instance, dangerous—to remain in the English community where they had been farming. So they had packed up betimes to return to France. They would support themselves in the same manner there until the restoration of their own estates could be processed.

Madeleine liked and admired them and was considerably touched when Madame Montefiore went on to say that they had stopped on their way to Dover to assure her that, as a newly widowed member of the family, she was welcome to join them should it prove convenient.

"I fear, *baronne*, you may find it uncomfortable in your own country for a time," she added sadly.

Madeleine owned that there had already been evidence of this. It came suddenly to her notice that none of her guests were dressed for mourning.

Madame Montefiore almost jumped at the mention of it. No, she could not too strongly advise against the folly of wearing mourning for such a one. Neither in England *nor* in Royalist France. She approved, however, of Madeleine's gray walking dress, from which Atty had clipped away the cherry-colored ribbons. "Sobriety is very much in order, however, for we must hope to make it understood that we feel great shame in our connection to such a villain."

Madeleine found herself beginning to give serious consideration to their invitation. She couldn't accept, of course, without making plain her intentions concerning Jack. Yet suddenly, in light of madame's attitude toward the baron, that didn't seem such an outrageous thing to do.

She began to feel a little hopeful. France must surely put her beyond the prying eyes of the English government. And the Montefiore home would give her a place where Jack could come to her in safety. Moreover, it would settle the troublesome question of waiting to remarry.

If Jack and she were to wed in France, there need be no announcement sent to the London papers. They would have a little time together in peace, and she could return quietly to England, no longer the notorious Baroness de Beauvoir, but the excessively happy and unobtrusive Mrs. Ashton.

She glanced up speculatively at Madame Montefiore, a little in doubt, however, as to how much help she might be on a farm. But she decided that it would likely not come amiss if her contribution were to be augmented by a few English pounds. Yes, she would go—provided she could do so with everything quite understood about Jack.

"Madame," she began tentatively, "I am deeply sensible of the honor you do me—to look upon me as one of your family— but there is something that you should understand before I accept your kind invitation. My marriage to your brother was one of arrangement and not affection."

"It is most often so among our class," nodded Madame Montefiore.

"There was a gentleman I should have preferred to marry, but his finances were not sufficient for the needs of my family."

Madame nodded again, clearly thinking she had conducted matters most sensibly.

"However, madame, I am deeply in love with this gentleman," Madeleine persevered, "and wish to marry him now that my family is no longer in need and I find myself unexpectedly free."

"It is natural," said madame, still awaiting the confession. Then distress suddenly flashed across her features. "This gentleman—he is not of your station?"

"Oh!—to be sure, he is!" Madeleine returned, a little startled.

"Ah."

"It is merely that I wished you to be aware of my sentiments and to know that I should wish this gentleman to visit me in France."

"But of course! You are young and beautiful, and it is natural that you should be in love. It is also natural that you should wish to marry again and that the gentleman must be permitted to court you."

Madeleine's relief was in no way reduced by her amusement at encountering—probably for the first time in her life—someone who thought everything she wished to do was quite natural and perfectly acceptable.

Her strain eased, and, with that much settled, she was able to pour out the entire story of her present difficulty regarding Jack and the investigation.

Her guests were so satisfyingly shocked and outraged when Madame Montefiore translated her words into more recognizable French, that Madeleine was feeling almost lighthearted by the time they all sat down to a cold meal. Suddenly her most pressing problems were in a way to being fully resolved.

Madame Montefiore had flicked away the difficulty of getting a message to Jack. "I shall carry your letter along and post it under my own cover from Dover," she shrugged. "It will be delivered even before you can prepare yourself to join us in Paris."

She was perfectly confident that the authorities would not attempt to follow her or search her possessions, but, seeing that Madeleine continued to show concern, she indulgently proposed a plan to put the matter beyond all risk.

"We shall write out your messages now," she said, "and I shall assist you. I have had some experience with such shifts—in fleeing from my country in the midst of revolution, you understand. This, I assure you, is not to compare. To start, you will use no names in your letters. You will merely say in the one, 'Pray give the enclosed message to our friend, the colonel.' Do you see, *ma chérie*, even if the authorities should wrest such a letter from me, they will not know what place to watch? I shall commit your cousin's direction to memory and afix it in my own fist once I am safely at Dover. I shall then post it, along with others of my own, and no one shall suspect it has to do with you at all. The enclosure must say no more than where you may be contacted in France."

The preparations that began with these letters escalated into a whirl of activity that was still well underway by midafternoon of the following day.

Madeleine had first approached Atty with a suggestion that she might prefer to await her in Curzon Street rather than remove to a strange country. But Atty was determined not to risk this opportunity for advancement under the guidance of a kind mistress. She said stoutly that she hoped to be able to give satisfaction wherever her ladyship should choose to live.

Madeleine laughed, smoothing back the girl's tan hair from her forehead. "I don't think you understand. I shan't be languishing in a grand house. I am going to become a farmer."

"My lady! You—you cannot! Your lovely complexion! And your *hands!* Your beautiful hands! Oh—but you are joking me again," Atty smiled, relieved by her own explanation.

"A little," Madeleine smiled back. "But it *is* to a farm that I am going. And everyone is expected to help."

All Atty would say was that she fancied she knew more about farms than about being a lady's maid—having been born and bred in Devonshire. And if that was what her mistress wished to do, well, then, she would help, too.

Roget, when asked if he would assume the role of escort and courier, was beside himself with pride and delight. Madeleine promised him a return passage to England, but he exclaimed, *"Mais non, madame la baronne!* It is to Paris that I wish to go, and to have my fare paid is more than my favorite hope!"

Madeleine said that in order to make an effective escort, it would be necessary for him to put off his livery and outfit himself as a gentleman. So they all went up to the baron's dressing room to see what could be contrived.

Since Roget was a tall, well-setup young man, the baron's coat strained dangerously at the shoulders and the pantaloons showed plainly that they would be much too short to be strapped beneath his boots.

Atty, however, sewed extensions on the straps, and it was agreed that it would be equally fashionable to wear them inside the sparkling Hessian boots, which he assured Madeleine pinched only a very little.

"You had better carry along your own shoes to wear in the carriage and during the crossing," she said doubtfully. "And pack yourself ample shirts, stockings, and neck cloths. There is no guessing how long we shall be. And you will need slippers and evening breeches and a black coat for dinner at the inns. We shall say you are my husband's cousin. From the list of names Madame Montefiore rattled off, there cannot be many Frenchmen who are not."

She turned to her maid. "And, Atty, a second pair of pantaloons rigged out as you have done wouldn't come amiss."

SIXTEEN

Madeleine went off then to see to her own wardrobe, advising Roget to help himself to whatever fobs, seals, and other adjuncts he thought necessary to complete the picture.

By early evening of the next day much of the packing had been completed, though there remained several small chores and errands still to be done. Roget was sent to discover if Charles was returned to town, while Madeleine put up a basket of food and wine to help lessen expenses on their journey. One hundred pounds a quarter would permit a prudent lady to live in modest comfort, but it was scarcely a sum calculated to accommodate one very long when nicked by the costly business of travel.

Roget returned just as she was finishing, but was able to report no success in Bury Street. It was the third time she had sent him that day, but Madeleine knew that the only message Charles could be depended upon not to ignore was one containing a veiled threat. And this she could trust only to verbal delivery.

She threw off the apron, which wrapped twice around her spare frame, and sent Roget to fetch a hackney and load into it what amounted to almost a year's supply of tea, sugar, and assorted spices.

"While I am gone," she said, presenting him with an ample purse when he came in again, "bespeak a chaise for a little after seven, then change into your gentleman's attire."

She hurried out to the waiting hackney and had herself driven to Curzon Street, where she quickly outlined her plans to her family and collected the remainder of the hundred pounds from her brother. Claudia herself had seen the futility of remaining in London while events were still so fresh in the eyes of society. They were already making plans to return to Yorkshire at the end of the month.

Madeleine nodded. "But Patrick, just as you are ready to go, pray send the tea and things to Cousin Fanny with my love."

She was back at Leicester Square in little more than thirty minutes, judging the hour before dinner as the best time to find Charles dressing for his evening entertainments. With all in train for a speedy departure, she was anxious to get underway before more complications could arise.

For one thing, she was becoming obsessed with the realization that only the next few hours held any further threat for Jack. Her letter hadn't had time yet to reach Hans Place. It was not wholly inconceivable that Jack might arrive betimes in England, in which case her cousin would unknowingly send him on to Leicester Square and straight into the arms of the guards.

She made a quick change into a forest-green traveling habit and told Roget and Atty of her plan.

"I daren't go without seeing Mr. Morland," she said, "and, though, I am confident he will be found at this hour, I am not so confident that he will respond promptly enough to a message to call on me. At all events, I wish to lure away our friends out there without further delay. Therefore I shall take one hackney to Bury Street and settle my business with Mr. Morland while

Atty sets out in another. You once mentioned having an aunt in Golden Square, Atty. You might as well go there and take leave of her. I know you should prefer to be doing this in Hans Place, but you do understand? . . ."

Madeleine supplied her with a few coins. "Fine. Even though I wasn't able to give particulars in the letter that's on its way from Dover to my cousin, I assured her that you are quite safe. I shall write again, including messages to all your friends, as soon as we land in France."

Drawing on a pair of black kid gloves, she spoke again to Roget. "As soon as the chaise arrives and our things are packed aboard, you may collect Atty and then call for me."

Everyone exchanged looks and nods. "Very well," Madeleine smiled, heading for the door. "If my luck is in, we shall all be together again in not much more than three quarters of an hour, and free to begin our journey."

Madeleine had no occasion to quarrel with her luck. She was shortly installed in a stuffy parlor by a disapproving landlord, who grumbled that he would see if Mr. Morland wished to receive her.

She knew she was acting with the greatest impropriety, to be calling at a gentleman's lodging without a companion, but her business with Charles was of too secret a nature to permit of such niceties. She shrugged away the landlord's scorn. On balance, it was rather a trifling consideration for one already suspected of selling her favors in order to betray her country.

She settled herself on the faded sofa and prepared for something of a wait. By choosing such an hour, the odds were heavy that she would be catching Charles in a state of undress.

It was nearly ten minutes before he burst into the little parlor, looking excessively harassed. "What the devil do you mean by coming here as bold as brass and sending up your name?"

"Afraid for my reputation, Charles? Or your own? How like you to make me a byword and then fear the association. Well, having also made England too hot to hold me, you needn't fear it much longer. A chaise will be at the door in a few minutes to carry me to Dover." She gestured at the chair opposite. "Sit down and be grateful that it didn't suit me to jeopardize more than your good name. It might easily have been your neck."

She had much to do to ward off an expression of contempt at the panic that leaped into his eyes. "Are you wondering how much I know?" she asked. "I know all."

She gave him a brief account of Marie's disclosure, explaining that, although they had revealed the baron's arrangement with his English collaborator, they had pretended not to know which of her admirers it might be. She told him of the list she had been required to give and that his name was on it.

"You stupid, *stupid*, little idiot! To put *me* on such a list!"

"Try for a little sense. Your attentions haven't been precisely *discreet*. Your name would have become wildly conspicuous by omission."

"Oh, be damned to you! Why did you have to blab out the tale in the first place?"

"Because I am frightfully selfish, of course. I didn't wish to go to prison and be burned to death just to spare you this inconvenience. If we are to speak of idiots . . . But never mind that. 'Forewarned is forearmed,' in the words of—well, somebody. The important thing for you to understand is that Sir Lloyd has stated it as his intention 'to leave no stone unturned.' A wonderfully apt association, now that I think of it. The point, however, being that they should have come round to you, whatever I did or did not say. They are investigating everyone who has ever called in Leicester Square. You've evidently been spared this long only because they are still concentrating on those in government or military positions."

She paused, leveling her gaze. "Which brings me to my next point. I am revolted by what you've done, Charles, but I haven't cried rope—and I shan't—provided you are willing to oblige me in one small matter."

His glance sharpening, he asked what she meant.

"My wretched maid told them of Colonel Ashton. Fortunately, she didn't know him by his correct name, and apparently she failed to mention sending him on to the Frost Fair. You may or may not be asked about a British colonel of my acquaintance. As long as you do not supply them with his name, I shall hold my tongue about you. Marie has agreed to say nothing—though she has, in any case, been sent on to France."

Charles rose abruptly. He would have bargained with her and gladly, except that Sir Lloyd had already confronted him at his country home and had *already* got Ashton's name.

After the incident at the fair, Charles would have been only too willing, purely on general principle, to see both Madeleine and her colonel in hell. But the prime opportunity to divert suspicion from himself had made it a double satisfaction to inform Sir Lloyd that Madeleine's secret lover just happened to be an intelligence officer on Wellington's staff.

Since that interview, Charles had read of the baron's death and breathed easier, believing there was no one left to connect him with the business. He had also supposed, with further satisfaction, that the same event must have left Madeleine thoroughly dished up. After weighing the situation, he had decided to return to Town and let it be seen how indifferent he was to both Madeleine's plight and the fact that such an investigation was taking place.

The world had rocked violently when he'd learned that Madeleine was standing in a position to accuse him. And, if it had rocked then, it now threatened total collapse. There wasn't a doubt that she would follow through on her threat, if not merely out of revenge, then in an attempt to ease matters for Ashton.

There seemed nothing for it but to silence her permanently. But Charles was by no means certain he could bring himself up to scratch. Given the time, he would have had no compunction whatsoever about hiring somebody else to see to it, but she was on her way out of the country. It would have to be done on the spot or lose the chance for good.

He began such a furious round of pacing that Madeleine felt compelled to ask, "Charles, have you understood?"

"Yes, yes, of course," he muttered distractedly.

"Then for heaven's sake stop displaying yourself before that window in the guise of a wild man or you'll be bringing down your own ruin."

He halted, as white as his neck cloth. "Are you saying you think they may have followed you here?"

"I am convinced of it. They follow me everywhere. My letters are intercepted. My servants—"

He sank down into his chair as abruptly as he had risen from it. "Oh, you Goddamned little scatterbrain! You've led them right to me! And for what? A paltry beggar like Ashton!"

"It is not good policy to be drawing comparisons of that nature, Charles. As for bringing you to their notice . . . Well, I must say I regret that myself. But the damage was done before I realized they *were* watching me. I'd sent Roget with a message to you yesterday, and having allowed them to see that much, it became all the more urgent to follow through and let you know how matters stood."

She watched the nervous way he was fidgeting with his quizzing glass and added, "But I've thought it through carefully, and there is no reason to fall into such a taking. They've known all along of my *supposed* partiality for your society. In view of that, they shouldn't think it too out of the way that I felt compelled to take leave of you before fleeing the country."

Just envisioning the position she had placed him in made Charles begin to feel that he might, after all, be well up to killing her with his own hands. Unfortunately, she had also placed him in the position of having to do it virtually under the eyes of the law. There was a chance, but only a slim one. He would have to prepare himself for flight as an alternative.

"Where are you going?" he asked furiously.

"To France."

"Hoping to meet Ashton," he said, his resolution as to his capabilities growing.

"That is not your affair."

"To think—this entire hornet's nest has come about solely through wishing to have the first roll with you, and Ashton has reaped the only reward. Or have you been his trull all along?"

Charles hadn't really expected her to answer, but, while she sat, staring stonily at him, he vowed to take her at least a time or two before making away with her.

"Very well," he snapped, "you've created such a devil of a coil, I've no choice but to bing it while I can. I'll be taking a place in this chaise you've got coming."

"Are you mad?" Madeleine exclaimed. "I—well, in truth, I can't help thinking that it *would* be your safest course to fly before they can submit you to a thorough investigation. But not all in a *scramble*. And rid yourself of the notion that you can come with me. For one thing, there is no room. I am traveling with two servants. For another, it would be tantamount to a confession, and you cannot suppose they should deal more kindly with you in France. If they didn't cut off your head themselves, they would return you promptly to England to be hanged."

"Oh, stubble it. It's not to France I intend going. And it's the only way to keep the look of a scramble out of it. You said yourself they wouldn't think it out of the way that you'd come to take leave of me. They'll think it all the more natural if they suppose you stopped to take me up."

"Well, whatever *they* may think, I've told you there simply isn't room."

"Then make room," he growled. "You've shown yourself ready enough to cast me to the wolves in order to spare Ashton. Now I am warning you. If I don't get clean away, I'll take an oath that I got everything I knew directly from your confounded, sneaksby intelligence officer."

Not for a moment did Madeleine think to doubt him. She had come suspecting him of something of the kind. But, apart from this, it did begin to seem that it might be safest in the long run to help him escape in an orderly fashion. The authorities would probably take to watching him now that she had called, suspecting, at the very least, that she was trying to convey a message through him.

"Very well," she agreed wearily. "Doesn't your brother have holdings somewhere in Kent? Do we pass near them on the Dover Road?"

She sighed, for Charles had gone off into another brown study. "Charles! *Is* there a turning off the pike road that leads to your brother's Kentish estate?"

"Yes. The crossroad to Queenborough," he replied absently.

"Fine. If I am asked at Dover what became of you, I shall say that I set you down there. Make ready, then, and be quick. I have both my watchdogs divided and occupied at the moment, but they will be united again once the chaise arrives. If we let it stand, one may slip off for instructions and be back in time to stop us in our tracks."

Charles went up to his rooms, reappearing in just a few minutes with only a small valise. The chaise arrived not long after, and they went out to it immediately.

As Madeleine stood, peering into its dark interior, trying to decide how best to distribute four bodies over seating for three, Charles pushed himself into the empty place beside Atty, then grasped Madeleine's arm with the obvious intention of pulling her onto his lap.

"Take your hand from me, Charles," she commanded in a sharp whisper, for she felt certain that there were curious ears somewhere in the shadows.

"Don't be a little fool," he growled. "It's the simplest way."

Charles was leaning partially out of the door, his attention fully on Madeleine. So it came as something of a shock to have his own wrist taken in a harsh grip.

Roget had not understood the words, but the tones, combined with the picture before him, had been sufficient for his understanding. He spoke quietly in French. "You will do as madame has bid."

"Who the devil's that?" Charles demanded with a start of fright.

Madeleine, her nerves taut, her sense of humor always pliant, had to struggle to keep her features in order. When she thought she could speak without danger of a fit of inappropriate laughter, she said in the best French she could muster, "He is the man in charge of my protection on this journey, so I advise you to do as he suggests."

"But who—? You said you were traveling with servants," Charles accused, barely making out an elaborately arranged cravat and a vastly proportioned nosegay (Roget's own contribution to his sartorial splendor).

"Charles, I have told you we mustn't linger here. It is Roget."

"Your confounded *flunky?*" he demanded and raged out in French at the shadowy form across from him. "I'll have you whipped for laying hands on me."

"Perhaps, *monsieur*, you will wish to do so when you recover. For if you do not release madame, I shall break your arm."

"Madeleine! For God's sake!" Charles exploded in a harsh whisper. "Are you going to stand there and listen to your damned skip-kennel threatening me?"

"Certainly. It would be a poor day's work to engage a man to protect me and then interfere with his first opportunity to do so. Make room, Charles, you know you wouldn't like to come to cuffs with someone of your own size."

"*Madame la baronne*, if you permit," Roget intervened. "You shall be too crowded. *Mademoiselle* Ahtee shall assume the forward seat and I shall repose on the floor."

Madeleine thought for a moment, sorely tempted, for she had no wish to be crushed so intimately against Charles.

"Oh, what the devil is this?" Charles demanded. "Saving even the *crumbs* for Ashton?"

That settled it.

"Thank you, Roget. I should be most grateful. Atty, take Roget's seat. Oh—and give him that cushion. Mr. Morland is not going the distance and shall not require it. Roget, if you place it behind your back and rest against the door, you shouldn't be too uncomfortable. Slide over, Charles, you see the arrangement."

And thus the uncomfortable party set out—over London Bridge, through the Green Man Turnpike, across the Surrey Canal.

Madeleine, sitting sideways on her legs in order to make room on the floor for Roget, shifted occasionally to ward off impending cramps and abused herself over her cheese-paring decision to reverse her order for a chaise and four.

Having indulged in a few tumbled calculations, she had concluded that there could be nothing accomplished by arriving at Dover before daylight. Nothing, except to spend funds unnecessarily at an inn. So it had seemed only practical to save the cost of two extra horses and travel with less speed. She had, of course, reckoned on their being able to nap throughout the long night.

Yet to alter arrangements at this stage would mean a lengthy delay while the baggage was transferred to a vehicle with a shaft designed for a team, thus making it unlikely that she would be any the sooner rid of her unwelcome guest.

But when more than half the journey had been accomplished without relief, and she was stiff and tired and thoroughly vexed, she glared over at Charles and demanded, "For goodness' sake, how much farther do you mean to drive with us?"

Charles had been wondering about this himself. His hope of being able to dispose of Madeleine along the way was not working out well at all. His pistol was ready in his valise, but his plan had hinged on being able to prevail upon her to engage a second vehicle so that they might drive in comfort. In such circumstance, he felt the pursuing authorities would continue after Madeleine's original chaise and leave him to murder her in peace.

He'd planned then to hide her body carefully and explain her absence later by claiming that it had been she who had engineered the system of a second chaise—apparently with the intention of making her escape. He would insist that she had left him awaiting her in the private parlor of an inn and had simply never returned.

All during the early part of the drive, Charles had been soothing himself by embroidering unpleasant little embellishments to his scheme. The least unpleasant was a decision to add that Madeleine had not only confessed her own guilt but had mentioned Ashton as her source of information.

But each time they stopped for a fresh pair of horses,

Madeleine flatly refused to be separated from her servants. In desperation, he devised an alternate scheme and tried to induce her to join him for refreshment at one of the posting houses. He could then slip out and bribe the postboy to carry off her chaise, thereby forcing her to accept his offer of another vehicle.

Madeleine, however, could not be tempted or cajoled into so much as stepping from the carriage in his company. All attempts at stronger persuasion were instantly quashed by her glowering footman.

Whenever she did alight to exercise her legs or to enter one of the inns, she took along her maid, requesting him to await her in the chaise, her request effectively reinforced by Roget's strong arm.

Madeleine had no suspicion of what was going on in Charles's head, nor any real fear of him in a physical sense. She was merely keeping her promise to Jack. But Charles, who knew nothing of this, was left to grind his teeth over the caprice that had allowed her to care so little for her reputation as to call blatantly at his lodgings one minute and, in the next, refuse to consider even a light repast in his company at an inn.

He had remained throughout in some doubt as to his actual ability to go through with his plan. At least as far as *killing* her. But he was fast becoming certain that he would be given no opportunity to put it to the touch. Even if he were willing to murder them all—maid, man, and postboy—it was not to be considered while that one particular coach reappeared so consistently behind them. No matter how often they halted for a change of cattle or how long they were kept kicking their heels for a malingering pike-keeper, each time the road straightened for a piece—always that particular coach. Never nearer, never farther away.

By the time they were drawn up at the Harbledown Turnpike, the last in their path before Dover, Charles knew there was nothing for it but to follow through with his emergency plan and arrange to have himself smuggled to America. He could only hope that the current mood over there would offer opportunity to an Englishman who had shown himself willing to betray his country.

Along with his pistol, Charles's valise contained all his available funds and valuable possessions, a precaution he had taken as soon as the investigation into the baron's activities had begun. While the ostlers were hitching up the final change of horses at Canterbury, he made his arrangement with the postboy who would guide them over the last stage.

A short while later, as their carriage topped a long upward grade, the postboy patted the pair of shiny, new, yellow Georges reposing in his pocket, and obeyed his instructions to "spring 'em past the next curve, then halt only long enough to count the legs of his mount."

SEVENTEEN

Madeleine joined her new friends in Paris, arriving only hours before His Sacred Majesty's truimphant return from exile in England. The city was a riot of celebration and packed tightly with dignitaries, armies, and curious citizens from every major power in Europe. England was perhaps best represented, and, as prophesied by Claudia, it looked as though all were in train for an extremely gay spring.

The festive atmosphere was stimulating, but Madeleine was eager to be off to the district where Jack would be expecting to find her. An advance party of the family had located a suitable farm in the province of Angoumois, near the confiscated Montefiore estates, so there was no real need to linger.

Roget would remain in Paris. Madame Montefiore's influence had secured him a coveted place as first footman in one of the city's most consequential houses.

He came to see them off, looking dashing in his new, extremely elegant livery. After assisting a rather apprehensive Atty into one of the cavalcade of carriages, he spoke to Madeleine in a low, concerned tone. "Are you quite certain, madame, that you wish this? I have had talk with one of the servants. It appears not at all a life for you. I, myself, will serve and protect you, if you prefer to rent a small house of your own."

"No, Roget, you must take advantage of this opportunity. I don't expect to be in France but a few weeks." She took his hand. "But thank you. For this and all your help. We shouldn't have had this successful journey without you."

Two nights later she dropped exhaustedly onto a narrow bed in a crowded chamber of the main farmhouse. She should have preferred to share a room with Atty, if share she must. But no. The Montefiores might have taught themselves to farm as laborers, but they retained unshakable attitudes concerning caste. The servants must be quartered in separate cottages near the main house.

So Madeleine found herself the chambermate of a morose female cousin of sixteen who spoke no English at all and, judging by several attempts to become friendly with her, precious little French.

The family breakfasted at cockcrow, gathered round a long, plain board table. Madeleine rose to the summons, stiff in every joint and feeling that she hadn't slept at all, but she was relieved to find that the other members, unlike her sleeping companion, were of a happy disposition. This was apparent at least in tone and countenance. But they spoke in such rapid French that she could grasp only bits of the table conversation and contribute nothing at all.

After the meal she insisted on giving a substantial sum toward hers and Atty's keep, saying that she doubted she would be staying long enough to become of real use about the farm. "Though, of course, madame, I mean to help in whatever way I can," she hastened to add.

Madame Montefiore hesitated. "I do not take this in payment, you understand, *ma* Madeleine. Regrettably, I must accept it as an *apport*. It is too much needed for items of food that we must purchase until the farm can be brought to support us. As to your help—that, too, I shall accept in the same spirit."

She called together several of the ladies, and a wild Gallic exchange took place. Madeleine waited, the object of much pointing and occasional scrutiny. Plainly, her fate was being decided. She began to hope nervously that it wasn't as horrifying as all that groaning and head-clapping seemed to suggest.

After a few more minutes of this, a buxom female, much of her own age, gestured for her to come. Madeleine followed her out to the hennery and was shown her duties in an attitude of enduring despair.

She guessed it was her look of delicacy, exaggerated at the moment by the weight she had lost during those weeks and weeks of anxiety. It put her on her mettle to be dismissed so summarily as a weakling. It was not the sort of thing she had been reared to do, and certainly nothing to her liking, but she fancied herself as capable of learning as any of them. So she entered the hen yard in a businesslike way and worked among its illogical inhabitants, sustained by her pride and what soon proved an invaluable sense of humor.

She had never supposed herself suited to a country life. After a few hours amid the colorful collection of birds in the sunny yard, she was certain of it. "What idiotic fiends you are!" she cried, appalled by such savagery when she scattered grain from a low pan. "There is more than enough for all of you! Good God, why take it as an excuse to try to kill and maim one another?"

Next she scraped the hen house floor with teeth-gritting resolution, then stole the daily quota of eggs from violently protesting hens, if not with professional sangfroid, certainly with praiseworthy courage. She even learned, after only a reasonable degree of shock, to rebuff the advances of a perversely amorous rooster who had settled on her as his object.

That evening, Atty, who was helping in the dairy, applied goose grease to her mistress's hands. "Oh, my lady." She sighed at their condition. "Didn't I say how it would be?"

Madeleine just shook her head and applied a little of the unsavory substance to her sunburned complexion, thinking how Jack would laugh to see her when he came.

But Jack did not come. And soon a month had passed. Madeleine walked as usual to the little inn near Ruelle that Madame Montefiore had suggested as the place of contact, but again no officer had inquired and no letter was waiting.

"Oh, I am convinced my letter to him must have gone astray," she said to Madame Montefiore when she hurried in. "I am going to write at once to Cousin Fanny and ask."

But she was assured by return mail that it had indeed arrived safely. Although "their friend the colonel" had not been by to collect it.

When another fortnight slipped away, Madeleine's fear was now for Jack's safety. All manner of possibilities passed through her mind until she could bear it no longer.

She learned that the British army was using Bordeaux as a major embarkation center. The Peninsular veterans were gathering there to be transported either back to England or off to new assignments.

"Madame, I feel a perfect wretch to be deserting my duties at such a time, but I simply *must* go down and try to get news of Jack."

"Calm yourself, *ma* Madeleine. *Certes* you must," Madame returned with great sympathy, begging her not to concern herself over the hens. "*Non, non,* and no more the butter. *Naturellement,* you must take your maid! *A coup sûr,* you must not think of traveling such a distance without the escort of a gentleman!"

"Atty, yes, but not one of the men," Madeleine insisted vigorously. "I couldn't think of it. Not when they are needed so urgently in the fields."

But madame was not to be overborne. If she could have been brought to overlook the aspects of prudence, those of propriety she could not.

In the end Madeleine submitted guiltily to accepting the

company of an elderly uncle, who sat beside her in contented silence over the entire eighty miles.

But, if not before, once in Bordeaux she couldn't be grateful enough for his presence. The town was as lively as might be expected of a place housing thousands upon thousands of victorious, war-hardened soldiers not yet accustomed to the leisure of peace.

Madeleine had learned to be at ease among military men, but she had never been exposed to large numbers of the army's rank and file. They struck her more as a mob of unruly rabble than Wellington's prize troops.

"*Oncle,* I am a trifle *effrayé* to walk the crowded streets amongst them. You must go out in my place," she explained. "Here." She gave him a purse bulging with coins. "They look as though they'd welcome more drink. Stand them to wine or ale and show this around." She unfolded a message written in English that he was to carry. It begged anyone acquainted with Colonel Ashton to accompany him to the lodgings of a lady who was urgently seeking news of him.

Two days of these efforts passed without results, but Madeleine, flinging open the door of her rooms at each sound of footsteps on the stair, soon became acquainted with a young officer who, even in her sunburned condition, was more than ready to give himself wholly into her service. From him, she was able to learn a little of what had taken place in southern France at the close of the war.

She sat across from him in her old-fashioned parlor and listened intently, filling the young man's glass the instant it became empty.

"Thank you, but no more, baroness," he laughed when she raised the decanter a fourth time. "Somewhere you seem to have got the notion that the army subsists on wine." He shifted into a more relaxed position. "No, we hadn't more than a whisper of peace until the twelfth of April. A dashed nuisance, when you think that a battle costing us forty-five hundred Allied soldiers was fought four days after Bonaparte's abdication."

This only added another to Madeleine's accumulating fears.

"But that means that Colonel Ashton would have been traveling through hostile territory during his return to Lord Wellington's headquarters."

"Well, yes—I daresay that's true enough," he owned reluctantly, then turned the conversation, correcting her on another point. "But it's no longer merely *Lord* Wellington, baroness. The great man was made a duke early in May."

Madeleine's worried gray-green eyes flickered with hope when she learned that it was for His Grace the troops were waiting. He was expected any day to deliver an address of official farewell. "I see," she said thoughtfully. "Well, *he*, if no one else in this place, will know what has become of the colonel. I promise you, sir, I shall have the ear of this much revered duke of yours if I have to cast myself on his neck to do it!"

In the event, this drastic measure wasn't necessary. The very next morning Madeleine's lieutenant burst in with news that he had located a major who would call round shortly with definite word of Ashton.

"Did—did he look grave when he spoke of him?" Madeleine faltered with a pounding heart.

"Not at all, baroness. To say the truth, he was a trifle unwilling to come. Said that it was probably just another of Jack's—er . . . that he supposed it to be a lady of only mild acquaintance with the colonel."

Just another of Jack's light-skirts . . . Madeleine completed the sentence in her mind, recalling how she had once expressed indifference over his activities in that area. She felt anything but indifference at the mention of it now. A flash of violent rage, to be precise. But she vowed instantly to overlook a hundred light-skirts, if only Jack were alive and safe, *and* ready to be done with them now!

The reluctant major made his appearance an hour later and was frankly startled to find the likes of Madeleine in such a place. He bowed elaborately. "Your *most* obedient servant, ma'am."

She set in at once, forgetting even to offer him a seat. He smiled a little, but answered her willingly. "Why, yes, as far as

I know Jack is perfectly fit. Unless," he added, with an attempt at archness, "he is prone to *mal de mer*. As it happens, I had occasion to shake his hand on the very day he embarked for America."

"*America!* Oh, no, no. That cannot be true!"

The major paused, then said civilly, "Perhaps not. Let us be clear on one point. Are we discussing *Colonel John* Ashton, brother to *Major Robert* Ashton? Both intelligence officers, you know. It's caused a deuce of a mix-up on more than one occasion. Of course, Robert is sold out now and returned to the family pile in Ireland . . . *Not* Robert," he said in answer to Madeleine's impatient head-shaking. "Well, then, baroness, you may be assured that good old Jack volunteered for service across the Atlantic. No question about it. Seen by myself and a dozen others, boarding a man-of-war bound for North American waters."

"But *why? Why* should he go there?" Madeleine demanded, still incredulous.

"We've been at war with the Yankees these two years, ma'am," the major replied politely, ready to accept that such a fact might have escaped the notice of a lovely civilian. Certainly *he* could think of no better reason for a colonel of the army to be heading that way.

Madeleine could think of none at all for Jack to have done such a thing, and throughout the entire ten-hour journey back to Ruelle, she alternated between a benumbed confusion and a biting indignation. "America!" she exclaimed, startling *oncle* out of a comfortable doze.

It was almost past her comprehension. She had learned through correspondence with her family that Lambert had been amongst the first volunteers to be transported to the American war. It was thought a good opportunity for a young officer wishing to advance as quickly as possible. But it was Lambert's intention to make a career of the military. Jack had said time and again that his only purpose for remaining in the army was to help stem the devastating progress of Bonaparte. Why, she even recalled his once saying that he didn't *approve* of the war with America!

Yet he had gone there. And gone *knowing* she must be on thorns awaiting him! And if he wasn't aware of the baron's death . . . Good God, that just made it all the *more* unforgivable! He must, in that case, be supposing her deeply embroiled in a scandalous struggle to free herself from her marriage—*and* by the rather *desperate* methods suggested by himself!

The only possible explanation to occur to her—and this far from acceptable—was that he had agreed to lend his aid in some particularly tricky business. But to be jeopardizing his life and all her peace in such a cause . . . and over something quite in opposition to his own convictions!

And *then* not even to have written to inform her of it—when she was sleeping among strangers on a lumpy mattress and toiling in the most offensive way. And enduring it all for no better reason than that *he* should have a safe place to come to her.

She couldn't deny that she should, in any case, have been forced to withdraw from society. But she might have gone into Yorkshire, with her *own* family! And there at least passed the time in comfort—with someone to talk to, and *without* those accursed fowls to plague her days!

Calmer reflection told her that Jack was incapable of such thoughtlessness. He must certainly have written and the letter merely gone astray. The major at Bordeaux had supplied her with the headquarters to which Jack was attached. The instant she arrived back at the farm, she gathered up writing materials.

But as she sat to her task, something else the major had said began to echo in her memory . . . *"Just another of Jack's—"* A memory that united involuntarily with Claudia's challenge to Patrick . . . *"Assure your sisters that you continued to fancy yourself in love with that Smith woman after you succeeded in bedding her a few times."*

No, no, no! Madeleine all but screamed aloud. Not Jack! Not her dear, loving Jack!

Yet, as she took up her pen, an innate caution prevailed, and it was not to Jack that she wrote, but to Lambert. She didn't know how she would ever live with it if such a thing could possibly be true, but she did know if she could live with it at all, it would be because she had preserved some shred of her pride and not thrown herself at the head of a man who wanted her no more.

Lambert must see Jack and learn his reason for going to America. And discover discreetly if Jack had in fact tried to write her.

Madeleine resumed her daily walk to the inn at Ruelle long before an answer could reasonably be expected. It was four months until it actually came.

She was eager and reluctant at once, and her breathing too rapid for comfort. She made no attempt to break the seal while still in town, but hurried down the lane that led to the farm, her heart beating in rhythm with her prayer . . . not her Jack, not her Jack, not her dear and very special Jack.

Yet she would not look until she was safely sheltered from all eyes in a little spinney.

"My dear sister," ran Lambert's reply. "I am sorry but it was not possible for me to see Jack since receiving your letter. I have been transferred some distance from Bermuda, where he is presently quartered. I don't know if I shall get back there again or not, but I trust I possess both your answers and a little more news into the bargain.

"I saw Jack not long before transferring away, and I fancy my first words were to ask what, by all that was wonderful, had brought him into our campaign. He merely shrugged, saying something to the effect that 'one must keep busy one way or another.'

"I didn't actually inquire whether he had written to you, but I did ask if he had heard *from* you. He replied that he hadn't, but that he had heard of your brush with the law and of the baron's death. He said everything proper concerning both."

Madeleine's hand was already shaking violently. She sank down onto the grass and laid the paper flat.

"If you are wishing Jack to know your new direction," Lambert went on, "I suggest you write to him at Bermuda. I expect he shall have something to tell you when he writes back, for I fancy we shall find him betrothed by now. He is billeted, along with another fellow (a bit of a chum of mine) in the home of a *very* wealthy family, with a *very* pretty young daughter. My friend (Evans is his name) was in the worst way in love with Miss Helpston and so, naturally, in the greatest gloom, for she took a fancy to our Jack straightaway.

"At my last opportunity to speak to Evans, he'd fallen into complete despair because Miss Helpston had plainly attached Jack as well (she is quite the reigning belle in those parts), and he was courting her with a vengeance, as you may suppose. Evans made his offer in spite of this, but papa told him flat out that he had already spoken with Jack and had given his blessings, to the tune of—oh, some outlandishly vast number of acres and a prime house for them in the midst of it."

Lambert continued with an account of his experiences in the West Indies, but Madeleine could no longer see to read.

For a long time after there were no tears left she remained on the soft floor of the spinney, no match for the corrosive thoughts that preyed on her while she lay, face pressed to the ground, too weakened by desolation to rise. She had known disappointment as a girl, but it was nothing. *Nothing . . .*

Not only was there the loss of Jack, the aching, aching loss of Jack, but the agony of realizing that the one man she had brought herself to trust had wanted no more than all the rest. In company with Charles, he had differed from the others only in the tenacity of his pursuit. Unlike Charles, physical conquest had been far from his only goal. He had not been content with merely her body. He'd wanted her very soul. A willingness to sacrifice anything and everything, even her loyalty to her family. That was what he had demanded from the outset. And what he'd got before walking away.

Something of reason finally prevailed to suggest that perhaps it had been an honest mistake on Jack's part. Perhaps he had merely misread his obsession and thought it love. He could not—surely he could not have been capable of deceiving her so cruelly for all that while.

Perhaps not. But whether he had deceived her or only himself, even reason couldn't deny that she had been right from the start. There were no fairy-tale heroes for real-life women to love. The Jack she thought she knew had stepped back into the pages of a book, and there was nothing left to believe in. Nothing at all, unless it were the cold, bitter philosophy that her mother had learned to embrace.

When at last Madeleine emerged from the small wood, the heat of her pain had drained from her, as had warmth of any kind. She walked to the edge of a small brook and bent to splash water on her face. She stayed for a moment, gazing down at the running water. Then she rose and walked briskly on her way.

It didn't take her long to realize that she wasn't even to have the consolation of removing from the discomforts of her present situation. Where was she to go? London—the only place she really cared to be—must be avoided until the coming spring, when the period of her questionable mourning had ended, and events, which had conspired to discredit her, were relegated to the past.

There was Yorkshire, of course, but Madeleine knew without a second's hesitation that she would prefer to labor in the fields with the Montefiore men than face her mother. Claudia had been right this time. Right all along. But Madeleine couldn't hear her say it. Not now. Not for a long, long while. And the others? . . . They had been entirely too understanding. She'd worn her heart on her sleeve like a flighty chit. Bubbled with talk of the perfections of her lover. No. No more could she bear the awkwardness of their embarrassment on her behalf.

There was nowhere. Nothing but to remain as she was. Six long, hard, lonely months to go. But it was better than destroying all hope of acceptance in London. Better than facing her family.

And so she stayed and continued to tend to her chickens. And to toss uncomfortably on her bed. And to take meals among contented people who chattered and laughed of things she could not understand.

But during the mild French winter her complexion returned to its usual smooth, creamy white, and, if her hands remained chafed, and callouses formed to replace the blisters, the months of exercise and good country food saw her back to her normal weight and accustomed glow of health.

And she could laugh again. Laugh at the antics of the children during play. Laugh at Atty's new command of French. Laugh at nothing in particular, in the rich, warm tones of her laugh of long ago.

Perhaps it was the contentment that made up the atmosphere of her daily world. She could not share deeply in it, but happiness was all around her. The Montefiores were particularly joyful now, as winter drew toward its end. Word had at last come that their confiscated estates would soon be returned to them. They moved about their daily chores with new zest, telling one another that the seeds they sowed this spring would be sown on their own land. And perhaps by the following year they would be able to hire laborers from whatever men the Corsican villain had left alive.

But the Corsican villain had more seeds of his own to sow. Very early in March word reached them that he had made good his escape from Elba and was landed in France. The news was disturbing enough to send one of the gentlemen to the surrounding towns each day in search of the latest word. By late in the month it was learned that the king's own troops, sent to defeat and recapture their former emperor, had instead thrown down their arms and cheered him. The king had already fled to Ghent, and Royalists throughout the country were once again hastily packing up to seek refuge in other countries.

The Montefiores set about this depressing task with grim expressions while two of their number headed out for the coast to see about the hire of a vessel that would get their party away.

"We must find a yacht," Madame Montefiore explained to Madeleine, "because we dare not travel up through France with Bonaparte already established in the Tuileries."

Madeleine had been without the need or the desire to spend from the income that her brother sent promptly each quarter day. So she offered at once to pay the hire of the yacht, urging that she should, in any event, have had the expense of her own passage back to England.

"Oh, *mais non, ma chérie*, it is not to England that we go this time, but to Flanders," said Madame Montefiore, explaining that it was to be the rallying point for the armies who would oppose Bonaparte.

"And it is not expected that we shall be forced to keep from home very long," she went on, "because the Corsican intruder has not the whole of Europe at his command this time. Our allies have already declared him an outlaw and are forming armies to join us in the fight. Even our own men, once they see us safely to a cousin with whom we may reside in Brussels, are going to join the Duc du Berri and his army."

Madeleine nodded approval of all madame had detailed so proudly and began discussing her own plans for returning to England.

"*Mais non, non, ma chérie!*" madame exclaimed again. "You must not even think of traveling through France. The last time that Bonaparte decided to make war with your country, he scooped up all the English civilians and put them into prison. You must remember, *ma bonne* Madeleine, that he has not the honor of your *Duc de Wellington*. His armies are permitted to take what they will—to rape and pillage without punishment. *Certes*, you *must* come away with us!"

EIGHTEEN

Madeleine had given no thought to the repercussions of war upon herself. There was nothing, past or present, to make it seem real to her. But she sensibly allowed herself to be guided by Madame Montefiore and agreed at once.

"However, there is no need for me to impose upon your cousin in Brussels. Once we are safely landed in Flanders, I shall simply pay extra to have myself taken across the Channel."

Madame Montefiore's face clouded. "Ah, *ma* Madeleine, I know you are eager to return to your own country. And I thought your plan to go this spring not a bad one. But you do not see that everything is different now. With Bonaparte in arms again, there will be fear and anger in London. Memories will turn back, *ma chérie.*"

Madeleine felt a wave of depression coming over her. She was not *eager* to return to England—she was frantic to do so. With the time to go home drawing nearer, she had thought of little else. And yet, not once had it occurred to her that the upheaval in France might stir feelings against her in London.

But madame's words brought it all tumbling in. Yes, of course, it would be as though a year had never passed. All the talk would again be of "that monster, Bonaparte." Of the treachery that had put him in power and had kept him in power and had now allowed him to slip back into power. And with this subject on every tongue, it needed only for the infamous Baroness de Beauvoir to show her face among them, and memories would indeed turn back to the treachery that had taken place on their very doorstep only a Season ago. God, if only she could rid herself of that hateful name.

But she instantly flushed guiltily at the thought. It had been a good name in France for hundreds of years. The family name of her very dear friend. Impulsively she caught Madame Montefiore's hand and gave it an apologetic squeeze, then walked to the window to stare out across the fields.

"Forgive me, madame," she said quietly. "I shouldn't be giving way to a fit of crotchets over such a trifling matter. Your loss is so much greater. Besides, I ought to have seen for myself that I am scarcely apt to make a popular addition to London society."

"Ah, it is so. But have I not also said that these difficulties cannot prevail? You have been dull here in the country. It is natural that you should be craving the diversions of society. But you shall see. Brussels shall be very much more gay than London this Season. And you shall be very much more *à la mode* to be going there instead."

Madeleine nodded politely but it wasn't long before she was obliged to concede that madame hadn't been dealing in the marvelous with such predictions. The Belgian capital was positively bursting with the fashionables of a dozen nations. And nowhere, except in London itself, could one have hoped to find a greater assemblage of England's *beau monde*. Nor could Madeleine have hoped to enter Brussels's society from a more consequential position. Madame Montefiore's cousin proved to be no less than the Duc de Montesquieu.

Madeleine found herself miraculously transported from a humble, cramped farmhouse to a palatial mansion overlooking the park. Not only was there no need to share a bedchamber, she was shown to an elegant apartment, boasting the added luxury of a private sitting room. The instant she was left alone, she threw herself across the wide expanse of feathery mattress and sighed.

Moreover, the owner of this fine bed, if brimming over with a not surprising degree of hauteur, was by no means unattractive. The *duc*'s figure ran to tall and lean, and his age Madeleine judged to be near, but not quite, forty.

She was in some doubt as to whether to offer such a man something toward her keep and asked Madame Montefiore's advice. "I feel perhaps I ought, and yet I shouldn't like to offend him," she said with a widening of her expressive eyes.

Madame smiled. "He is more likely to roar with laughter. *Non, non,* Madeleine, do not trouble yourself with such thoughts. He is quite the wealthiest nobleman in Brussels."

Madeleine couldn't help being relieved. She'd insisted on paying a sizable share toward the yacht that had carried them from France, and with so many Royalists again on the scramble, the fee had not been small. Nor, she thought, glancing round, eyes still wide with the wonder of her transformation, could be any contribution toward this style of life.

But if madame had been correct in assuring that the *duc*'s situation made him supremely indifferent to concerns of finance, she had overlooked the possibility that he might not be above accepting another form of compensation for his hospitality.

His wish to be welcomed into the beautiful rooms provided for Madeleine's private use was hinted at almost from the start and soon took the form of frank suggestion.

Fortunately, for the preservation of her newfound comfort, Madeleine possessed an easy skill in dealing with such suggestions, and no awkwardness resulted from her smooth rebuffs of these ducal advances.

Old experience made her equally skilled in the practice of economy, and she managed, out of resources that were only a fraction of the sum she had been spending as the baron's exquisitely gowned wife, to accumulate a wardrobe that suffered no loss of elegance for its simplicity.

Unfortunately, both skill and expenditure went in vain, because the approval of English society, at which these efforts were aimed, was not to be won by charming and subdued dress. The doors of her own countrymen remained closed to her, and those members of fashionable London who did not actually cut her directly extended none but the chilliest of bows.

Driving through the town one afternoon in her carriage, Madeleine turned to Madame Montefiore with a slight shudder. "There aren't words enough to tell you how grateful I am for your wise counsel, madame. It couldn't be plainer what a desolation my life should have been in England. Here, at least my status as a guest of the Duc de Montesquieu assures me a reception in the homes of the Dutch, French, Germans, and Belgians."

She was being no less than realistic in allowing the reason for her reception in these houses, but once received, Madeleine's own attractions and winning ways brought her an enviable degree of popularity. Invitations flowed in with gratifying regularity. She enjoyed her customary throng of admirers, never wanting for an escort day or night, all her dances bespoken only minutes after she entered a ballroom.

Life was indeed very gay, and even her pinings for home were, to some extent, assuaged. England was at least well-represented for her in an enviable supply of suitors from the British Army of Occupation, which had been stationed in the district since the peace of 1814.

If these gallant young officers thought her a spy, they evidently found it a point of honor to be fearless in the face of the enemy. And when certain English ladies frowned upon their attentions to one of such questionable reputation—well, one smile from the incomparable Madeleine made up for a thousand such frowns.

The *duc* complimented her. "You have made a quick success, Madeleine," he said, then complimented her further by offering a carte blanche.

Madeleine slipped into Madame Montefiore's chamber later that night to discuss the matter. She had passed enough time among the continental aristocracy not to be greatly surprised by her friend's views. "Ah, you must understand, *ma petite*, that your consequence as the *duc*'s acknowledged mistress will be far greater in many ways than as the legal widow of a baron."

With little reputation left to preserve among her own countrymen, Madeleine would have been less than human not to spend a few minutes in contemplation of the sumptuous comforts that could be hers for life. The *duc* had naturally promised a handsome settlement.

Also to be considered was the rather fearful possibility of incurring the *duc*'s wrath by a refusal. He could ruin her just as easily as he had helped to establish her in the only social avenues she had left.

In the end, however, she shook her head, and madame nodded. "Perhaps you are wise, *ma* Madeleine. For in possessing no husband at the moment, there will be no one to give a name to your children."

Madeleine agreed, with a twinkle, that the arrangement did hold this disadvantage.

The *duc*, however, did not agree to this or anything else. "Nonsense," he said, once convinced (and Madeleine spared no effort to convince him) that there was no question of personal dislike. "You are thinking with the morals of the bourgeoisie."

Madeleine made no reply, just looked off to the side, smiling to herself in a way that had stirred the blood of more than one jaded gallant.

"It is true, you are English," the *duc* excused, trying not to let that smile bewitch him further. "But that cannot wholly account for such stupidity. There are a dozen English ladies, of fine families and noble birth, in Brussels at this very minute, who would not cavil to accept the arrangement I have offered you. *Mon Dieu,* you would have almost everything."

Madeleine turned an alluring green gaze on him and said smoothly, "Yes, *monseigneur,* but it is to the '*almost* everything' that I object."

She had judged that in such outrageous presumption lay her one hope of putting him off without losing his approbation. She found to her relief that she had judged rightly.

After a brief look of astonishment, he threw back his head and laughed heartily. "Ah, no, no, *chérie!* Surely, even one of your *agacerie* cannot hope to attain marriage with me. Why, do you not realize, my adored Madeleine, that I could command the hand of a princess?"

Madeleine did realize it, but she just glanced away and smiled her smile again, knowing she was on safer ground to have the *duc*'s mind occupied with trying to evade *her* designs.

And, quite as she had hoped, suddenly he desired nothing so much as to end the discussion and go from the room.

Madeleine waited until the door closed behind him, then rose, pinched the lifeless chin of the marble statue that had been overlooking the proceedings, and went up to change for dinner.

But she found herself beneath those same unseeing marble eyes a week later, no less astounded than the rest of Brussels would be, because the *duc* had summoned her there to make a formal offer of marriage.

How all of Brussels knew only a few hours later, Madeleine could not have said. But that they did know was beyond doubt. Even Lady Caroline Lamb, who had been creating a considerable stir with her transparent gauzes, was cast into the shade, as everyone pushed to get a better glimpse of the lady in chaste white robes who had caught the uncatchable Duc de Montesquieu.

Belgian doors opened wider still, but the English, although impressed, showed themselves less inclined than ever to accept their beautiful representative back into the fold, the general opinion holding that she must surely be an even greater adventuress than at first supposed.

Madeleine had accepted the *duc*'s offer, but not without further piquing her consequential suitor by begging a few hours to consider. When she returned to receive his ring, she found him even more nettled because, in his complete amazement at being put off, he had forgotten to declare two important conditions.

Madeleine said with a low laugh that he must, of course, mention them now.

He took several turns about the room, his countenance a mixture of chagrin and indignation. Finally he told her that the meticulous etiquette obtaining at his level required that she pass one more year of widowhood before remarriage.

"Yes," he snapped harshly, "I can see that that doesn't trouble you. Nor does it trouble me to wait a year—or *ten*—for the wedding. But I wish you to understand that I shall not wait for *you!* I expect to assume my privileges within an hour of signing the marriage contract."

Madeleine knew this was not an uncommon practice or particularly frowned upon, even in England. From her own point of view, it was merely something that must be faced sooner or later. She nodded her assent.

Somewhat mollified by her lack of hesitancy, the *duc* added, in a more friendly spirit, "The other point is quite a minor one. Merely that I shall require you to remain faithful for the period of one year after the marriage—whether or not you are got with child before that time."

Madeleine agreed again. However little it might signify to him—and indeed, it signified less to her—he could depend upon her remaining faithful, in that respect, for the rest of her life. Whatever had awakened in her at the Queen's Arms had died again at Ruelle. His Grace would benefit from her experience only in that she would come to him without fear, ready and able to "endure." And that merely because it was the only way a female could have or be anything in this world.

The *duc* nodded his satisfaction and stepped forward to kiss her. To this, however, she did not agree. "No, Rodrique—I trust I may address you so now? I feel I am owed a condition of my own. We shall wait until the signing of the marriage contract for this, as well."

He was naturally nettled again, but this time it was mingled with a fascination at her sheer impudence. He bowed ironically and said he would set forth immediately to have the documents drawn.

Madame Montefiore was transported with joy at hearing the news, but she came to Madeleine's chamber a few days later wearing a worried frown. "Oh, *ma chérie*, I have just heard. If only there were someone to act for you here. The time that will be lost—having to send the contract to your brother in England. It is not wise to give a man so much time to cool."

Atty was engaged in brushing Madeleine's glossy dark hair, grown well below her shoulders since leaving England.

Madeleine met her friend's eyes in the looking glass. "Oh, I doubt we have much to fear on that head, madame. It has been my experience that they do not cool *before* they have what they want."

Madame had no argument with such a fundamental fact. Her concern rested on the possibility that Madeleine would find herself unable to resist her noble lover for such a length of time.

Madeleine laughed dryly. "On that head we need have no fear at all."

"Ah. It is a pity. You do not care for him at all, then."

"But I do, truly. I find him excellent company and vastly amusing. It is a deal more than I dared hope in my next husband." She glanced quizzically over her shoulders. "Good heavens, don't be pitying me because I am not in love with him, madame. When he has already indicated that his interest in me will be wholly spent within two years."

"Ah. You must not be offended, *ma chérie*."

"Not at all. I respect him for his openness. *And* for his ability to judge his feelings so accurately," Madeleine added, turning slightly so Atty could begin piling up her hair. "Truly, I am more than content with his arrangement. He may tire of me as soon as he likes. The important thing is that I shall go on being a *duchesse* for the rest of my life."

"Well, if it is as you say, *ma* Madeleine, then it is well to see you thinking so sensibly. But still, I feel something. Something of a discontent in you."

Madeleine hesitated. "Yes. I think you will understand, madame, that I mean no insult to this fine country. But I cannot help regretting the loss of my own."

"Ah! It is natural. I was afraid it was of your officer that you still think."

Madeleine's gaze focused on her own reflection. Her officer. Yes, she had been thinking of him. She thought of him constantly. Infuriatingly. Especially when she would catch herself having just spent hours refashioning a happy ending to her rarefied fairy tale.

She laughed. "Heavens, no. Why, it has been well over a year since I saw him last. I doubt I should even recognize him after all this time."

Madame nodded her satisfaction, but she should have been very much dismayed only a few days later had she noticed, when the *duc*'s coach paused for cross-traffic, how quickly Madeleine's gaze was arrested on one particular scarlet coat amid a great collection clustered at the corner of the park.

Madeleine was not only dismayed but remained in a rage with herself for hours afterward, recalling how apparent must have been her look of shocked alarm. She was in no doubt at all that Jack had as easily noticed her. For a time she felt insensibly imposed upon. As though his being in Brussels was somehow infringing on her rights.

Yet, when she paused to consider, there was nothing at all

surprising in his presence. Underlying the gaiety of Brussels, there had been a sense of apprehension that had not eased until the arrival of the Duke of Wellington. And even then, with Bonaparte's vast and well-organized troops increasing along the border, it was continually lamented that the cream of the British forces should be miles away, en route from America. Every effort to return them in time had been made. And made successfully, it would seem, if Colonel Ashton's appearance were any indication.

This thinking was confirmed a few days later when another scarlet-coated gentleman called on Madeleine.

"Lambert!" she exclaimed, rushing into his waiting embrace.

Her younger brother was encamped near Ghent and had obtained a day's leave to visit her. Madeleine insisted on begging off from the engagements that evening so that she might spend what time there was quietly alone with him.

During their private dinner Lambert glanced about him and remarked, "Well, Mady, you've caught the grand prize this time, haven't you?"

Madeleine smiled. "What did you think of the *duc?*"

"A likable enough fellow. But are you really going to be happy living over here? I shouldn't have thought it."

"I rather think the circumstances justify the effort, don't you?" she said playfully, toasting him with a goblet fashioned from gold. "The worst thing is that I am such a fright at languages. *Now* I must try and learn Dutch and German. Just enough to be polite, but I have far from mastered French. Rodrique was used to find it amusing, but he has already begun to rip up at me. Madame Montefiore coaches me every day for hours, but—"

Lambert broke in on her light talk. "Mady, I told you that I stopped home before making the crossing, and—"

"And you learned what you didn't realize when you wrote to me of Jack," she supplied. She had been fearing he would insist on alluding to it. "Yes, love, but don't tease yourself. It was much better for me to hear it without roundaboutation." She paused, then added, "He is in town, you know. With his child heiress in tow."

"Miss Helpston? Here?—"

"Why not? All the world and his wife seem to have flocked to Brussels. And I daresay Jack would not wish to be separated from his—well, *perhaps* she is his wife already. But I must say she doesn't give the appearance of one. Not the way mama still hovers about her."

Lambert clapped his forehead ruefully. "And *I* came rushing down especially to warn you that Jack was apt to turn up. So, you've met them already."

A spasm swept through her at the thought, but she said airily, "No, no, I was merely attending the same state function. *Meeting* anyone requires a monstrous effort at the squeezes they hold here. We never came closer than opposite sides of the ballroom."

"You can say what you like, Mady, but it's a devil of a thing. For this to be taking place right under your nose. And I can see plain enough that you're feeling it, too."

Yes, she was feeling it. Though she had promised herself a thousand times since those moments in the spinney that she would never permit Jack or anyone else to hurt her again. But just the sight of him . . .

And then having to watch him with his new love. A pretty, little fair-haired thing in sprig muslin. Yes, she'd felt the sting at every turning. And a positive agony at each familiar gesture. The way his eyes would half-close when he listened attentively—the little crinkles at the side. The way he'd take her arm so confidently to guide her through the crowds. And his ready laugh whenever she said something that amused him. Oh, dear God, but that hurt most of all.

Madeleine was hard put to know how she'd got through the evening. Try as she would to concentrate on anything else, somehow, out of hundreds and hundreds of human forms, her eyes seemed constantly to fall upon Colonel Ashton in his exquisite ball-dress uniform. Something she, for all they'd been through together, had never been privileged to see. The fine,

fine netting of his pantaloons, starkly white above the black of knee-high boots, clinging and rippling over the long, hard muscles of his thighs as he danced on and on. Quadrilles, waltzes, contradances . . . another thing she had never shared with him. Never so much as even one dance together in all that time.

Madeleine glanced up and caught Lambert watching her with a troubled frown. She laughed ruefully and bid him try another scalloped oyster. "You mustn't fret for me," she said. "It isn't wonderful that my first sight of them together should have churned up old memories. I shall come about. One does." She looked down the long table sadly and added, "I think I regret most of all that we had to lose the friendship along with the rest. We were, you know, very, very good friends."

"Listen, Mady, dash it all. This *duc* of yours must have other houses. A round dozen, I'll be bound."

"And how do you imagine I could explain a wish to retire to one of them when Brussels is the very center of the world at the moment? Rodrique very much likes a full and active social life. And if he knows anything of me at all, it is that I do, too." Her fingers tightened round her golden goblet, as if trying to draw strength from it. "No, I shall stay and manage very well. And really, like yourself, Jack was probably in town only for the day. Chances are I shan't even be disturbed by having to see him again."

She made this speech solely for Lambert's peace of mind, and he accepted it for hers; neither of them believing it for a minute. Both knowing well that Jack received his orders directly from headquarters, and Wellington had established his in the Rue Royale, only across the park from where they sat.

And if that weren't enough to make Jack a familiar figure about town, there was Miss Helpston's presence to bring him on the run whenever his work permitted. So Madeleine steeled herself for constant glimpses of him—in the street or across a reception hall.

She didn't think it necessary, however, to steel herself for actual speech, being quite convinced that he must find her far too great an embarrassment to dream of coming near.

Yet, at the very next affair, she was alarmed to see him weaving through the jam of people on a course calculated to bring him directly to her side.

NINETEEN

The *duc* was off in the card room and Madeleine standing amid her usual crowd of admirers when Jack reached her. Although weak with an inner shaking, she heard herself say in a perfectly calm and cheerful tone, "Ah, Colonel Ashton. What an age it has been, to be sure."

"Your servant, baroness," he replied with a bow, then extended his hand. "My dance."

"Oh!—no, no, my friend. I should be delighted, of course, but I am promised—I am quite sure to—"

"Captain Fulsome," Jack supplied. "Yes. He gave me his turn."

This speech was received by Madeleine's hopeful beaux with a chorus of gasps mingled of shock, incredulity, and envy.

"*Did* he?" Madeleine laughed gaily. "How very unhandsome of him."

"No, you mustn't be imagining him at all willing," Jack returned in the same spirit. "More a case of being so thoroughly beholden to me that he found himself at a stand."

A waltz was striking up, and without further comment, Jack nodded to the other gentlemen and swept Madeleine onto the floor.

There was no one to hear their conversation now, and their eyes met and held for a somber moment, Madeleine all too conscious of the tense strength in the arm that encircled her. At length she could stand the electric silence no longer.

"Well, Jack?"

"Well, Madeleine?"

He said no more. Her body moved supplely in response to his hand on her back, while her mind worked frantically to create unbendable lines of defense.

But why was he doing this? She had at least expected some effort at explanation. Some attempt to fob her off with a plausible tale.

A voice, loud and tumultuous within her, cried, Oh, God, if only he would just explain it all away. If only he could. At the same time her practical self was screaming from what seemed an incredible distance, bidding her not to be an idiot, warning that it was in just this way that foolish females made victims of themselves.

Wish and warning alike seemed pointless, for he remained tensely silent as he guided her round and round a floor so brightly polished that it mirrored the hundred or more candles blazing above them overhead. But there was an energy in the hand that held hers, a passion that made its heat felt right through their interlocked gloves.

Was that his game? she wondered, her mother's words to Patrick invading an overworked brain. (" . . . you will eventually seek your wife from among the innocents just out of the schoolroom, and spend the rest of your days humiliating her with your infidelities.")

Madeleine looked away into the crowds, a slight flush rising to her cheeks. Had her shocking behavior at the Queen's Arms brought him to the decision that she wasn't fit to bear his name—and yet pleased him in a way that he wished to indulge in it again? Was he thinking that now, with them both safely committed to others, it might be possible to renew only that portion of their relationship? Heaven only knew she'd given him reason enough to suppose her the most lustful female alive.

Round and round they turned, beautifully, gracefully. How magnificently he waltzed. But *what* did he want? Why in God's name did he not *say* something?

In a moment or two he did, his deep voice almost shattering

her nerves when it sounded in her ear. "I've neglected to congratulate you on your betrothal. A life's ambition, I shouldn't wonder."

Madeleine was almost amazed to hear herself respond so casually. "It is not generally the thing to congratulate the lady, but I have no objection to preening myself a little on the accomplishment. Thank you."

And am I expected to thank him, too, for jilting me and making it all possible? she wondered, strained to the point of collapse by the effort to maintain her poise, so intently on guard for his next words that she failed to notice he was leading her steadily to the edge of the dancing area.

She started and looked up at him in surprise when he brought her smoothly to a halt, then took her elbow to guide her through the assembly gathered round the dancers.

"Where—where are you taking me?" she demanded in confusion.

"Back to Fulsome. I promised not to keep you for the entire dance if it proved unnecessary."

"Upon my word! You creatures seem to have got the idea that I can be passed amongst you like a bottle of wine!" she exclaimed, indignation tangling with an effort to grasp the significance of what was happening.

And once again, because he had undermined her concentration, she lost awareness of her surroundings and didn't realize, until much too late, that he was moving her on a straight course toward an English lady of her acquaintance, who acted instantly on the opportunity by giving her the cut direct.

Madeleine flushed crimson with a combination of fury and humiliation. Fury, because she had always used care to avoid putting herself in the way of such snubs. Humiliation, because Jack had been the shocked witness to that very blatant affront.

He drew her between himself and a nearby colonnade, shielding her from the vision of passersby until she could regain her composure. His expression was at once sympathetic and regretful. "I'm sorry, Mady. I let you in for that, I know. I'd heard you weren't being received in some quarters—I just wasn't thinking."

"Oh, well, as one spy to another, I daresay you can understand these things. I fancy you might meet with quite the same sort of rebuff in Bonapartist circles."

"Spy? The devil! Are you saying this has still to do with that de Beauvoir business? After all this time?—"

"I can only wonder what you *did* suppose," she retorted, still excessively ruffled.

He made an impatient gesture. "Any number of things. God knows you've always been confoundedly careless of your reputation."

Her eyes blazed up at him, but before she could reply Captain Fulsome succeeded in working his way to her side.

"Gad, Ashton, didn't place any real dependence on your letting her go half-through. Very much obliged, I assure you."

Jack nodded to the captain, bowed to Madeleine, and strode off into the crowd.

Everything was happening too fast for Madeleine to be able to sift through the several emotional assaults she had experienced over the last minutes. Jack was moving away. Captain Fulsome was trying to lead her back to the dance floor. She was conscious of a deep sense of loss, liberally salted with irritation. For a moment there was an almost overpowering urge to hit Captain Fulsome with the first thing to hand, but her thoughts were so jumbled that it seemed easiest to just give way to his nagging efforts and allow him to pull her where he would.

But by the time they had circled once round the dance floor, it required all her control to keep from wrenching out of his arms and thrusting her way through the crowds in pursuit of Jack.

Something was wrong! Something was dreadfully wrong! She saw in a staggering flash that Jack's explanation for returning her to the captain didn't jump with any of the possibilities she had considered. Certainly not the most conceivable. If his object had been to reestablish their former intimacy, it made no sense to refer to the remainder of their dance as *unnecessary!* He'd offered no excuses, made no advances. Even if he'd sensed her underlying hostility, it would have been more suitable to say "useless."

There seemed only one reasonable explanation. And, though she could hardly credit it, even the remotest chance that it might be so had the effect of turning her half-mad. Could he possibly have been giving *her* the opportunity to explain? Waiting just long enough to see if she would—or *could?*

She blanched white. If that were so, it could only mean that he hadn't abandoned her. That something or someone had caused him to believe that it was *she* who had been playing fast and loose. Oh, God in heaven. And that being so, could anything—*anything* —have made further attendance more "unnecessary" than her continued silence?

Her heart pounded wildly beneath the waistline of her white lace ball gown. It was by no means certain, but there could be no rest—no peace—until she knew. She must see him again and demand that he tell her what he had meant by it all.

The most exacting search of the rooms, however, yielded nothing but the unassailable fact that Jack was no longer beneath the roof.

Nor did she meet with greater success on arrival at a ball given by the Marquise d'Assche on the following evening. But she was hopeful of seeing him there eventually, for the *marquise* was able to boast the attendance of the Duke of Wellington and, as far as Madeleine could determine, nearly the whole of his staff.

By midnight, however, Madeleine was ready to own her endeavors hollow and should have counted the night a total waste except for the extraordinary event that took place next.

She was exchanging unenthusiastic badinage with her regular gathering of cavaliers when, inexplicably, two or three of assorted military rank seemed to grow visibly taller as they stepped smartly aside. She next found herself staring at what was currently the most famous nose in Europe.

The Duke of Wellington moved comfortably through the short path that had been made for him, a jovial expression on his distinctive countenance, the Duchess of Richmond on one arm and Lady Mount Norris on the other. Neither lady had ever cut Madeleine. Scarcely possible since neither had ever been presented to her. Her list of acquaintance, before leaving London, had never run to such lofty spheres as these.

One of the young officers, responding instantly to a silent communication, presented the Duke to Madeleine, and he, in turn, introduced her to his pair of flanking matrons.

Madeleine bowed gracefully and said everything that was proper, though every nerve in her body was poised expectantly.

"Ah, baroness," said the Duke, taking her hand and shaking it vigorously. "I have been wishing very much to make your acquaintance. So that I might thank you personally for your assistance in our last campaign."

Madeleine didn't need the warning pressure of the Duke's hand, still clasping hers, for she had been braced for something out of the way from the moment of his arrival. She didn't betray by word or look that she hadn't a notion what he meant.

But if Madeleine showed no surprise at this startling statement, she was the only member of the small party who did not. The Duke laughed loudly, causing heads to turn from as far as twenty feet away. That, at least, was a fairly common occurrence. His laugh was as remarkable as everything else about him.

"I can see you are all wondering how this delicate little lady could have served in such a rigorous business," he chuckled. "Well, there's no need to be trying to imagine her at the head of a troop of cavalry. Her work was done in London. Yes," he smiled reminiscently, "quite a thing that. It was just after she married one of our strongest Royalist supporters (or so we all *supposed* that wily rascal de Beauvoir to be) that she tumbled on to what he was at.

"Not knowing quite how to set about reporting such an event, she contacted an old friend. One of my boys in the intelligence department. Of course, we might have had the baron laid by the heels right then, but it seemed a far better plan to make use of such a stroke of luck. So, with the baroness's help, we saw to it that her rogue of a husband received all the information he wished. Information that somehow always proved to be quite the reverse of fact."

If Madeleine were not now more intent than ever on finding Jack (for she didn't doubt for a minute that she owed the Duke's intervention only to him), she might have spared the time to reflect on the eccentricities of a world that could turn her overnight from a villainess to one of the most petted and courted ladies in town.

The Duke's mendacious tale spread with unsurprising speed, growing with each telling, until Madeleine began to wonder if she might yet find herself credited with the single-handed defeat of Bonaparte himself.

Invitations poured in, and not only was she besieged with embarrassing apologies from members of her former set, but she became the most sought-after guest of England's most prestigious hostesses. Not the least notable was the flattering letter that accompanied an invitation from the Duchess of Richmond, hoping she would find it possible to drop in at a ball she was giving only a se'ennight hence and claiming their too recent introduction as the cause of soliciting her at so late a date.

Madeleine hurried to her writing table to scratch out a hasty acceptance. If there was hope of finding Jack anywhere, it would be there. Not only was it to be the grandest ball of the Season, Jack had frequently mentioned being on terms of friendship with one of the duchess's military sons.

But as she sorted through the remainder of her letters and invitations, she came upon something that was very far from welcome. Or at least she felt the timing to be most inopportune. It was her marriage contract, back from Patrick, along with a note assuring her that all was in order and congratulating her on a truly extraordinary settlement.

Also included in the packet was a letter from Claudia, almost beside herself with delight at Madeleine's truly gratifying achievement. It quite made up, she went on to say, for Dorothea's uninspiring match with Mr. Hunter and the two almost wasted Seasons Jane had passed. For there was still much talk of that unfortunate affair concerning the baron, and poor Jane had not been received as they had hoped on account of it.

Madeleine smiled, thinking of the enthusiasm with which

Jane would soon be received. Once the news of her sister's brilliant military triumphs spread across the Channel. And, of course, Claudia would not be missing any opportunities to say, "My other daughter, soon to be the Duchesse de Montesquieu . . ."

But Madeleine's smile swiftly faded when her gaze fell again on the document that would not only represent a binding commitment to the *duc*, but would instantly inaugurate her submission to him as a wife in all but name.

She pondered over it for a moment, then walked briskly into her dressing room and tucked it away in a trunk, beneath garments she had considered unsuitable for use this year. She simply could not sign it until she had seen Jack. Even if he didn't want her any more, or if he himself was too committed to allow of a future for them together, she felt it completely beyond her to enter into that sort of intimacy with the *duc* while Jack remained so near.

If near he was! Madeleine could find no evidence of it. She had accepted all invitations to parties taking place in English homes, now plentifully available to her, and, by combining them with those of her foreign acquaintance, came near to exhausting herself in the attendance of as many as seven affairs a night—ranging from a dizzy round of state functions to one theater party or musical evening after another—hoping, hoping, always hoping.

But Jack was not to be found.

When he failed to appear even in the Duchess of Richmond's overflowing rooms, Madeleine cast her pride to the winds and inquired directly of Captain Fulsome where Colonel Ashton might be found.

The captain chuckled. "His friends had better hope that he cannot. Be found, I mean," he added. "The entire intelligence department is off in France, trying if they can learn where Boney means to strike. You see, the Duke has us spread too thin, not knowing—"

Madeleine turned her attentions from the captain's explanation of the difficulties of defense, her own thoughts centered on what a dangerous business it was for an Englishman to be in France at such a time. It had once been possible to fob her off with talk of routine and tedium, but she had learned by now that there was very little in Jack's work that wasn't undertaken at the constant risk of his life.

Her worried gaze caught sight of Miss Helpston, and for the first time she felt a connective link. Certainly the poor child must also be weak with fear over Jack's safety.

She glanced away, aware of a pang of conscience. For why else was she searching for Jack if not to take him away from his bride-to-be, if she could manage it at all?

It had all seemed perfectly reasonable a few minutes ago. She loved Jack as she would never be capable of loving again. If she had lost him through an unfortunate quirk of fate, then it had struck her as only fair that she should have him back.

But suddenly she was no longer so sure of the rights of it. She supposed she had not been taking the attachment of such a young girl as very serious. Yet a moment's recollection should have shown her that she had been frightfully hurt at even a younger age. In her case, it had proved a lucky escape, but it had, nevertheless, caused a shock and disillusionment that had threatened her entire life.

And now this girl was believing in Jack and expecting him, with good and sufficient reason, to marry her.

Madeleine's reflections were interrupted all at once by a murmur of urgency that had begun to fill the room. She turned to seek the cause. Captain Fulsome had disappeared and dozens of minor dramas were taking place all about her. Officers who only a moment ago had been dancing and flirting wore strange expressions. Some grave and tense, others curiously exulted. And everywhere ladies, young and old, were clinging to a scarlet sleeve for a last word of reassurance.

The war! It had begun.

TWENTY

The city became a concert of rumors. Madeleine could discover only one undisputed fact. Bonaparte had crossed the frontier that morning and was somewhere to the south of Brussels. To the Belgians, whatever their sympathies, he was considered invincible, and they held fearfully that only time stood between him and the Namur Gate.

Most of the English countered stoutly that it was the Duke of Wellington who stood between. But even among the English there were croakers: "The Duke, it must be remembered, has never actually confronted Bonaparte himself."

By the following afternoon the rumbling of cannonade began and, with it, the terror of realizing how incredibly near one stood to mass devastation. By nightfall talk turned to escape.

Shortly after daybreak on the next morning Madeleine stood at her chamber window and watched as a terrified troop of Belgian cavalry galloped through the city, shouting wildly that the French were on their heels. The roads to the north carried away hundreds of refugees in their wake. Yet no French appeared to justify the mass desertion.

Those civilians remaining in Brussels seemed suddenly to live in the streets, business, social functions, activity of every kind forgot. Everything but a continuous rushing about, collecting or conveying the merest scraps of information. And that with nervous, suspicious caution. Anyone too inquisitive was in danger of being thought a spy—anyone too communicative, a possible traitor.

In such an atmosphere, only the very few actually receiving tidings from the lines could be trusted to pass on genuine fact. And fact, when it could be had, seemed always to place Bonaparte closer and closer to Brussels.

The wish riding topmost in Madeleine's mind now was that Jack *was* in France. Far into France. Safely unaware that the war had begun. A war in which men shot at one another with guns so cruel they could make their presence felt miles away.

But it wasn't long before there was more to concern her. Several regiments of British infantry marched into Brussels and halted to verify orders. Lambert, though much occupied with his new duties as aide-de-camp, found time to seek her out and beg her to wish him luck in his first crack at Boney.

"Oh, dear God! I thought you were to remain in Ghent!" she cried.

"Mady, sometimes you can be a perfect ninny. Why the deuce should we remain in Ghent when it is plain as a packsaddle the battle is going forward somewhere to the *south?*"

"Oh, I don't know," she said irritably, keeping a fearful grip on his arm. "I thought you must stay to guard the French king!"

He kissed her cheek hurriedly, detached himself, and dashed down the stone steps to his waiting mount.

Madeleine watched from the door, supposing she should be comforted that so many men were marching out to defend the city. She wasn't. Not a bit. She found it only a depressing sight and was able to think of nothing but that they were marching directly toward those guns. Those hateful, hateful guns.

Soon she was able to see the effect of them on human flesh. The streets began to fill with wounded, many having staggered or limped throughout the night, all the way from Quartre Bras. Others less fortunate arrived in unsprung carts.

Madeleine ran down the steps to assist one who had fallen before the house. And from this instinctive act, she, along with many ladies like herself who had never encountered more than a minor cut or scrape, began what was to seem an endless career of administering to appalling wounds and broken bodies.

With the wounded and those who carted them in from distant fields came alarming statistics and hair-raising descriptions of the formidable army at Bonaparte's command.

Colonel Jones, left in military command of the city in the Duke's absence, was flooded by English citizens requesting passports. But Colonel Jones would give only lectures on patriotism and national pride.

Despite these bracing speeches and lack of passports, great

rushes were made to secure canal transport out of the district. And, failing that, any other means of getting away. There was no longer a chaise or a fiacre to be hired, or a place on a diligence to be had. The cabriolets and calèches—even the wagons and carts of private owners—had all been bespoken, if available at any price. Horses that could be purchased were purchased for outrageous sums. And many that could not be purchased were stolen. Stolen by formerly respectable members of society turned desperate to save the lives and safeguard the chastity of their wives and daughters.

The Montefiores began packing again, as did the *duc*. But, for Madeleine and others with loved ones at the battle, there could be no thought of flying now. Madame filled her ears with horrific tales of Bonaparte's soldiers. So disciplined in the ranks. So murderous and cruel when turned loose upon a populace.

Madeleine was white with fear but she shook her head as she rushed away to round up sheets that could be cut into bandages.

She was at least fortunate in that the *duc* assumed her only purpose for remaining was that her brother was engaged—and so offered no serious opposition. But he insisted on leaving behind a light coach, an undercoachman to drive it, a manservant to cook, one footman to serve her in the house, and another armed with a pistol to help guard the horses.

Madame Montefiore made a last attempt when the coaches were at the door, saying that she was certain if Lambert could be consulted, he should wish to know his sister was out of danger.

Madeleine took her hand. "It is more than that, madame. Even if Lambert weren't in the fighting, there is my officer. He is here—there. Somewhere! But if it were for neither of them—many of those poor wounded have dragged themselves back with the main object of sending final messages to loved ones in England and Scotland. They must not come all this way only to find too few that are able to speak their language.

It would be—" She broke off, feeling the familiar sting of tears welling up. "I shall remain, madame, and there's an end to it!"

Madame Montefiore nodded sadly and walked out into the pouring rain to her coach. Madeleine hurried into the streets with Atty and two footmen bearing a makeshift litter.

She had begun this gruesome occupation with terror in her heart. Terror that she would be unable to fight back the nausea that threatened constantly to overcome her. That the next cart would bring Jack or Lambert, maimed or dying. That a sudden onslaught of savage French soldiers would appear on the road before her.

But fatigue soon brought her to a state of mechanical activity. While at work she thought of little but the poor creatures who accepted her aid so gratefully.

Not that she could help but look up at the sound of joyous cheering, "*Bonaparte est pris! Le voilà! Le voilà!*"

She watched a brilliantly arrayed general pass through the street, riding with unimpaired dignity despite being tied to his war horse and surrounded by a jeering crowd. One of the English ladies working nearby had been presented to Bonaparte while he was content to be known as First Consul. With a disdainful shake of her head died the fleeting hope of a speedy end to it all, and Madeleine resumed her work with the same set expression.

On the following day her attention was caught again by riotous shouts. But these were of despair and horror. "*Les Français sont ici!*"

The sound of shutters being fastened filled the air. Yet women with children in their arms burst screaming from other houses, only to join the thousands running through the avenues in various and unconsidered directions.

When an intelligible explanation could at last be had, Madeleine learned that a civilian, venturing into the Forest of Soignes, toward the battle, had come flying back to spread the alarm that an enormous army of French soldiers were marching toward the gates and would be within at any moment.

She felt her blood run cold with fright as the stories told her by Madame Montefiore raced through her mind. Yet as great as her fear was the anguished realization that the English army must be completely annihilated. There was no question but that they would have fought for the city to the last man.

There was small hope of escape at this point and less incentive to make the attempt. So she worked on, forcing the future from her thoughts and trying to bring peace to those whose minutes were numbered in any event.

A short while later the French marched in, in vast numbers. But disarmed and under guard. Merely prisoners being taken to the barracks of the *Petite Château*.

When dusk fell, Madeleine ended her tour of duty and walked wearily home. She entered the *duc*'s great, empty house with Atty and the pair of footmen, too tired and anxious to eat.

Atty, sharing her room in this emergency, fetched her up a small pot of tea without being asked. Madeleine smiled gratefully. She had offered to let her go with the *duc* and his party but she was glad beyond words to have her here. Not that she had ever faced the necessity of remaining alone in the house. She had been flooded with invitations when it was learned that the *duc* was removing his guests to the country.

But Madeleine preferred her lot, being equally able to pace and vent her feelings without occasioning comment as to face her fears for Jack and Lambert in long periods of silence without risk of giving offense.

She swallowed the hot tea and climbed directly into bed. She had no clear memory of how long she had lain awake tormented by grim apprehensions, but somewhere about midnight she was jerked from an anxious slumber by a loud knocking on her sitting-room door.

Atty, also awakened, met her alarmed gaze in the pale moonlight. They both stiffened as they recognized the urgent voice of one of the footmen. He spoke too rapidly for either of them to be able to translate his words but it was plain that he had come to inform them of yet another calamity.

Madeleine sprang from the bed, pulling a wrapper over her nightdress as she ran barefooted into the adjoining room. She opened the door a crack and bade the tall young man to tell her more slowly what was the matter.

"Oh! Oh, dear God!" she cried when she had understood. "Yes, yes, of course! Atty, my purse and hurry!"

A peasant had come to the rear door saying he had a wounded English officer in his cart. One that claimed to be the brother of the *duc*'s affianced wife and that ten gold pieces had been promised for conveying this officer and a few of his comrades to this house.

Madeleine flew down the stairs and through the house to the service entrance, where she found the cook in his nightshirt and the other footman with only a dressing gown pulled over his breeches. She rushed forward to the peasant, easily recognizable by his sabots and red night-cap, and caught his startled hands in a fervent gesture of gratitude, assuring him that he should have his reward as soon as the men were carried into the house. She turned and ordered the embarrassed cook, who was trying to cover his undress with a large apron, to give the man a flagon of wine and anything else he wished, then hurried out into the moonlit courtyard to the cart.

"Lambert! Oh, Lambert, my *dear!*" she cried as she caught sight of him heaped beside his comrades.

"Now don't fly into a pucker," he said hoarsely. "My mare went over with me. It's just a broken shank. Hurts like the devil but it'll mend soon enough."

"Oh, my poor Lamb, of course it does," she said, taking his hand.

He grinned, wincing with his pain. "You haven't called me that since I was in short coats."

"You would fly into such a pet over it," she smiled back through the tears clinging to her long lashes. She had seen so many ghastly wounds and missing limbs that her heart had been in her throat since first hearing he had been brought in a cart. Next there was relief and, after, an odd sense of guilt for being so very grateful that her brother's injury would heal and leave him whole.

She let go of his hand as the two stout footmen lifted him

onto the litter they had fashioned for their work in the streets. "Mind his break," she said. "We had better keep them all below stairs. It will be easier to care for them."

She had Lambert carried into one of the smaller saloons, nearest the kitchen and laid down on a couch already draped in a holland cover. "Wait before getting the others," she ordered. "No need to maul them about twice. Push back the furniture and fetch truckle beds. Where is Atty? Oh, there you are. Kindle a fire while I fetch pillows and blankets. He is chilled through. They must all be so."

"No," Lambert croaked weakly from the couch. "Water. Water first."

Madeleine left Atty to continue with the fire and ran to the kitchen, sending the cook out to the men in the cart with a jug of water while she conveyed a large cupful back to Lambert.

Soon all the men were settled in the room together, wrapped in blankets and drinking hot soup that had been laced liberally with port wine, a comforting fire crackling in the grate.

Madeleine sent the cook to guard the horses while the coachman, who had already been called several times to set broken bones, came in to see to Lambert's leg. It was useless to expect one of the exhausted civilian surgeons to come before morning, but not once had they failed to nod approvingly after an inspection of her coachman's handiwork. So, leaving him to deal with Lambert, she and Atty set to work on the others.

"Did you see to that blackguard's blood money?" Lambert asked, as the coachman's practiced hands examined his break.

"Yes, to be sure," Madeleine said, not looking up. "But why do you call him that when he was kind enough to carry you back?"

"Kind! If you didn't chance to be betrothed to a Belgian *duc* . . . That pesky devil meant to drag the boots off me. I'd have preferred a swift bullet, but I had nothing to bargain with. We'd *already* been gone over and fleeced—in the *most* agonizing way—by two sets of Prussians!"

This time Madeleine did look up. "Lambert! In the name of God, are you saying your own allies found you in this state and could think of nothing better than to steal your belongings and leave you to suffer?"

"That's exactly what I am saying! Of course, those of us who put up a struggle were *not* left to suffer!"

"Oh, dear God!" she exclaimed, her hands flying to her face at the grizzly picture to be inferred. "Oh, is such a thing *possible?* Hadn't they enough of killing?"

During the half hour Madeleine worked over the soldiers she heard a deal more to appall her. She was almost stunned to learn the war was actually over. Her hopeful inquiries throughout the last three days had so often met with disappointment that she had stopped asking and just steeled herself to a seemingly permanent state of misery and fear. The cannonade had ceased to sound at dusk, but so it had upon the two previous evenings. Tonight, however, they had ceased for good and all, because the battle had ended at just that hour. Ended in a complete and unalterable victory for the Duke but with the bodies of forty to fifty thousand men lying dead or wounded over eight square miles.

Lambert and one of the other men, both veterans of the Peninsular campaign, agreed that they had never seen such a sanguinary affair as this battle fought on the fields just beyond the village of Waterloo.

The instant it had fully sunk in that it was truly over, Madeleine demanded to know why they should have been lying wounded on the field hours later.

She learned that no efforts were made to get the wounded in once darkness fell. And to her further horror, that the fields were so laden with bodies that it might easily be days before the comparative few whose business it was to see to the wounded would have time to find them all. In the meantime, they could expect to find themselves tumbled about and searched, over and over, and silently stabbed to death if it seemed expedient.

Then they must hope to survive not only the wounds themselves, but the weather. The soldier-looters were only after money and valuable trinkets, making officers the primary targets at first. But the Belgian peasants took all from everyone, stripping both the dead and the wounded to the skin. Taking even teeth from the mouths of the corpses, because dentists paid well for the raw material to make up false sets from real ones.

"Lambert, this is horrid. *Horrid!* Why don't the British soldiers search the fields immediately, when they know such things are going forward?"

"Well, they are searching the fields," he laughed mirthlessly. "Along with the rest—and with the same object. At least those among them with stout hearts. For one thing, the looters are killing each other for the spoils, and for another, the Duke deals harshly with violators in his army. We had two come up on us. Didn't offer us violence, but they wouldn't lift a finger to take us in. Couldn't risk it being known they were away from camp. They'd have given us a drop of water, at least, if there had been any to be had. But all the wells in the area became contaminated during the fight."

Madeleine helped her patient to lower himself onto a pillow and leaped to her feet. "Lambert, will the Duke have returned to his headquarters here in Brussels, do you think? I must know immediately how Jack has fared, and—"

She broke off, seeing the expression on her brother's face. "Oh, no! Not *dead?* Oh, Lambert," she pleaded, her throat already constricting painfully. "No, no. Pray do not tell me he is *dead*."

Lambert rolled his head. "I don't know, Mady, but—It was shortly before I took my own tumble. I was carrying a message from Sir John to our brigade major, and Jack was riding toward our position. Doubtless bringing orders from the Duke. He—he stopped a bullet. That much I know. I saw him drop over backward from his horse. He was still alive and trying to struggle up, because a French cavalry charge was heading right at him. It—it was too late. He hadn't a chance of getting clear. Just seconds later a ball exploded in my path. My mare reared and came down on my leg. I might have been trampled by the same lot, but the mare scrambled up, unhurt, and I caught her tail. I remember dragging along for some distance and nothing else until I came to my senses. It was just turning dark."

Madeleine had been gathering up the medical supplies and returning them to her satchel as he talked. She strapped it shut and looked down at him, her face ravaged with grief. "Where? Tell me where it happened."

"*Mady!* Good God! Have you taken leave of your senses? *You* can't go there! It—it's *ghastly!*"

"No, wait," she said, paying no heed to his protest. "You must tell one of the footmen. They will be more familiar with the district, and your French is better than mine. Atty, find Hugues and tell him to come at once. Then order the horses put to and begin loading the carriage with the litter—blankets, a pillow, clean sheets. Food, wine, and water. Several jugs of water. Cook must help. Oh—and Gustave must find lanterns and two more weapons. Pistols are best. But anything if they aren't to be had."

"Mady," Lambert exclaimed, trying to sit up. "Did you not hear all we told you of what is going forward out there? You—"

"Yes, I heard!" she snapped savagely. "Do you think *that* could do anything—*anything*—but make me *more* determined? *Lie back!* Now understand me, Lambert, and don't waste my time. I am going. You can spare me hours of searching by telling Hugues precisely *where* you saw Jack fall. But make no mistake. I *will* search. The entire eight miles, if I must. Now if you won't help, you may close your lips and go to the devil!"

TWENTY-ONE

Twenty minutes later Madeleine was seated in her coach with both footmen behind, each armed with one of the *duc*'s dueling pistols. Atty had been willing to come, but space was limited. "Besides," Madeleine had told her, "you must stay and rest, in order to be fit to assist Cook to care for Lambert and the others in the morning."

Often the horses had to be slowed to a walk. The roads were unbelievably rutted and covered with debris. Near the villages of Waterloo and Mont-St.-Jean they were thoroughly congested with activity because of the field hospitals established there.

Madeleine's palms were dug sore with the pressure of her nails as she put emphasis to the prayers running through her mind from the moment of setting out: He must not be dead! Oh, God, don't let me find him dead!

Her first sight of the battlefield, when at last they reached the district Lambert had described to Hugues, was almost enough to extinguish all hope. Bodies of men and horses from both sides of the conflict lay heaped in all directions. Ghastly was the word Lambert had used. Madeleine thought it not nearly strong enough. She was sure, at any other time, she should have fainted clean away from the sights that met her eyes. But she had no time to faint. She must find Jack.

She left the coachman with his large pistol to mind the vehicle and supplies while she set out to walk the fields with the two footmen. Between them, they bore hampers of food, water, and several blankets. Madeleine carried her satchel and a lantern.

The moon was bright enough for them to pick their way through the field of trampled corn. The lantern was needed only for detail. She had explained that they must look for a uniform very like her brother's except with silver lace instead of gold and with two epaulets rather than one. She gave orders to stop for anyone they found alive.

"However, we must keep closely together and not linger long," she added. "If it is at all possible, we shall carry them to a field hospital later."

They were able to make swift progress over a great area where the uniforms were mainly French cavalry or the blue of British artillery. The first of the wounded they encountered groaned that he had already been plundered and begged them not to jerrycummumble him about further. Madeleine spoke up to reassure him, then bade the footman cover him and give him water. They left him with a cup of soup, meat, cheese, and wine. The next was a French officer, and the footmen looked at her uncertainly.

"Yes, yes, of course," she said impatiently. "We are not here to fight a war. Give him what he wants and tell him we shall try to come back for him."

They found two others alive and dealt with them accordingly, adding a few drops of laudanum to the water of one. But at each scarlet-coated officer that lay dead, Madeleine's heart pounded in terror until his features proved unfamiliar. Seconds later she'd be overcome with pity and guilt, realizing that someone loved this man and would have viewed his body with as much anguish as she had relief. There was so much that was impossible to comprehend in the human heart, and the strain was beginning to wear hard on her. Then, as she moved behind a stand of burned trees, a voice spoke out of the shadows.

"Stand back! We're armed!"

She knew that voice. "Jack! Oh, Jack," she sobbed.

"What the—*Mady?*" demanded the voice.

"Yes, oh, *yes!*" she cried, rushing forward, the lantern held high that she might see where he lay.

But he was standing when she reached him. He had been crouched, the serviceable end of a broken lance held in a menacing grip. He lowered the weapon, but his expression was anything but welcoming.

Madeleine noticed vaguely that the little clearing was filled with wounded soldiers, some stretched out on the ground, others propped in sitting positions against the trees. But she paid no heed until her scared eyes had run twice over every inch of Jack. Had she beheld him before her sensibilities had become blunted to the sight of men returning from the ravages of battle, she might have fallen into despair at just the sight of his uniform, gashed and tattered and soaked with blood. But she had learned not to prejudge a man's condition by such signs. Sometimes the most superficial of wounds bled profusely, and often the blood encrusted on a uniform was not the product of its wearer at all but of a comrade he had aided or a mortally wounded horse he had been pinned beneath.

Instead, she directed her search to more tangible evidence of Jack's condition. His face bore several bruises and nasty scrapes, but his eyes were clear and his hands steady. She saw that his shirt was missing from beneath his ragged coat and guessed he had used it to make the bandage showing through a jagged rent running the entire length of one trouser leg.

The footmen hurried up behind her, already uncorking the jug and filling a cup with water. Gustave offered it to Jack, but he waved it away. "See to the others first. They're in worse case than I."

Madeleine made no attempt to remonstrate with him. She had seen him before during an emergency, when he had become very much the colonel. She nodded to Gustave, adding, "But hurry," then ordered Hugues to unpack the food and distribute it among those able to eat. Glancing at the lance in Jack's hand, she said, "Oh, and give us one of the pistols. When you have seen to these men, you had better keep together and try if the coach can be brought closer. We crossed a track not far from here."

If the footmen thought it odd that their master's promised wife was looking with such warmth upon another gentleman, they gave no sign of it. They had, in fact, discussed Madeleine over their supper wine and were entirely too impressed with the steel and compassion that made up their little English mistress to feel she would ever be properly appreciated by the *duc,* a man well known for his views as to the limited value of females in general and beautiful ones in particular.

Jack accepted one of the pistols and threw down his lance. Fortunately, the shot Lambert had seen go home merely nicked the fleshy part of his shoulder. And somehow he had survived first the slash of a saber that laid open his leg in what proved to be a long but mercifully shallow wound and then a thorough knocking about from the French cavalry, when it charged over the position where he had fallen from his horse.

But his wounds apart, he'd been able to snatch no more than naps since Bonaparte launched his campaign three days back. And he'd spent the last several hours in the exhausting project of collecting and defending the wounded men he'd been able to locate. He was sore and tired and host to an excruciating headache.

His expression, as he glared down at Madeleine, reflected all this. And his tone was condemning when he broke the brief silence that had followed her orders to her footman. "This is no place for you. For any woman."

"It became a place for women," Madeleine returned tensely, "when the able-bodied men who might have mended this *appalling* situation chose to ignore it."

"Evidently you're not aware that 'this appalling situation' is damnably dangerous!"

"Oh, good God, Jack. It is *because* of the danger that I am come. Lambert told me of it and that you had been shot and trampled. Was I to ignore the chance that you might be lying here helplessly? In peril of having your throat cut or of being stripped roughly and left to succumb to the elements?"

"You might better have considered what such marauders would think to do if they had happened upon you," he said, then shook his head with tight-pressed lips. "It's Dutch comfort you've brought me, Madeleine. I've had enough to do to keep them off these poor devils, who hold far less allure."

"You have a *pistol*."

"And much use it will be if there are more than one."

"Oh, in the name of God, are you saying you should have preferred to stand guard over these men—possibly for days—armed with nothing but a—a *staff*? I have a coach and three strong men. We can remove them to a field hospital."

He sighed. "No, no, everything is appreciated except your presence. If you had used your head, you would have sent your coach and three strong men and stayed at home."

Madeleine was herself much strained by lack of sleep and overwrought nerves. Jack's reception, after all she had endured to find him, had been chipping away at her control. She was stung by this last into hissing, "And how—you arrogant ape—would they have *recognized* you?"

His features relaxed just a fraction. "Alive I should have been happy to introduce myself. Dead, it shouldn't have signified."

"It should have signified very much to me, drat you. I'd have gone demented, sitting back there, not knowing."

His gaze raked her face with a frown, then he turned from her. "Well, since you are here, we must set to work and make the best of things. I collect there are medical supplies in that satchel you carry. Arrange them so I can find what is needed by the light of the moon. We cannot have that lantern once your servants quit us to fetch the coach. I dragged these men into the shadow of these trees so that intruders cannot see how many or how well armed we are. So far, all would-be attackers have decided the obvious risk was not worth the questionable gain. But we'll not convince them of that if they catch so much as a glimpse of you."

Madeleine swallowed her sense of ill-usage. He was right. It was no time to be brangling. But she walked over to where Gustave was still circulating the water cups. There were three. She took one and carried it to Jack.

"You have been stoic long enough," she said, thrusting the cup into his hand.

While he drank, she laid out a blanket on a patch of moonlit ground and fell immediately to organizing the various items from her satchel. When Jack stepped over to examine one or two of the articles, she told him of the four men they had come upon in the fields. "I think we should have them collected and carried here. That way they will be protected while awaiting their turn. Besides, from what I saw of the crowded state of the hospitals, none of these poor men may expect to get immediate attention. If I start now, we shall be able to send them along at least somewhat patched up and more comfortable."

Jack agreed to her plan of having the other men brought into their circle but frowned over her intention to undertake the nursing of wounds. "That is no work for you, Madeleine."

"Is it not? Then I wonder that I and every other lady in Brussels should have been so indiscreet these two days past."

He regarded her thoughtfully, then shrugged and led her to a sergeant of artillery and helped her to remove the makeshift bandage he had used to stanch the bleeding.

Madeleine began at once to cleanse the alarming wound, which encompassed almost the whole of the man's massive chest. Jack watched her carefully until assured that she hadn't overestimated herself, then went off to prepare a draft of laudanum and water.

"Drink slowly," Madeleine warned the sergeant when Jack held the cup to his feverish lips.

The footmen, having completed their ministrations, stepped up for instructions. Madeleine kept her eyes fixed but said briskly, "We must have this man and one other—the colonel shall say which—carried over into the moonlight beside the blanket. I shall be tending to them while you direct Georges to this place. Fetch the rest of the blankets from the coach when you return."

Jack raised a detaining hand and addressed Madeleine. "You asked for *one* of the pistols earlier. Have you two by you then?"

"*Three*, Jack!" she exclaimed, insensibly grateful for this opportunity to please him.

"Right, then. I must have another. The mate, no doubt, to this," he said dryly, leveling before him what he guessed to be one of the *duc*'s richly ornate dueling pistols. "Looters will not be expecting to find servants in possession of anything very valuable. Their livery should be protection enough for your footmen. Just warn them not to interfere in anything untoward they may chance to see."

As Madeleine began to tangle and abuse two languages in order to convey his message, Jack rolled his eyes in impatient amusement, then waved her to silence and delivered it himself in his flawless French.

Gustave handed over the pistol with a grin and went to help Hugues collect the man Jack said must receive attention next.

When both Madeleine's patients were in place, the lantern was extinguished and the footmen sent off. She worked swiftly and efficiently, cutting away clothing, cleaning wounds, covering them liberally with basilicum ointment, and then replacing the dirty, ragged shirts, which Jack had used as temporary bandages, with clean compresses tied firmly in place by sheeting that had been torn into strips.

Jack stood by, lending a hand when she needed him to help wrap a body wound. But for the most part he just watched while partaking hungrily of the food Madeleine had brought. Now and then his gaze shifted from her busy hands and rested on her face, fixed in an expression of taut resolution.

The coach arrived and departed again for Mont-St.-Jean as soon as Madeleine indicated that the men she had been seeing to were ready. Two others were carried to the working area, and the footmen went off to hunt down and carry back one of the men they had left waiting in the fields.

Jack stole out a few minutes later to investigate a sound, but was soon restationed beside Madeleine with the news that it was merely a cow strayed into the area.

When she had done all she could for an unconscious private with a grievous stomach wound, Madeleine slithered round the blanket without even rising and set right to work on a young officer of cavalry. She cleansed and bandaged his right arm, which had been badly mauled by a saber, then tied it tightly against his body to prevent further bleeding. As Jack lowered the young captain again, Madeleine was already applying ointment and sticking plaster to one of many cuts and scrapes about his neck and face, but she caught sight of a fleeting grimace of agony and demanded, "What is it? What have you not told me?"

The young gentleman flushed through his pallor. He had begged Jack not to mention his leg wounds. Madeleine guessed how it was and ran her eyes over his lower body. In the uncertain light, it was difficult to judge, but she thought there might be an injury beneath a small rent in his trousers near the knee.

She smiled down at him. "Come now, captain. These nice notions won't do. I promise you, I've become very accustomed to the sight of great, hairy limbs. Or are you afraid I mean to strip you? You needn't be, you know. I shall merely cut away one trouser leg. Is this where you were injured?" she asked, indicating the suspect area.

At this point, Jack addressed the captain. "You'd do well to own up, Brown. I know her well enough to promise you she'll plague you to distraction until you do."

Captain Brown smiled feebly. "I did catch a bullet there, baroness, but it has scarcely bled at all. I shall do until the surgeon can see to its removal."

"Oh, yes, to be sure, for I am no dab at extracting bullets," Madeleine rallied him. "But it is often the outer flesh causing the pain. I could perhaps ease that for you."

"Thank you, but I've had very little pain from the shot. It is my ankle that is wanting to burst through my boot. I—"

"Broken? My coachman—"

"No. Just ricked, I think. I was able to stand on it for a while. Really, ma'am, you mustn't concern yourself. It's nothing you can manage here. And—and, if you please," he added hastily, as she splashed some water in a cup and took up a small bottle. "I'd as lief not be given laudanum." He flushed again and mustered a meager laugh. "It—it is only that I don't want to wake to find they have taken my arm."

Madeleine saw that he was in genuine terror of this and said sternly, "You are teasing yourself to no purpose, captain. Your arm is going to heal famously. I've seen far, far worse, and there wasn't the least talk of removal."

Nevertheless, she did not pursue the matter of the laudanum but desired Jack to substitute brandy for the water in the cup. Again Captain Brown protested, claiming he had never been able to acquire a liking for the stuff.

Madeleine would not be overborne on this head, however, merely saying that she knew of no reason one must have a liking for his medicine. She bestowed an approving smile on him when he drained the cup and set calmly about cutting away his trouser leg, adding that it was something that must, in any event, be done before the bullet could be drawn, and he might depend upon their going about it with less patience at the field hospital.

She cleaned and wrapped his knee and continued with the work she had begun on his face until the footmen brought in another man. Glancing over her shoulder, she said, in an urgent aside, "Jack, you must realize how long he may be obliged to wait for relief at the hospital. Permit me the lantern while my footmen are here to support us. Just long enough to cut away this boot. You shall see how very quick I can be. I must have done a dozen like it already."

He nodded and lit the lantern for her. She placed it near the captain's leg and set right to work, while Jack stood quietly, marveling, as he had in the past, at the odd bundle of contradictions that made up the lovely creature before him. Not that he was in any way amazed that Madeleine had been willing to lend herself to such a project. He had always known she possessed a spirit of high gallantry. He was, however, a little surprised at the degree of stamina that evidently lay beneath her look of fragility. Hugues had told him of their schedule over the past two days.

And he was impressed, extremely impressed—considering her spasmodic absorption of all things academic—to see that her willingness to help had been joined with the kind of attention that could make that help of real value.

When she had done, Madeleine held out her hand wordlessly and received a small cup of brandy from Gustave. "Now, captain," she urged, holding it to his gray lips. "Take this and no fuss."

The captain had no fuss in him at the moment, and he raised a hand with knuckles whitened from the fist he had clenched throughout and took the cup thankfully.

"I know," she soothed, her expression pained with sympathy. "But you will realize the relief of having that wretched boot off soon."

The captain nodded and drank off the contents in silence, but when the footmen were getting him onto the litter, he held out a hand to Madeleine. "There are no words to thank you, baroness. If I had not already believed the Duke's accounts of your heroism during the Peninsular campaign, I should have no doubts of them now."

Madeleine colored slightly and smiled. The instant he was out of tongueshot, she turned to Jack. "I realize, of course, I have you to thank for that. It was excessively generous in the circumstances."

Jack shook his head. "Merely a matter of righting a wrong. You didn't deserve their condemnation."

"Nor do I deserve the praise I am receiving now. So that, too, is wrong."

"Just accept it as an equalizer for the months of unfair censure," he returned, stifling a yawn.

"You are fagged to death," she said, almost accusingly.

"I am, of course, and the food has served only to make it worse. That soup of yours must have been half port."

"Not quite," Madeleine smiled, then ventured that it would be an excellent opportunity to attend to his own wounds now. "Really, the most serious cases have been seen to."

But Jack shook his head again. "A waste of time. I intend having a bath the minute we get back to town. I shall do until then."

The next pair of men were carried over, and the routine was unvaried until the last of the soldiers had been collected from the field. At this point, Madeleine instructed her footmen to drive along to the hospital. The process would not take nearly so long if Georges were not delayed there, waiting for someone to lift the wounded men from the coach.

The only sound of approach during the next half hour was preceded by the clopping of hooves and rumble of wheels, giving the comfortable assurance that it could only be the servants returning from a run to the hospital.

And, indeed, Gustave's voice spoke out from the edge of the trees, announcing with all the form he might have employed at the drawing-room door, that he'd brought a person who had inquired for the *baronne* at Mont-St.-Jean.

Madeleine hadn't a guess who might have done such a thing,

but the mystery was swiftly solved when an Irish voice penetrated the darkness.

"Oh, me lady, is it that you've found me master?"

"Right here, old fellow," Jack called back.

"Thanks be to Gawd," O'Hare gasped, making his way carefully through the shadows. He unrolled a light cloak he carried under his arm and tossed it to Jack, who put it on in place of his torn and bloodstained coat.

O'Hare inquired into Jack's injuries and was given a concise description. Madeleine listened, as she worked over the wounded French officer, and was much relieved, for she had been filled with concern, yet dared not try Jack's patience.

O'Hare seemed to relax, too, and addressed her in his usual cheerful tone. "Faith, but it's a remarkable thing, me lady. This being twice now that I've run mad alooking for me master, only to find you've been afore me and had everything in hand."

Madeleine merely smiled and offered him some of the brandy, which he gulped appreciatively. He went on to explain that, after a useless trek over several fields, he'd been searching the hospitals, when he'd recognized the markings on the *duc*'s coach. He'd been unable to communicate with any of the servants, beyond the mention of her name, but the coachman had nodded and pointed in this direction. So, having no better prospects, he'd followed along on his horse.

Madeleine tied off a bandage and told him how it was that she'd known where to look. O'Hare sighed over Lambert's misfortune, nodding. "Ay, but there's evil doings abroad, me lady. Even the soldiers are keeping close-packed in their camps."

Madeleine had strong opinions as to where the soldiers ought to be, because of the evil doings, but she kept silent, and in less than an hour, the last of the men were carried out of the clearing and loaded into the coach.

She rinsed off her hands. Then, as she covered her mud and bloodstained gown with the cloak she had removed during her work, her eyes lifted, under a veil of dark lashes, and locked with Jack's.

TWENTY-TWO

Well, this was what she had wanted, Madeleine told herself. It was what she had searched the town night after night hoping to achieve. Jack, and a chance to talk with him. She could easily ask O'Hare to step away and claim the few minutes of privacy she had been seeking. Yet she just stood, staring.

It seemed wrong—impossible—to raise issues of personal happiness in this atmosphere of death and misery.

Finally she lowered her eyes and moved to take a seat beside Jack on a fallen tree. Dropping down, she said exhaustedly, "We can do no more, but there are others who can." With the thought, a frown settled on her features. "I find it almost unbelievable that the Belgian peasants should be as cruel as Lambert described. The townspeople of Brussels have been boundless in their generosity and compassion. You may be sure they will come or send carriages the instant I tell them what is going forward—and naturally the English ladies I have been working with."

Jack nodded and they fell into silence until the rattle and clop of the coach returning from its last run to Mont-St.-Jean brought them to their feet.

During the tedious progress back toward Brussels, Madeleine supposed Jack asleep. Yet he responded instantly to her murmur of alarm when the coach drew up suddenly at a crossroads about a mile short of town.

"It's the lane where my lodgings are located," he said. "No need taking your coachman off his route. I can share O'Hare's horse from here."

Madeleine's alarm merely refocused. "But your wounds! I was to have seen to them once you had your bath."

"O'Hare is more than capable."

"I daresay. But I was expecting we'd talk after."

His laugh was cold. "Has it taken you all this time to concoct a plausible tale, Mady?"

"It has taken all this time to *find* you," she fired back, then laid a hand on his arm. "Oh, Jack, let us not begin pulling caps. Or even say anything more just now. Come along and we'll settle it after we are cleaned up and comfortable."

"Come *along?*" he repeated. "Is it possible you've been envisioning me snugly tucked up in Montesquieu's house?"

"Oh, stop. I shouldn't have suggested it, except they are all gone into the country, and I already have something of a hospital on the lower floor. Lambert and two of his comrades."

"Well, you shan't be adding me to your *ménage*," he cut back, reaching for the door.

"Wait! If you insist on this, we'll drive you to your lodgings. But I want your promise to meet with me later today."

"Leave be, Mady," he returned tonelessly.

"No. And you cannot want that either. You must have wished to sort this out when you asked me to dance."

"Not 'wished.' Driven by curiosity and temptation was more the way of it. But I saw the futility almost immediately. *And* the folly of putting myself in the way of such temptation. My thanks for your efforts tonight, but I'm burned to the socket and should like to get on to that bath."

She felt a small stab of pain. Yet she could understand the indifference in his tone. Fatigue had brought her close to a sense of it herself. It made her able to see the wisdom of postponing their talk. They were both too exhausted, too emotionally ragged to delve into whatever confusion lay between them. But Jack's words about temptation echoed in her thoughts. He hadn't been out of the country *all* that time before the war. He had been avoiding her. And the jut of his jaw offered no hope that he wouldn't do it again. Maybe even quit the district altogether.

"Very well," she sighed, flicking a hand in defeat. "But you are in no case to ride . . . *And* you will be sparing us nothing, Jack," she added crisply, seeing his hand on the door handle again. "I shall instruct my coachman to dog you every step, if you persist in such nonsense."

Jack rolled his head to the window in a world-weary gesture and signaled for O'Hare to lead on.

It was almost a mile before they drew up again at a small wayside inn. He climbed stiffly down, turning back only for a brief salute, before disappearing behind an iron-studded door.

Madeleine fought off a fresh wave of exhaustion just long enough to take careful note of the turning, once they jolted back onto the main road, then fell back in her seat, dozing uncomfortably until the change of sound beneath the wheels heralded their return to Brussels.

It was full daylight now, and she began trying to rub enough wakefulness into her eyes to carry her through this one last task. Giving a light tug on the check string, she directed Georges to halt beside the tent hospitals that had been erected near the Namur Gate.

The response to her description of conditions on the battlefields was all that she had anticipated. More than enough to make the following hours of sleep, if not untroubled, at least undisturbed by qualms of conscience.

It was just after four when Atty reluctantly woke her with the tea that she had requested before coming up to bed.

Madeleine had to force herself to sit up, but she was determined not to let the day slip away—and, with it, what might well be her only opportunity for cornering Jack.

Two cups of strong tea managed to drive off the sleepiness that was stinging her eyes, but a feeling of deep enervation lingered as she stood, wrapped in a sun-gold dressing gown, beside Atty at the wardrobe.

The day was more than warm. That didn't help. Nor did the memory pictures that continued to flash through her brain. The sights and sounds of the last few days. And now once again the matter of Cecilia Helpston, which had been cast, unresolved, into the lumber room of her mind.

She listened absently to Atty's recommendations concerning apparel while her thoughts dwelled on this last. But after a moment she shook her head. Whatever claims the girl might have on Jack now, she had none on the past. Jack had a right to know he had not been betrayed, and she to learn what it was that had destroyed her only hope of real happiness.

She raised a tired hand to Atty. "No, find me the gray that you cut the ribbons from in London. That seems best suited to the occasion." She was thinking of more than the depressing aftermath of war. "Oh—and just sandals," she added. "It is too warm for stockings."

Leaving Atty to collect and follow with her clothes, Madeleine went down the back stairs to where she had been bathing in order to spare the overworked servants hauling hot water up two flights.

They were grateful, of course, but even Atty had wondered what caused her mistress so much amusement over taking her bath in that small, dreary room off the kitchen.

By half after five, Madeleine had bathed, dressed, and looked in on Lambert and was waving away Atty's warnings that the air often turned chilly after sundown. Full dark did not come on until nearly nine. She would be back long before.

She stepped out of the house, feet and ankles bare except for small gray sandals. Not even a shawl to relieve the plainness of her gown, and yet as alluring a picture as she had once made in the somber hues of Harrogate. The soft, clinging dove gray fitted perfectly now, over the fuller, more rounded figure she had regained in France, and her own vivid coloring seemed only more pronounced by contrast.

At the foot of the steps she breathed relief and blessed her luck. There was a fiacre just setting down its passengers at another of the imposing mansions along the way. Even if everyone but Cook and Atty weren't sleeping the day through, she owed it to Rodrique not to use his servants for such an errand.

The rough drive was passed with as near a blank mind as she could manage. Soon she was pushing back the heavy, iron-studded door that Jack had used earlier in the day.

She was greeted in the tiny foyer by a plump woman, still wiping away the remnants of flour from her hands. A kindly woman, who hurried away with quick sympathy when Madeleine identified herself as Colonel Ashton's fiancée.

She reappeared in less than a minute, beckoning from the head of the stairs. Obviously there was no parlor in which they could talk.

Madeleine smiled her thanks as the woman threw open a door, urging her forward with a romantic gleam.

And there was Jack, looking dashing again. All in scarlet and snow white except for black boots, sparkling with polish and spurs. It seemed she hadn't come a moment too soon.

She dropped her gloves and reticule onto a small chest as the door closed quietly behind her and nodded in response to Jack's none too flattering laugh.

"*Fiancée*, she told me," he said, turning to pour from a bottle on the mantel. "I must say I was somewhat taken aback."

"Were you? It was in the certainty that Miss Helpston would *not* come here that I fobbed off your landlady with the tale."

His back still to her, he downed the contents of his glass. Refilling it, he said, "Quite right—even if her mother were not by to curb such an improprietous impulse."

"Quite," Madeleine returned drily. "So you might have guessed it could be none other than the indecorous Madeleine."

"So I might. Wine?" he asked calmly.

"Thank you."

She waited until he handed her the glass before saying, "As it happens, I don't think I was seen. I came in a hackney. But, of course, I had no hope of finding this place so quiet. Are you alone here then?"

"I've been sharing the inn with two other officers, but one is off organizing the pursuit, and Fulsome is en route to Ghent with a dispatch for the French court."

"And you, apparently, are preparing to be off somewhere yourself."

"No. Just back from giving in my report at headquarters."

He removed the glass from her hand, setting it on the table, and encircled her waist with just the spread of his fingers. "So, you see, my temptress, we have plenty of time. Did you manage to find another complacent nobleman?"

One hand strayed up to caress a breast, but Madeleine twisted sharply out of his hold. "I didn't come here for that, you conceited rakehell!"

There was considerable agitation behind her anger when she turned again to confront him. Despite the calculated insult, he had actually aroused her. That quickly. That easily. Responses she had thought wholly dead were evidently only too alive where he was concerned.

He handed back her glass with a wry smile. "What, then? Still determined on an explanation?"

"Yes. But not to give one."

He frowned. "A game, Mady? You'll have to supply me with the rules."

She walked a short way off. "I can overlook that rude implication a moment ago. Because I suspected you of wishing that and no more when you borrowed Captain Fulsome's waltz. I was so confused by it—and all that followed—that I could think of no better reason until you had gone."

She fixed a smoky green gaze on him. "I fancy you know better than I why I was unable to find you again until last night. At all events, I did see—or guessed at least—that you had somehow got the idea I'd let you down. I did not, Jack. And I want you to tell me why you didn't go to Hans Place for my message. It was ever our arrangement, and—"

"Mady," he broke in, his expression a mixture of annoyance and concern. "Don't go on with this. I haven't a clue as to your purpose, but what you don't realize is that your every move was observed and recorded after the authorities released you. I didn't go to Hans Place because the report told plainly that you'd made no effort to leave a message there. You didn't go yourself. You didn't send a servant. Not even a letter."

She gasped. "They showed you the report?"

"I demanded it. I wouldn't believe what they told me."

"But they oughtn't to have told you anything!" Madeleine exclaimed, outraged. "Sir Lloyd assured me that the details of an investigation are confined strictly to official circles."

"I know nothing of your arrangement with this Sir Lloyd,"

Jack returned angrily. "He was gone from Town. And with him the report you speak of. It happens I didn't see that. Only the one involving matters after your release. Although I should *think* an order signed by Wellington rather gave me entrée into those 'official circles.'"

Madeleine looked round in her confusion and moved instinctively to a chair pushed under a small table by the window. Drawing it out and dropping down, she pressed the nails of both hands to her forehead in an effort to concentrate.

"I don't understand—any of this, Jack," she said, looking up. "I was released *before* you returned to England. In order to have such a document by you, you must have learned of the affair while still in France."

Jack propped himself against a bedpost. "Oh, yes," he murmured with a dry laugh. "A dispatch rider arrived with orders from London to detain me for questioning. It seems Morland recommended me as a prime suspect."

"Charles?—" Madeleine's large eyes widened. "But he *couldn't* have! Unless—" She broke off as Jack nodded, his expression even more cynical.

Well, there it was. She had her answer. Charles, of course, had bubbled her thoroughly again and produced an effect that even he had not anticipated. Obviously his disclosure had caused no hardship at all where Jack was concerned. Just caused him to come to London, armed with that order from Wellington. And simply because she had taken such excessive care to avoid Hans Place, she had lived through hell this year and more.

But a flash of anger pierced her depression, as another thought struck home. "And naturally you also saw that I had called at Charles's lodgings—"

"And sent your servant there a half dozen times."

She made fluttering fists of both hands. "Oh, Jack, really. I'll allow the earlier misunderstandings about him to have been entirely my own folly. But I should think that you had had proof enough on *that* score. How *could* you assume again that we were lovers?"

"I didn't assume it. Naturally, I was forced to consider it as a possibility. To allow that—well, that your recent awakening might have caused you to view him in a new light." He shrugged. "But really, at that point, it didn't seem to matter. As you say, it was far from the first time you'd put me in that position. There has always been something to astound or hurt or wonder about. And *always* Morland at the center of it. If it was never quite what it seemed, it did invariably serve to place me in an insulting—thoroughly *stupid* position. No. By then I cared only that you had gone off without a word—*knowing* I must be on the way to you. There was no question that you might have supposed me dead, or you shouldn't have remained so stubborn about my identity in that idiotic business over Edelmar Croft."

"And naturally it didn't so much as occur to you that it might be *because* I knew you were on the way to me that I went off as I did," she threw back angrily.

"On the contrary, that was precisely what *did* occur to me. I don't pretend to have arrived at your exact reasoning. But I learned that your family were in Town. It suggested the even more likely possibility that you might have reversed your thinking in favor of them again and were merely flying rather than face me with it. That Morland was not the *cause* of your departure, but merely an instrument to facilitate it."

"Oh, *how* could you think such a thing?"

"Easily. It wouldn't have been the first time you'd mizzled away with that in mind."

She stared back blankly, then exclaimed, "From Harrogate?—Oh, God in heaven, Jack! There was no similarity at all! No longer a question of promises made years and years before I even knew of your existence! And Menard was already dead. There wasn't even a question of scandal or the settlement money."

"Perhaps not, but from what I understand of your mother, there was and always had been a question of title and consequence."

"It is not my *mother* we are discussing."

"No, we are discussing my thinking at the time. Your aunt lamented on more than one occasion that your mother's views had been drilled into you from birth. It wasn't inconceivable that you might have been worked around to take advantage of your new freedom to make the sort of match she'd always wished for you. For her sake—the sake of your sisters. Finding you comfortably betrothed to Montesquieu seemed to settle the question."

He began to pace, a look of irritation etched on his brow. "But what are you at now, Mady? Reasons can no longer signify. Yet obviously you want me to believe that you were prepared to go through with our arrangement. That I misjudged the entire situation. Why?"

"Because it's *true*, drat you. Not only did you misjudge the situation—but *me*. Did I really deserve so little trust?"

He halted to face her. "It was more a lack of confidence. Good God, at the Queen's Arms you struggled almost until the last to preserve your mother's approbation—your social status. I told you at the time that I was at the end of my patience. Only then was an agreement wrenched from you. And there was no forgetting the heat of *that* moment."

"Not just an agreement, Jack. A promise."

"And what store was I to set by that? You also promised not to entrust yourself to Morland. Yet only minutes after my return I was informed of your flight with him to France."

Madeleine looked thunderstruck and cried, "*No!* To France?—It isn't true!"

"Oh, what the devil is this? It was all down in black and white by people with no ax to grind. I tell you, Mady, you were followed."

"*Yes*," she ground out with asperity. "Yes, I was followed! Of *course*, I was followed."

"I see. You knew. It was merely that you didn't expect they would tell me of your activities."

"Indeed I did *not*. Since most of my 'activities' were directed toward keeping them from even learning *who* you were!" She shot out of her chair and stood, partly turned away. "I—I was terrified for you, Jack. You don't know what it was like. The things they asked—and said. I thought if they discovered you were an intelligence officer, they would be convinced that the information Menard received had come from you—that you would be arrested and possibly hanged."

Glancing back, she caught his expression and snapped, "Yes, I see *now* how stupid were my efforts. But how was I to guess you had no need of them? That you apparently needed no one but your duke to shield you from all harm?" She thrust a knuckle between her teeth for a moment, but came back bristling. "And it *might* have been that even your duke would have found it beyond his power to save you if Charles had made good his threat to name you as his source. It—it was he all along, you know."

"I guessed as much. Knowing what you'd told me of his hold over Beauvoir."

Madeleine turned back abruptly. "And did you also decide I must have been involved in *that?*"

"Don't be a ninny. You know as much of political intrigue as I do of needlework."

"As *I* do of needlework, for that matter," she murmured, taking some comfort from at least this much show of faith.

"I was even convinced you were in the dark about his involvement," Jack added bitterly. "Now you speak of his threat to embroil me. He couldn't have made it *during* your arrest. Yet you rushed to him directly after."

"Oh, no, no. Menard's cousin explained all that just before my release. It was *because* of that that I went to Charles. And then that he made the threat!"

"Damn it, Mady!" Jack thrust his hands into his trouser pockets and stalked back to the bedpost. "It is just this sort of thing that is making it as hard to believe you now as it was then. A chaise—a chaise *already* loaded for a flight to the continent—arrived at Morland's door less than an hour behind you. The two of you emerged only minutes later and set out."

TWENTY-THREE

Madeleine threw back her head, causing her attractively piled coiffure to spill a dark, curling tendril along one hollowed cheek. She drew a long breath and dropped again onto the chair, lacing her fingers tightly together on the table. "Will you permit me to explain in a more orderly fashion? Perhaps then you will find it possible to believe me."

He nodded grimly, and she took her narrative back to when she'd first learned that she was being followed, telling of her fear that he would fall into the trap, her dilemma about getting a message to Hans Place, and finally of the Montefiores' offer of a home.

"I wrote out your letter then, and madame posted it from Dover. I was on my way to join her in Paris when I stopped off in Bury Street. I *had* to stop. For one thing, to explain to Charles that I'd thought it safer to include him on a list of possible suspects. I knew, if he were left to believe I had exposed him deliberately—and they managed to bring it home to him—he wouldn't scruple to drag me down, too. And of equal importance—or so I thought—was the fact that he was the only one (apart from my family) aware of your true identity."

She paused, glancing up from the intense study she had been making of her hands. "It was then—after I'd warned him that he was soon to be questioned—that I threatened to expose him if—"

Jack's hands flew from his pockets and he took an instinctive step forward. "*Threatened!* Great God, you knew him to be guilty of a hanging offense and you *threatened* him!" He swept a hand through his hair. "The wonder is he didn't strangle you."

His swift movement caused Madeleine to turn to him, unthinking, her own hand half suspended in appeal. She brought it back to the table with a light shrug. "Not really. You know what a frightful coward he is."

"Yes, and that none *but* a coward would try to save his skin by such means."

She made a slight gesture. "Perhaps you are right. I didn't consider. Possibly because there was no real danger of it. Not with the chaise due to collect me at any minute and the government men below. He knew of that. It was through learning that I had been followed that he became so unnerved and insisted I give him a place in my carriage. It was *then* that he threatened to take an oath that you had been his source of information if I did not."

Jack gritted his teeth, and she added swiftly. "There was no danger in that either. I took great care not to be alone with him at any time. Even for refreshment at the inns. Not that it occurred that he might harm me in such populated surroundings, but I do *try* to keep my promises."

"And did it not occur either, when you boarded the packet with him at Dover, that he might cast you into the Channel? For God's sake, Mady—"

"No, it did not, because I tell you, I did no such thing!"

"The report said plainly—"

"Jack, I don't care a fig *what* the report said. Charles left me at a turning just past Canterbury. They apparently just assumed we were both bound for France and gave over the pursuit."

"Well, they didn't. That's not how such matters are conducted. They continued all the way into Dover, where one claims to have kept an eye on you and your maid and the other to have trailed Morland while he went off to book your passage. Both remained on shore not only to observe the three of you boarding, but to see your vessel well under sail. It was when they told me of this that I demanded to see the report. You may be sure I studied it minutely, searching for the least sign of loose speculation or doubt."

Madeleine had turned her gaze to the window, an odd, wholly humorless smile compressing her lips. "I could think this rather a rare joke, if only if hadn't happened to break my heart," she murmured. Looking back, she added with cold irony, "It was not Charles that they so efficiently observed escorting us on board. It was my footman. Yes," she nodded, as

Jack's eyes widened. "Yes, my footman. Dressed in Menard's finery to lend consequence to his role."

"But how the devil did he get there? There was no mention of a footman. The passengers—all seats—were accounted for. The chaise collected a maidservant in Golden Square and went directly to Bury Street to take up you and Morland."

Madeleine nodded again and described the arrangement they had made for seating in the carriage. "And, yes," she sighed, "Roget is of a size with Charles. Naturally they did not see Charles jump out along the road, and apparently they did not see Roget get in at Leicester Square." She looked down at the table, the same ironic smile underlining the unhappiness in her eyes, as she added flatly, "Undoubtedly because I took especial care to lure them away from the house, thinking that you might turn up."

They both seemed to be gazing into the glare of revelation for a moment.

Then Jack walked over and took her shoulder in a painful grip. "Damn it, Mady, I'm sorry. But I wish to God you'd referred them to me straightaway. Let me deal with them myself. In my own behalf *and* yours." His grip eased. "I know, I know," he said in answer to his own thoughts, "you were in the devil of a hobble and managing the best you could. The confounded thing is that the resulting tangle . . ." He moved his other hand in a motion of useless rage. "I can say no more than that the circumstances made it impossible to believe otherwise."

There was another long pause before Madeleine reached up and covered the hand still resting on her shoulder with her own. She pressed them together with her cheek. "Well, I expect there is no one in a better position to understand that. Never once did any of this enter into my calculations, to justify your conduct when you failed to turn up at Ruelle. Or when I discovered at Bordeaux that you had gone off to America. . . . Or when I had Lambert's letter about Miss Helpston. Odd, how we are made. Love seems never to be able to overcome reason except to our detriment. As a girl I trusted Charles in the face of every possible evidence that I should not."

They fell silent again until Madeleine removed his hand with a quick squeeze and rose. Jack detained her. "And—"

"And that is why I came," she said, still keeping her manner brisk. "I was—as you said—curious. And, of course, I couldn't bear for you to go on believing as you did." She glanced away. "Now everything is tidy again."

Jack took her by the shoulders and stared hard into her face. "Yes, and although you're looking mighty unhappy at the moment, I want you to take a few minutes and think. A really honest evaluation. Ask yourself—given the choice at this stage—would you really pass up the rather rare opportunity to become a duchess in order to struggle up the ladder with me?"

"Despite what you may have learned about my mother's ambitions, or I have caused you to think of me, Jack, I don't need a few minutes. I would pass it up to live with you in abject poverty."

He continued to stare. "Are you sure, Mady? *Truly* sure? Because I am going to bring you face to face with those words."

Her eyes flew up. "But you cannot. What of Miss Helpston?"

"Hedging?"

"*No*. But—but I should like to think I have enough honor not to set myself up against the child you are promised to wed." She looked away. "Though I don't think I have." Then quickly back at him. "What I cannot believe is that *you* have not."

The smile was gone as swiftly as it touched his eyes. "I can only say that I'm mighty grateful not to be tested on that point, Mady. As it happens, I am not in honor bound."

"Not?—Yet, only moments ago—When I spoke of her as your betrothed, you—Yes, you answered quite as if it were so."

"I did. A cowardly thing, I know. Taking refuge behind the skirts of a female. But I was still a trifle shaken by the events of these past weeks. I felt I might do worse than ensure a little protection against this unexpected visit of yours."

Madeleine was a trifle shaken herself and not fully able to take it all in. She raised her hands to her face while she steadied her breathing. Then dropped them just to stare wide-eyed before collapsing against him, saying in a low, unfathoming tone, "Oh, Jack. Protection against me, when all I want to do is love you forever."

"It was the *ways* you have always wanted to love me forever that were causing concern. First as my friend. Then as my mistress . . ."

She responded in spite of herself with a laughing sob. "I should still like to be your friend. Always that. But if you are truly free, I should also like you to make an honest woman of me as soon as may be arranged." She hugged herself tightly to him, still a trifle unsure. "Yet how in the world is it *possible?* The girl is here. In Brussels with you. And Lambert said you actually spoke with her father."

"I could wish Lambert a little less busy, but it's true enough—said that way. The fact of the matter, however, is that her father approached me."

Madeleine looked up questioningly. He shrugged. "He seemed to feel he had cause to inquire into my intentions. I shouldn't have thought it, but I fancy Ceci might have influenced him there. She, too, has been a trifle spoiled into expecting her own way in most things."

Madeleine thought this a little unfair. Unless it were to be now, she couldn't recall ever having got her way in anything of importance. She supposed he was referring to those conversations she had begged him to put off in the past. But the past held no interest for her at the moment. It was this conversation now, and she wanted him to get on with it.

He smiled at her decision not to rise to the bait. "Oh, I won't tell you I wasn't tempted by his proposition. I was looking for a future that wouldn't involve London. It seemed improbable that you would remain out of the country. And Ceci is amusing—"

"I noticed. A perfect *bel esprit*, if your continued laughter is anything to judge by."

Jack ringed his finger in the loose curl that was still dangling at the side of her face. "Not quite. And in no way a satisfactory substitute for you. No one ever could be, you know."

Madeleine sniffed and held silent. It was either that or burst into a mad bout of abandoned tears.

"And that was the main reason I didn't close with Helpston's offer there and then," Jack went on. "I explained—in something of a gross understatement—that my affections were engaged. That it would be a while before I could in fairness offer myself as a husband to any lady, much less one so young and romantically attached. Which brought me to my second scruple. I felt—still feel—that Ceci's attraction was more caught up in my work than me. Fascinated—oh, in much the same way as young Henry. I meet with that a good deal."

Madeleine was in no state to quibble with his modesty. She could only hope that he was right in his assessment of Miss Helpston. Her youth argued at least that he might well be.

"So, I suggested that we let matters rest until a few months after the war. Giving Cecilia a chance to see me in a more humdrum existence and both of us an opportunity to reevaluate our sentiments."

He paused to gather Madeleine closer in his arms, his breath stirring through her hair. "But as you probably know from Lambert, the dust barely had time to settle over there before this business with Bonaparte fired up. And then, in all *improbable* places, I ran smack into you. I told both Ceci and her father, shortly after our waltz, that I would not be returning to Bermuda. I was no nearer recovery than the day I'd left London over a year ago. Since that time, I took care to keep out of both her way and yours. Or tried."

Madeleine just continued to hang limply in his arms. Eventually she raised her face in obedience to his finger beneath her chin and let him kiss her. It took quite a few kisses before she could believe it was all really happening. She had dreamed such unlikely things so many times.

Finally she drew back reluctantly and sighed. "I've left my driver to await me below in the coffee-room. Or the taproom—if they have one. If not, I expect he can be found in the kitchen. I daresay I should go along now and—"

"Go *along?* You're wide of the mark, if you fancy you are *ever* going back to that house."

She couldn't help a small laugh. "Now, now, colonel, you must know I have no other purpose than that I've left everything behind me. Not the least of which is a brother—and surely you'll agree that Rodrique must not be deserted without so much as a letter."

"A letter he may have. But you'll write it now. O'Hare shall see to its delivery."

He returned her gently to her chair. "It's best that you remain out of sight of the Brussels set until I can arrange a quiet marriage and an unobtrusive departure. So you might as well put up here. O'Hare can arrange to have Lambert carried out and comfortably transported in the morning. That settles that problem, and he can serve as chaperone, as well."

"Scarcely an efficient one—all in splints and unable to rise from his bed."

"I can think of nothing else to make his presence at such a time even tolerable."

He moved off and began gathering writing materials from a small case. "His comrades can be taken to hospital facilities in town, and your maid—is it the English girl that traveled with you to France?"

Madeleine nodded, beginning to feel the ease of old familiarity seep through her.

"Very well, O'Hare shall escort her here, as well. After she has packed up your belongings."

He returned, setting down a freshly mended pen, paper, wafers, and ink pot on the table in front of her. "I notice you are not wearing that boulder of a ring I saw on your finger when we danced."

"Not since the outbreak of war."

"That, naturally, should be left behind, but instruct your girl to leave anything else he has given you."

"There has been nothing but trifles. Flowers, sweets." She met his eyes and added, "I was not his mistress, Jack."

The look he returned was laced with irony. "You needn't say. If you had been, I'd stake my life a betrothal should never have come about. The man's a legend in this town. However, the fact that a betrothal did come about makes the matter of other presents an accepted practice."

There was a hollowness in his tone, and Madeleine, in no doubt of what was really on his mind, replied levelly. "Yes, other presents and other things. But there have been neither in this case, Jack. The marriage contract is not signed."

"Not? Nothing? . . ."

"Not and nothing."

There was quite a long silence while a slow smile built itself onto his features. Then all at once he laughed and pulled her from the chair and into his arms. "Mady, Mady, my endlessly unpredictable love, I don't even mind telling you that *that* is a deal more than I bargained for. I shan't ask how you contrived it. That somehow it *was* you that contrived it, I haven't the flicker of a doubt."

He kissed her and set her back in the chair, a laugh still lingering in his voice. "By God, I begin almost to pity your *duc.*" But he became businesslike again and added, "You may complete your letter to him while I settle up with your driver and give O'Hare his instructions."

"Good heavens, that doesn't give me much time. And I shall also have to say something to Madame Montefiore."

"Well, be brief. You may write to her in greater detail tomorrow, along with anyone else you wish to take leave of in Brussels."

Madeleine drew a sheet of paper before her. "This is probably the first thing to which she will not reply, *'C'est naturel.'*" She paused reflectively, stroking her cheek with the feather edge of the pen, then smiled as she began to write. "And yet, she may at that."

Jack left her to go downstairs but was back in less than twenty minutes. "How are you doing?" he asked, not bothering to close the door behind him.

"Just a minute more." She scratched out a last line and fixed her signature. "No sand," she shrugged with a teasing smile, perfectly aware of his impatience and fairly sure of its cause, as she waved the paper slowly back and forth to dry the ink.

"Amazing. Positively amazing that you have attained this age without being soundly beaten," he observed.

She flashed him another smile while she affixed a wafer to the folded sheet, then passed him both letters.

He was back in only seconds, locking the door behind him and striding purposefully into her laughing embrace.

"Outrageous goat," she whispered as he kissed her face.

"Still no regrets?" he whispered back.

"I? None. Though I shall, of course, be at some pains to convince my mother that there is more consequence in turning down a duke than in marrying one."

"An excellent point."

"Umm," she agreed between kisses. "Where am I to sleep tonight?"

"In here, of course."

"Your landlady?"

"A sensible woman."

"I'm grateful there is to be at least one beneath this roof."

He had turned her away from him and was kissing her neck and ear as his fingers unhooked the back of her gown and went on to unfasten her stays with all the deftness and familiarity of a lady's maid. It reminded her of another matter they would have to discuss.

Then both garments dropped to the floor. Her shift was lifted swiftly over her head, and he began to caress away the marks left on her skin by the stays, his lips tracing the course of his fingers.

Madeleine turned into his arms, a slight moan crushed by his lips as she was lifted out of the swirl of clothing at her feet and carried to the bed.

It was over quickly. Too quickly. And Jack was looking down at her laughing. *Laughing.*

"I was just reminded of an old joke," he explained. "A man who takes a woman while still in his boots is said to have made her a duchess."

"If you're thinking that another good point for my mother, I can tell you she will not be the least impressed."

Jack disappeared beyond the bed curtains with another laugh.

Madeleine heard his boots hitting the floor with relief, for she didn't feel at all like a duchess. More like a bird suspended in midflight. She watched him return, reminded once more of those beautiful statues—except for a bandage here and there. She wondered how he had contrived to become so completely bronzed. Swimming, she supposed.

He slipped between her outstretched arms and buried his face in the loose hair spread out beside her. His lovemaking this time, though no less fervent, was more patient, leaving her in a more receptive state for any further jokes he may have recalled. But there were none. Just several soft kisses before he suggested that she begin thinking about a honeymoon.

"I thought perhaps I was having it."

"You're entitled to another after the wedding."

"Then there is only one place. The Queen's Arms in London."

"We can go there, of course. But just now, I fancy you could choose from the whole of Europe."

"The Queen's Arms in London," she repeated firmly. "And I should like to begin at once looking about for a house for us to rent."

"Should you? I had supposed you might prefer to purchase one."

She paused, frowning a little curiously at him. "Well, I should, of course, but if we dig so deeply into your capital, shall we not find ourselves a trifle pinched? Especially since I evidently caused you to lose those positions in London."

"Oh, a position will pose no problem. Wellington has interests in several areas to suit me. Not that it is strictly necessary. You are forgetting that I have been able to add to my capital for two years from a lieutenant colonel's pay. But I wasn't thinking of that for the house. I sold the Irish estate to my brother and thought we'd use the proceeds from it. Although I trust you realize we are discussing only a very *modest* house."

"Oh, what does that signify? One all our own." She paused. "Yes, and I don't even mind telling you, my fine buck, that *that* is a good deal more than I bargained for." She laughed. "You

may consider our little account paid in full. What fun. But then
we shall have to plan on staying at the Queen's Arms some
little time, Jack, for naturally we must look carefully over everything available before choosing."

"Somehow that comes as no surprise."

His tone was joking, but she thought he was looking a little
concerned. She settled her head on his chest. "Oh, my precious love, it is more than most people ever even dream of
having."

"Yet I cannot quite forget that it is rather a bagatelle to what
you cast to the winds only a few minutes ago."

"I had not thought you such a goose," Madeleine laughed,
tweaking one of the hairs on his chest. "Well, if I ever have any
regrets, I shall remind myself that our more moderate living is
an excellent hedge against ending back in Harrogate for a
course of the waters to cure me of the gout."